THE NEIGHBOR WAR

ONLY IN ATLANTA #2

KATIE BAILEY

Cover Design by
CANVAPRO

Character Art by
KRISTINACHISTIAKOVA, DARIARIABETS VIA
CANVAPRO

ELEVENTH AVENUE
PUBLISHING

1

COURTNEY

I love lists. Lists keep things organized, keep my thoughts in order.

For example, here's a list of things I find more pleasant than Aiden Shaw:

Mosquito bites. Sunburn. Paper cuts. Rush hour traffic. Telemarketers. Lukewarm coffee. Period cramps. Picking up dog poop. Mouth breathers. Acid reflux. Boob sweat. People who drown kittens.

Okay, okay, maybe not the last one... I'm not a psychopath. But still, the list is very clear: I do not like Aiden Shaw. Not one bit. And to be extra clear, he doesn't like me either. It's the one and only thing we agree on.

It's also the reason I'm about to do something I never, ever do: Grovel.

"Pleaaaaaaaaaaase," I wheedle as I bat my eyelashes at my boss, Philippe. Who I may or may not have a teeny little crush on. But, that's neither here nor there. This is necessary eyelash-batting, mission critical. Philippe frowns, and I add a little pout. "Pretty please with cherries on top."

"No." Philippe is oblivious to my light flirtations, which really shouldn't surprise me. The guy's never shown any interest in me whatsoever—why would he start now? He adjusts his silk tie, runs his fingers through that curly hair of his, then dips a spoon into a vat of simmering soup. He makes a big show of gagging. "Puh! More salt!"

"Yes, boss." One of the sous chefs practically salutes, wiping sweat from his brow before tending to his broth creation, which smells like heaven.

"It's an emergency," I say desperately. But, Philippe isn't listening.

"You! Tidy up that hair!" Philippe barks at a trainee waitress who's just entered the kitchen with a towering armful of dirty dishes. "I'm running a fine dining establishment, not a hoochie bar."

"S-sorry," the waitress chokes before depositing the dishes in the sink. "I'll fix it now."

"That, you will," Philippe snaps. "And then, get to table seven and take their drink order before they die of thirst. No customer will die on my watch, I will not have blood on my hands! Do I make myself clear?"

The poor girl nods and scuttles for the door—no doubt running for the bathroom to fix her already perfectly presentable ponytail and wipe away her forthcoming mascara tears. I must find her later and tell her that Philippe really isn't as bad as he seems. Most of the time. And also inform her about the super duper lacquer hairspray I found at Walmart, in that old lady section that sells rollers and blue rinse. Lifesaving stuff in a hot, humid work environment that wreaks havoc with hair.

Philippe claps his hands at the retreating waitress's back like he's shoo-ing a stray cat. Then, he faces me again. His slightly-too-small, forest-green eyes (not that I'd ever tell him that. Hopefully our children will have my eyes.) flash. "I don't think your neighbor dropping in for dinner is considered an emergency, Courtney."

"What's a hoochie bar?" I ask innocently.

The bus boy behind me titters, but turns his laugh into a cough when he sees our boss's glare.

"Don't change the subject," Philippe says, flicking a dish towel at me. "I'd help you if I could. But we have a full house out there, and we're a waitress down."

Of course. Diana had to go and have an emergency appendectomy, today of all days. Some people are so selfish.

"Doesn't working here for seven years give me some kind of veto power?" I try one last course of action. And tack on a silent, *especially seeing as I'm insanely overdue either a pay rise or a promotion. Both, actually.*

But, the guffaws from the peanut gallery of chefs behind me don't inspire hope.

"Absolutely not," Philippe snaps. "Now go and serve that man and his date before I fire you."

"You won't fire me," I say, sounding much more confident than I feel.

It's an art I've perfected over the years—don't let anyone think you want or need anything, or you risk looking weak. A good concealer will easily disguise the bags under your eyes that your sixty-hour work week has given you. Bags you could pack for vacation. A vacation I could really do with, right about now.

"Can't you just give me the rest of the night off?" I plead. "One measly little night?"

"No."

"For girl problems?"

"Advil's in the bathroom."

"Sudden case of the stomach flu?"

"Don't puke on anyone. Now, get out there!"

"I'm going to report this place for workers' rights violations," I mutter as I push open the kitchen door and stalk onto the restaurant floor.

3

I pause behind an eight-foot-tall display of calla lilies to tie a crisp, white apron over my black dress. Then, I peek out to survey the scene.

The dimly-lit restaurant smells like melted butter, garlic and wealth. Crystal glasses clink and opulent chandeliers glimmer overhead, reflecting the flicker of candlelight from the tables. The resident pianist has her eyes closed as she croons *Comment Te Dire Adieu* from the corner stage. I don't know a word of French, but I could sing every one of the songs on her playlist at this point.

Petit Soleil is one of Atlanta's premier gourmet restaurants, and I know it's difficult to get a job here. Yeah, it's a little stuffy, prim and proper, but the tips are great. And Philippe—despite the one-sided, unrequited, kinda pathetic crush I've harbored on him since the day I started working—is a decent boss.

Despite having to consistently paint my appearance to polished perfection—and perma-smile through bleeding, blistered feet—it's the best way I can save enough money to achieve my real dream: running my own business full-time, and being a badass girl boss.

But again, I sound more confident than I am. Nothing about me is what anyone would refer to as "badass". I enjoy reading romance novels and watching old teen movies, jogging and experimental (read: disastrous) baking. I mean, I own two golden retrievers! I'm about as badass as a cup of decaf Earl Grey tea sipped out of an oversized pink mug while snuggled under a handknit blanket.

Yet, I know in my heart of hearts that I will be an incredible businesswoman—badass or not. I've saved and scrimped for years so I can do the whole thing alone. In true girlboss fashion.

The last thing I want is to have to rely on an investor or bank loan. So, becoming a shift manager is—has to be—my next stepping stone. The income boost will allow me to work less hours and dedicate more time to building my company. And then, once my business starts making money, I'll be able to leave my job and run it full-time. Maybe in a year. Or two.

In the meantime, though, I'm stuck putting in long, long hours in heels and hosiery, offering only the best in customer service. Currently, I'm a hostess. Which means that my job involves a lot of smiling real pretty and taking coats and pouring Perrier.

But, of course, Diana had to go in for surgery—leaving me to cover her tables—on the one night my arch-nemesis decided to dine at my workplace.

What I wouldn't give to be the one on an operating table right now. I'd sacrifice my appendix in a heartbeat. Anything not to wait on Aiden freaking Shaw—the man who can set me ablaze with a single look.

Due to rage, not desire. FYI.

Sacré bleu. (Okay, so I've picked up a bit of the language working here... mostly French swear words from the chefs).

I don't know what I did to piss off Karma, but she sure does seem to hate me.

I take a deep breath as I approach Aiden's table. Jerk-face looks disturbingly handsome in a light blue suit that I might have to accidentally spill red wine on later. Ugh, the man is all dark, tousled hair and incredible jawline and dazzling smile and pure, utter evil. If he wasn't my best friend's brother, I'd guess the devil himself spawned him. But, I've met Mr. and Mrs. Shaw, and they're a pair of harmless, vegan-sandal wearing, pottery-making hippies who were unlucky enough to have only a 50% success rate with the children they birthed.

Reproducing is a serious gamble with odds like that, if you ask me.

Aiden is seated across from a ravishing blond woman in a low-cut silver dress. While my own frazzled blond hair looks, and feels, like straw most of the time, this girl has a flowing crown of spun silk. I kind of want to ask what shampoo she uses, but this is hardly the time for that.

Aiden leans forward with a coy smile and says something that makes Blondie collapse into a fit of giggles. Maybe he told her he's balding and is wearing a toupee.

One can only hope.

"Good evening, sir. Mademoiselle." I barely manage to choke out the guest greeting Philippe forces us to use. "Welcome to Petit Soleil."

Aiden turns to face me and I'm gratified to see a glimmer of shock cross his annoyingly pretty face. Unfortunately, it passes all too quickly, and he shoots me that cocky smirk I've come to know and loathe. Probably glad of the unexpected opportunity to torture me.

"Courtney?" He raises his smug eyebrows extra-smugly. "You work *here*?"

"No, I was just having dinner and my lobster was taking ages, so I decided to make myself useful," I say benignly, filling their water glasses.

Aiden rolls his eyes, but Blondie claps her hands.

"You're funny!" she squeals. "I'm Breanna."

"Nice to meet you, I'm Courtney." I refrain from asking her what on earth she's doing on a date with Damien Devilspawn. I'm at work, that's the professional thing to do.

"How do you two know each other?" Breanna asks.

Because I make it my business not to know anyone like Aiden, I say, "we don't."

"She's friends with my sister," Aiden says at the same time. We glare at each other for a second, then he adds, "but we don't know each other well."

"We're just neighbors," I emphasize. Widen my eyes to

6

silently signal to Breanna that she should run for the hills while she has a chance to flee.

Unfortunately for her, she doesn't take my helpful cue. Instead, she raises an eyebrow and drums her pointy fingernails on the table. Fixes me with a *look*. "I don't think I'm following."

"Two houses, right next to each other," I explain.

"I know the dictionary definition of the word, *thanks*." She sounds the opposite of thankful, but you can't win 'em all. "I mean, are you neighbors, or friends with his sister?"

"Both."

"And you don't know each other?"

Aiden picks up his fork and examines it like he's never seen a fork before in his life. His pained expression—like he'd rather be anywhere else on earth—brings me incredible amounts of joy. "Courtney and I don't have a personal relationship. We're just acquaintances through other people."

"And address proximity. Can't help who you live next to, amiright?" I add with a strange, jolly chuckle and a wink-wink-nudge-nudge motion that I'm sure makes me look like a broken Santa Claus toy.

"You sure can't," Aiden says, surprising me.

Wow, turns out we agree on two things. Who knew?

He bites his lip like he's physically biting back a smile, and I realize that his previous expression was not one of pain. It was mild inconvenience, mixed with mild amusement. Here I was, thinking I was having an impact on him, making him sweat on his date, and it turns out that he's *enjoying* this!

I rock back on my heels and take a huge breath. Remind myself that I am not inferior because I'm waiting on him. I'm waiting on him because I need every last penny from this job to help me pursue my dreams.

Breanna looks at me like she's sizing me up, then wrinkles her nose in distaste. "Did you guys used to date or something?"

"NO!" We both yell, earning ourselves a shower of dirty looks from nearby diners. Out of the corner of my eye, I spot Philippe. He's redder than a tube of Angelina Jolie's lipstick, and when I catch his eye, he mimes slitting his throat.

Uh oh. May have forgotten where I was for a moment.

"Definitely not," I say in a much calmer voice. I add a soothing smile for good measure. A true customer service professional at work.

"Why are you grinning like a circus clown?" Aiden asks with a wicked, infuriating smile that makes me want to smack him. Just once. Just to see how it feels.

"Because your face is funny," I retort, balling my hands at my sides.

Screw professionalism, the gloves are coming off.

"More to the point," Breanna pipes up, pointing a perfectly manicured fingernail at Aiden. "Why would you take me to the restaurant your ex works at?"

"She's not my ex." Aiden's voice is super calm and relaxed, like he's chatting about football scores or the merits of club sandwiches over BLTs (turkey, mainly). But, he taps his fork on the table to punctuate each word. He might sound casual, but he means business. "We would never be together."

My stomach constricts involuntarily, like that fork stabbed me right in the gut. "Yeah, because heaven forbid anyone could ever be good enough for Aiden Shaw."

The words fall out of my mouth, but the second they're hanging in the air for all three of us to hear, Breanna turns bright red.

And I realize I've not only said the wrong thing, but the worst thing possible.

Shoot. I meant to say it lightly. Flippantly, like a joke. But, it came out in this weird, seething tone that evidently painted me with a bright scarlet letter. Branded me as the woman scorned.

Before I can take back my words, Breanna rounds on Aiden. "Is this some kind of joke to you? Or some kind of revenge date to make *her* jealous?" She yanks a thumb my way as her voice escalates. Heads across the room turn.

"It's just a coincidence, Breanna," Aiden says. His voice is low and soothing, butter melting over warm toast. But, I don't miss the muscle twitch in his jaw.

No longer enjoying yourself, are you, homeboy?

"As if this is a coincidence!" she squawks.

"Please stop shouting," he continues. "Courtney is just my neighbor. Not my ex-girlfriend—"

"You told me you liked me!"

"Shh!" an elderly, bespectacled man hisses from the next table.

Oh dear. This is getting out of hand. Time to reel this big ol' fish back into the boat. Stat.

"My apologies, sir. I—" I begin, but Breanna cuts me off.

"No! MY apologies!" She pushes her chair back from the table and stands up.

Aiden stands, too. Puts a gentle hand on her arm. "Breanna, please sit down," he says reasonably.

Does nothing fluster this guy?

Breanna glares at Aiden, and for a moment—just a fraction of a millisecond—I think she's going to acquiesce. Sit. Or, make an excuse to go to the bathroom, and let the situation dissipate.

Instead, the world abruptly tilts on its axis and launches us into a parallel reality.

I'm not exaggerating. Because what unfolds next is too good to be real. So good, I'll be mentally replaying this

9

moment for years to come. A veritable Prozac pill of a memory I can pop at any time to lift my spirits.

"My apologies for believing anything other than the rumors I've heard about you, Aiden Shaw!" Breanna shrieks as she yanks the elderly diner's plate of creme caramel from his table.

She reaches a hand into it, scoops up a huge chunk of the wobbly, pudding dessert, and lobs it RIGHT AT AIDEN'S FACE.

COURTNEY

Splat!

The creme caramel collides with Aiden's eye—our Breanna here has the arm of an MLB pitcher—and splatters tremendously in every direction. As if in slow motion, little droplets shower the surrounding diners.

And then, everything happens all at once.

A woman two tables over screams as she fishes a decorative cinnamon stick out of her hair. The old man whose pudding just turned into wearable art shouts for a manager. His wife begins to cry. An Instagram-model type who managed to narrowly avoid the custard shower is filming the entire scene with her phone. *Note to self: look her up on social media and ask for the footage later.*

"That's for using me as a pawn in whatever childish game this is," Breanna yells, then slams the plate back down on the elderly man's table. He jumps a mile, but Breanna doesn't care. She simply points at Aiden, lips curled in a malicious smile. "Your dessert's on him."

Touché, Breebree. I always appreciate a good pun.

Aiden stands stock still, mouth open, blinking in horror.

Like some kind of custard-covered, angry meerkat in a designer suit.

Somewhere in the far, deep and dark recesses of my mind, I know I should do something to diffuse the situation.

Sit the guests down. Get Aiden a cloth. Direct Breanna somewhere out of the way to cool off.

I know I should.

The long-suffering pianist (bless her) continues singing above the chaos—she's moved on to a heart-wrenching rendition of *Je Ne Regrette Rien*.

The song title means "I regret nothing." Which is ironic, because I know that, later, I'm absolutely going to regret what I'm about to do.

But I can't control it. I'm utterly powerless. I don't know whether I'm delirious from lack of sleep or just happy that, for once, Aiden is getting his comeuppance for being a womanizing so-and-so. But, the situation suddenly seems too funny. Way, way, way too funny.

The bubbling gurgle boils over in my stomach, rises up, and erupts from my mouth.

And I laugh.

Everyone stops shouting and starts staring. As Aiden turns to look at me, a glob of creme caramel slides off his cheek and spatters on the floor.

I laugh harder.

Then, my hands fly to my mouth, clamping down like a vice. But, the damage is well and truly done.

Aiden trains his glinting eyes on me. "Oh, think that's funny, do you?"

"Yes." I look at him defiantly.

It's a mistake. We hold eye contact for one moment. Two moments. Three. Four.... Everything else fades into the background. I'm vaguely aware of Philippe doing damage control—offering free wine, cool washcloths and lavish apologies to the patrons. Even Trainee Waitress is mopping the floor.

But, all I can see is Aiden's midnight blue gaze, zeroed in on me like a sniper rifle.

Time stands still as we stare at each other, a battle of wills that neither of us is prepared to lose. My skin flushes under his fiery glare and I grit my teeth. Steel myself. I will not crack, I will not crack, I will not—

"See! I knew it!" Breanna screeches, jolting me back to the present. Back to the chaos. "You're standing there, staring at her, when you should be apologizing to me! You —" What follows is a string of choice four-letter words and hand gestures that would sound like one big, long *beeeeeeeeeeeep!* on TV. If you catch my drift.

"S-sorry," I choke out breathlessly, tearing my eyes away from Aiden's and spinning to look at her.

"What are *you* sorry for?" Breanna curls her plump, pink top lip in a sneer. "You know what? You can have him. You two deserve each other!"

"We're not—" Aiden starts, calm as ever.

But, Breanna isn't in the mood. "Screw you, Aiden Shaw!" she shrieks, then makes for the door.

Aiden doesn't move to follow her. He keeps looking at me, blue daggers sending icicles across the room.

I shake my head at him. Turn around to look for a broom, a mop, anything to help the situation. But, before I can do a thing, Philippe appears at my side. He grabs me by the elbow. "You!"

As my boss frog-marches me to the kitchen, the gravity of the situation presses down on me. I inadvertently caused a food fight. In a three-Michelin-starred restaurant.

Merde.

Cold sweat pricks my forehead. "Philippe—"

He holds up a hand. "No."

13

I follow him into the kitchen, trying to ignore the stares of the chefs and pot washers. It's so quiet in the usually-bustling kitchen, you could hear a pin drop. My face floods with blood.

"Am I fired?" My voice comes out all croaky.

Philippe smoothes his silk tie. Closes his green eyes for a moment, and sighs.

"Darling girl," he says in a tone that suggests he thinks I am the exact opposite of a darling girl. "Is the Pope Catholic?"

I gather my things.

3

COURTNEY

I arrive home to find a pest on my front porch. Not a mouse, or a cockroach.

Much, much worse.

"You've got the wrong house," I snap as I walk up my driveway, shoving a wayward strand of hair out of my face.

It's mid-October, and the breeze carries the smell of crisp, fallen leaves. It would be a lovely night... if it weren't for the fact that I just got fired.

I blink fiercely as I walk, silently willing my tears to dry before I get close to Aiden. I smooth my hair and skirt, then jut out my lower lip and puff a breath upward to assist the tear-drying process. I'd rather strip naked and streak around the neighborhood than admit to Aiden that I've been crying. I never cry.

But, tonight was humiliating enough to spring up a well of hot tears. Not only did I embarrass myself in front of my colleagues, boss, and nemesis, but then, I spent an hour begging Philippe for my job back. Not even the shift manager job he's been dangling over me like a carrot for months, but my *hostessing* job. I groveled for the second time in one evening, and therefore broke my own promise to myself twice.

But, desperate times call for desperate measures. And I am Miss Desperation. Living at 1 Desperate Road, Desperationville, Georgia.

Unfortunately, Philippe was immune to my groveling. He stared at me sternly and said he had no choice. What kind of example would that set to the other staff? I tried to explain that it wasn't my fault. Convince him that Breanna was clinically insane and Aiden was a deranged stalker.

When that didn't work, I pulled the underhanded card and blinked big eyes up at him, claiming that, by firing me, he was depriving me of my livelihood, my hopes and my aspirations. I may have quoted Yeats at one point—*"Tread softly because you tread on my dreams"*—which might've been a tad dramatic.

But, what's the point in knowing poetry if you can't quote it once in a while?

Sadly, my soon-to-be-ex-boss responded to my impressive literary prowess by handing me my backpack and a portion of the evening's tips. Then, he showed me to the door. The back door.

Which meant that I had to climb over several stacks of leaky garbage bags in a dank alleyway to get to my vehicle. Gross.

And to top off the evening, Aiden is now leaning against my front door, blocking me from entering my own home.

As I get out my keys and jangle them in the hopes that the noise might scare him away like the mangy, stray cat he's currently impersonating, he smirks. "We've lived next to each other for years. I'm pretty sure I've got the right house, Corny."

I narrow my eyes, nostrils flaring. That particular nickname came from the three-year-old son of our mutual friends, Pete and Mia. But, while little Oliver can call me "Corny" anytime he wants, Aiden can most definitely *not*. When he first overheard Ollie's unfortunate mispronunciation, you should have seen his face—lit up with sadistic glee.

He's called me "Corny" ever since. Which is a tad maddening.

Even more maddening, I can't help but notice how Aiden is now pudding-free and freshly showered—his dark hair is even still a little damp. He's changed into athletic shorts and a stupid too-small white t-shirt that shows off too much of his stupid, too-big tan biceps. Double gross.

Okay, fine. Not gross at all. In reality, his t-shirt fits really nicely and his biceps look very... ideally bicepy. A good size for a man's bicep. But, Aiden is the enemy, so he and his well-sized biceps are not ogle-worthy. Ever.

"Excuse me," I say, crossing my own bicep-less spaghetti arms over my chest.

"You aren't excused," he smirks.

"You're trespassing on private property."

"On the contrary, I'm just paying my *neighbor* a *neighborly* visit. Seeing as we apparently don't know each other, I thought it might be time."

"Oh boy, lucky me." I bunch my fists and do a little mock-cheer, *Bring It On* style. *I said brrrr it's cold in here!* Then, I smile a perfectly angelic smile up at him. "So, did you bring me some dessert?"

His expression remains neutral, but in the flicker of the streetlight, I see a shadow cross his expression.

Feeling a flash of delicious victory, I smile even more sweetly, rubbing salt in the wound. "No? None left?"

Sure, it's a bit of a low blow, and I'm not usually a mean person, I promise. But, Aiden deserves it. He got me fired, remember?

Unfortunately, Aiden doesn't seem put out by my

attempt at a crushing remark. Instead, he grins right back, showing a full set of gleaming white teeth. *All the better to eat you with.* "Brought your mail. You'll find my dry cleaning bill enclosed."

He shoves a handful of letters my way and I cross my arms behind my back, staring at the papers pointedly. "How thoughtful. But again, wrong house."

"Oh!" Like the fabulous actor he is, he feigns confusion. "So, a Miss Courtney..." He squints at the top letter with fake concentration. "*Martha* Turner doesn't live here?"

"She does. But she wasn't the one throwing pudding around. That would have been your date. Remember her? Or has she already become a nameless, faceless addition to the Ghosts of Aiden's Girlfriends Past collection?"

Aiden's mouth twists into a smirk. He has such full, soft-looking lips. What a shame those good looks were wasted on him. "If you want a spot in the collection so bad, you just have to ask, Corny."

I take a deep breath. *In, then out, Courtney. Focus on not punching him in his stupid pretty face. Assault charges are the last thing you need right now.*

"I wouldn't go on a date with you if you were the last man on earth. I'd rather eat a slug. In fact, I'd rather get a tattoo of a slug on my forehead. While eating a slug. And sitting in a bathtub of, er..."

Aiden cocks a dark brow. "Slugs?"

"No." I shoot him a death glare. "I was *going* to say eels. Electric eels."

"No, you weren't."

"Ugh, just get out of my way, slugboy!"

"Now, why would I do that?" Aiden says thoughtfully, tapping his chin. His navy eyes are fixed on me, and my stomach lurches as his gaze prickles my skin.

Ever notice how romance novel heroines always

compare blue eyes to water? How they make grand statements about drowning in a man's ocean eyes? I've never understood this. "Eyes you could drown in" should describe your mortal enemy's gaze, not your potential lover's.

Aiden's eyes look very drownable right now. Raging with riptides to pull you under and dash you against the rocks repeatedly until you bleed and die. Savage, unrelenting and turbulent.

I intend to stay safe and dry on shore, thank you very much. Maybe put up a few "Danger! No Swimming Under Any Circumstances!" signs for good measure.

"Aiden." I rub my temples and close my eyes so I can avoid his gaze for a few moments. I feel a splitting headache coming on, and I need a glass of wine. Just one. And right now, my path to my sauv blanc is being rudely interrupted by over six feet of brawny man behaving like a toddler having a tantrum. "As much as I appreciate you dropping by to torture me, I do not have the mental capacity for this conversation right now. It's not my fault that your date thought I was your ex. You were the one who took her to the restaurant I worked at. You were the one who said you knew me."

"First off, I had no idea you work there. Secondly, I do know you, you lunatic. You've been my neighbor and self-proclaimed nemesis for, like, four years." He leans backwards, rests his broad shoulders against my front door, then adds the word "unfortunately" under his breath.

"Well, you didn't have to tell Briella that," I counter.

"Bre-*anna*."

"Bless you."

Aiden opens his mouth, then shuts it again. He runs a hand through his hair and tugs on the ends. Looks me up and down before shaking his head. When he finally speaks, it's in a tone that could only be described as frosty. "Why

19

did you say that I think nobody is good enough for me, Courtney?"

I blink, surprised by both his question and his use of my actual name. Of all the things that happened tonight, he's concerned about *that*?!

"Because you go through women like I go through towels. Use once, maybe twice, then grab a fresh one," I burst out. "You deserved what happened to you tonight. Frankly, I'm surprised that it didn't happen sooner."

"Is that what you think of me?" Aiden's voice is suddenly low and weighty, his handsome face creased in such a deep frown, I almost want to smooth it out with my fingertips.

But, I obviously don't, as feeling up your enemy's face in the middle of a stand-off is probably an ill-advised tactical move.

"Yup." I take a breath and fix him with a glare. *Don't let him get inside your head.* "And I'd be overjoyed if you and your exceedingly large head would move out of my way."

Aiden smiles suddenly, all traces of heaviness gone. It's the smile of a shark, luring you into his lair. "I'd suggest you ask me to move a bit more nicely. But as we don't know each other, it would be inappropriate for me to be doling out helpful advice. Right?"

I glower at him. Of course he has to go and turn my own words around on me.

I don't reply. He doesn't move. We're both frozen on my front porch, glaring daggers at each other in the darkness. I tilt my chin up as I hold his stare, which is so chilly it's Antarctic.

My daggers are sharper, buddy. I can go round two on a stare-athon. In fact, I can stare all night. Alllllll night long.

Unfortunately, I open my mouth to breathe, and at this

exact moment, an aphid flies right into it. I sputter and spit the bug out. Gross.

Aiden laughs like the big jerk he is, but thankfully, he steps out of my way.

"Here." He pauses on the top step, jostles the letters in my direction. "You know I'm not actually giving you a dry cleaning bill."

I do know. Franklin, our darling but increasingly senile mailman, is forever mixing up our houses and delivering us each other's mail. And, while I know the letters in Aiden's hand belong to me, I also don't want to take them. One, because I am a child. And two, because what if the letter I've been waiting for has arrived—on this night of all nights —and I actually have to read it with no idea of what I'm going to do next?

I pause for a beat too long, and Aiden raises a brow. "Your mail."

"Ah. Um. Yes." I take the stack gingerly, like I'm expecting the letters to be fresh-from-the-oven, casserole-dish hot.

"You're welcome."

"I'm not saying thank you until I double check that there isn't actually a dry cleaning bill in here."

I swear I see his lips twitch.

"Maybe it's an eviction notice," he says in this low, gravelly tone that makes my toes curl. *Not* in a good way.

"Or, maybe it's the planning permission for the thirty foot wall I applied to build between our houses so I never have to see you again." My smile is positively saccharine as I flip him the bird. "Thanks for stopping by. *Sweet* dreams."

Aiden rolls his eyes, then mimes being stabbed in the heart. "Ooof," he groans as he walks away. "How will I ever recover from that one?"

"I hope you don't," I call after him.

After the human house pest leaves, I let myself into the house. Slam the door behind me.

The second I'm inside and safely alone, I sink to the floor and rifle through the letters Aiden gave me. I've tried, many times, to explain to sweet Franklin the mailman that my house is number 32, Aiden's is number 34. But, he simply doesn't get it. Or understand how unnerving it is to have to exchange mail with the enemy on a biweekly basis.

I spot the telltale letterhead and my heart slams as I open the envelope.

"Dear Miss Turner. Please find enclosed your business license and an invoice…"

I drop the letter to the ground, waves of hot and cold traveling through my body. If I'd received this letter yesterday, or even earlier this afternoon, I would've been thrilled. But, as it stands, I'm now jobless and no longer a hopeful, soon-to-be shift manager with big (and attainable) dreams.

Which means that my business license—and the accompanying invoice—are pretty much just laughing in my face. I'll find another way, I'll have to. I'm used to taking care of myself at this point.

I press my lips together, determined, and sort through the rest of the letters, checking to see if Aiden really *did* put a dry cleaning bill in there. The man is literally that entitled —like the universe revolves around him, like it keeps spinning so he can wake up every morning and make people miserable with the fact that he's breathing.

My entire body is still buzzing with energy from our interaction. I've never met anyone else so insufferable. Ever. My blood is a million degrees and you could probably fry an egg on my face.

But, at least I stood my ground so he didn't have the

satisfaction of seeing me crack like said egg. There will be tap-dancing penguins colonizing the North Pole before that happens. Mark my words.

The frantic pitter-patter of overeager paws thump in rhythm with my rapid heartbeat, stirring me from my thoughts. Butch, Cassidy, and my new pup, Sundance, come running to greet me and the doggos jostle for my attention, jumping and licking and nuzzling.

I gather my babies in my arms, rubbing my cheeks into their soft fur and receiving their kisses gratefully. Cassidy and Butch are my pride-and-joy golden retrievers, and Sundance is the sweetest little dachshund you ever did see.

If nothing else, at least my animals love me. And I love them.

They are, after all, the reason that my dream is to build my Life is Ruff business empire—i.e. Rent a commercial space and expand my dog walking side-gig into a full-fledged, full-time doggy daycare business, complete with pet grooming and boarding options. My mission is to give all pets—no matter their health, abilities or appearance—the love and care they deserve.

I walk to the bathroom and the three of them follow. Wait patiently as I scrub off my makeup, braid my hair, change into PJ shorts and a baggy t-shirt. They're the only ones I let see me like this, and they still love me. Proving my theory that animals are superior to humans.

See, animals are simple. They depend on you to feed them and take care of them, and they love you unconditionally in return. Humans, on the other hand, are a minefield that you cross at your own risk.

In general, I'm not a risk taker. As the old saying goes, "prevention is better than cure."

Last thing I need is more meds around here. And, speaking of meds...

"Come on, boys!" I call. "Time for your shots."

Like the little troopers they are, Butch, Cassidy and Sundance line up in the kitchen as I open the fridge. They know the drill. One jab equals one bacon cruncher.

Easy math.

I poke all three of them and only Sundance, the littlest and least used to our routine, wriggles.

As soon as I put the needles away, I lean forward on the kitchen counter and cradle my head in my hands. I love my pups so much, and the thought that I might not be able to save the money for Life is Ruff? Well...

Cassidy presses against my legs. He's so attuned to my every mood, every emotion. It would be the sweetest thing in the world if it wasn't so sad that the being I'm closest to has four legs and terrible breath.

"What am I going to do?" I whisper as I scratch Cassidy's chin.

He looks at me solemnly and I crouch down so I can bury my head into his fluffy neck. Breathe in his sweet, doggy scent like the weird dog person I am.

After a few silent moments, I nod. "You're right, Cass."

Cassidy is always right, a veritable oracle of wisdom.

As much as I want to hide under a blanket and watch *Clueless* on repeat and cringe when Cher falls in love with her stepbrother (seriously, I have no idea how I can love a movie with a questionable plotline so much... probably young Paul Rudd. Sigh.) I need to get off my butt. Stop feeling sorry for myself, and make a list. Time to get back on top of everything that's pushed me down today. Girlboss style.

First, I am going to check my schedule for tomorrow and line up my dog walking clients. Dog walking is my day job, and I realized long ago that it's the perfect introductory step to opening Life is Ruff. My loyal clients will make for a built-in clientele when I expand.

Now that I've been let go from Petit Soleil, *sans* manager job, I'm roughly ten steps back on my plan to fund my dream. If I have to rely solely on my dog walking income, I'll need to go out and find more clients, and also ensure I provide top-notch service to keep up my good reputation.

Tomorrow, I have a rottweiler, a dalmatian, and a sweet mutt with wonky ears. I also have an introductory meeting with a big-wig potential client who has two sweet and fluffy bichon frises. If I can secure her business, it'll be a big step in the right direction.

Next, I will put on my big girl panties and scrounge up the money to pay the invoice. I have my business license now, for better or for worse.

And last, but certainly not least, Google will become my best friend as I search for a bakery in the area that's open late.

Because revenge can be oh-so-sweet.

4

AIDEN

"What the—?"

I cringe as my foot splatters into something soft, warm and sludgy. I close my eyes for a moment. Count to three.

Then, I look at what I've stepped in and sigh. Loudly.

It's too early for this. I haven't even had coffee yet.

Everyone who knows me knows that there are three things in life I truly love: my sister, my house, and my sneakers.

My sister is self-explanatory. I adore my friends and family, and I'm lucky to have both quality and quantity of each, but my little sister holds a special place in my heart. Special, in that she can manipulate me into doing just about anything she wants, and I let her. Maybe it's the protective big brother instinct, but I'd take a bullet for her without blinking.

My love of my house is a bit more complicated. I believe in prioritizing people over possessions, friendships over material things. But, I also grew up in a third floor walk-up with a shockingly friendly drug dealer downstairs and a bedroom window that looked out onto an alleyway often frequented by a particularly amorous homeless couple.

My parents used to say "love conquers all." And I love my family with all my heart, I really do. But, by the time I was eight or nine, I was also painfully aware that love didn't put milk in the fridge or shoes on my feet. Deep down, I think I love my house because of what it represents—that I have a good job, a stable income, and a roof over my head that doesn't smell like incense from the psychic down the hall.

And then, we have shoes.

The psychology buff in me thinks this is a byproduct of my scarce upbringing. But, in a more practical sense, I see shoes as an investment. I often spend my lunch breaks surfing StockX (it's like Wall Street for shoes), searching for rare pairs of kicks.

It's my nerdiest trait, and all my friends laugh at me. I know it makes me sound like the shallowest man on earth, but my shoe collection is my pride and joy. Everyone knows that.

Even my neighbor.

Which is precisely why I know that she's behind the chocolate cake—Devil's Food Cake, to be exact—that's now plastered all over my work shoes. Italian suede dress loafers. Ruined.

I swear quietly and step out of the sticky mess. The last thing I expected was to find an unreasonably huge sheet cake on my front porch in place of my doormat. Then, I spot the card.

Dessert's on me this morning. Nothing sweeter than getting to know your neighbor.

Despite myself, I snort with laughter.

Well played, Turner. Well played.

As I'm reading the note, Courtney Turner herself pops into view, walking her three dogs—two dopey, sweet golden retrievers and a tiny dachshund with a wicked underbite.

27

Both her pale hair and her square, white teeth glint in the tepid fall morning sunshine.

"Morning, neighbor!" she calls with a jaunty wave. "Beautiful day, isn't it?"

"It sure is!" I shout cheerily, shooting her my best *Mister Rogers' Neighborhood* smile. Despite what Courtney said last night, I *do* know her. Better than she thinks. Well enough to know exactly what's going to bother her the most right now.

And, juvenile as it is, bothering her is pretty high on my agenda right now.

I pick up the cake, which has a huge foot imprint in it. "Someone left me a delicious cake. I think it's from Amanda down the block. I always thought she had a crush on me."

Amanda Down The Block is not a real person. But, Courtney's one of those busybody types who knows everything and everyone, so this is going to bother her deeply.

I smile as I watch the frown line pucker between her eyes. *Gotcha.*

"Pity about your shoes, though. Looks like you need to watch your step in the future." She smiles again, more forced this time.

I look at my feet, shrug like I'm not in mourning. "Oh, these old things? They were on their way to the charity store anyway."

I'm lying. I bought these shoes two weeks ago, and I've worn them precisely twice.

"No, they weren't." Courtney's eyes gleam with mischief.

I raise my brows. "You've been paying attention to what I wear?"

"No." A blush blooms on her cheeks, petal pink at first, then deepening to a strawberry shade that makes me avert my eyes. I don't want to feel all warm and soft inside when I

28

look at Courtney, or think about how her blushing cheeks are the same red as her lips. She may be beautiful, but she's practically a domestic terrorist.

What I *do* want is to feel vengeful. About the fact that, in the last twelve hours, the woman has ruined my favorite suit, my new shoes, and what could have been a perfectly pleasant second date with Breanna.

Who she totally baited last night with that "no one's good enough for Aiden Shaw" spiel.

I grit my teeth. She doesn't need to know how much that stung.

"Well, I better go," I say as I open my front door. "Shoes to change, Amandas to thank. Maybe I'll take her on a date to Petit Soleil. I heard the food's good there. I've never managed to try it."

That particular sentence is a winner, and I'm rewarded with a spectacular scowl.

"BYE!" she yells, rather aggressively for 7am.

"Have a blessed day," I reply. Shoot her a flirty wink. Then, I close my door and clench my fists in a little victory cheer.

This morning's round belongs to me.

5

AIDEN

The first time I laid eyes on Courtney Turner, my first thought was "I'm going to marry that girl someday."

The thought came to me completely unbidden, out of the blue. I've never looked at anyone and thought anything like that before. Marriage was never something I wanted to pursue. I simply wasn't the settling-down, long-term-relationship type.

But, there she was, striding up her driveway, the wind whipping her pale hair around her face. Her long, slender fingers clutched the bottom of a cardboard box like she was holding onto it for dear life.

It wasn't just that she was beautiful—plenty of women are beautiful. It was something else. Something about the defiant tilt of her chin, her arrow-straight spine, her glimmering light eyes that were equal parts sharp and curious.

I wondered if she was the new owner—the house next door had been for sale for a while.

Without wasting a second, I grabbed a bottle of wine and made a beeline for her house. I wanted to give her a real Southern-hospitality welcome, let her know I was next door, should she ever need anything. If things went well, maybe we'd end up sharing the bottle. Get to know each other in a nice, neighborly fashion.

In the interest of being entirely clear, I would've gone over with a housewarming gift no matter who my new neighbor was, or what they looked like. My momma raised me right.

But, sharing wine with Courtney was not on the cards that day. Or any day, for that matter. What actually happened was as far from my fantasy as could be. And to this day, I have no idea why.

I'll admit that my game was off. Big time. Usually, I'm pretty smooth with women. Charming, some might say. But Courtney? She took my breath away. No makeup, sloppy sweatshirt and all. I've never met anyone who made my heart race like that on sight alone. And it didn't hurt that she wore a sweet pair of Jordan 1s.

But then, it all went wrong. Very wrong.

As I walked up her driveway, she gaped at me. Open-mouthed, like a trout. Then, she bit her lip and steeled me with the scariest look I've ever seen.

"Are *you* Aiden Shaw?" she demanded. Like my name was a four-letter word. When I said yes, I was Aiden Shaw —something I hadn't known until then could be considered an irredeemable flaw—she pursed her lips. "Well this would be just my luck."

And, if that wasn't enough, she proceeded to thrust the cardboard box into my arms before sauntering into her house without another word. Leaving me speechless and staring in her driveway. Holding a (very heavy) box of her things.

Then, she poked her head out the front door and called, "come on, then!"

Like she expected me to carry the box inside. I'm not

sure if it was shock or abject curiosity, but I obliged. Carried her box to her doorstep.

Instead of thanking me, she simply nodded. Then closed the door in my face.

That day, as I stood there, entirely stunned and wondering if she'd been raised in a barn by a pack of wild monkeys, I realized the chances of my marrying Courtney Turner were lower than a fur coat making it through a PETA rally unscathed.

And ever since, she's proven herself to be entirely maddening. A thorn in my side, a pain in my behind, a swollen, infected bee-sting kind of presence living next door. But, the funny thing is, despite how hard I try not to think about her, the woman lives in my head rent-free. Right next to the "Hide yo' kids, hide yo' wife" video.

So, the more she insists on hating me for no apparent reason, the more I delight in winding her up.

And that's how the neighbor war began.

A war consisting of four years of mail mix-ups and stealing each other's parking spots, of words slung back and forth over the garden fence, and insults (from her) met with shameless flirtations (from me) that leave us both red-faced and aggravated.

Until last night, though, I had no idea that she truly had such a scathing opinion of me. That she legitimately thinks I'm some loser womanizer who goes around hurting people for fun.

It's all I've been able to think about all morning.

"Morning, Mr. Shaw." Kayley, my assistant, sounds extra perky when I walk into the office. Her eyes are all blinky and wide. "Need help with those?"

"Nah, I'm good. And, please, call me Aiden. Mr. Shaw is my grandfather." I move my triple shot Americano into one hand so I can set down the tray I'm carrying. "Got your extra-hot, skim, no-foam, vanilla whatsit, and that mocha thingy that Patricia wanted. There's a tea in there for Steve, too, and I couldn't remember what Denise likes so I just got her a cappuccino."

"Thank you, um, Aiden. That's really nice of you."

"I wanted you all in top form for our strategy meeting at 10, and that sludge in the break room is undrinkable," I say brusquely. I like buying coffees for my team—they all work so hard—but I don't want to look soft, either. It's a balance.

"Absolutely." Kayley squints at me, her expression indecipherable. "You okay, Mr... uh, Aiden? You look tired. Late night?"

Gee, thanks, Miss I-party-all-night-and-still-come-to-work-fresh-faced-the-next-day.

Oh, to be twenty-three again.

"I'm just peachy," I reply.

Kayley raises her eyebrows. Bites her lip.

"What?" I say. Have I missed something?

"Aiden," Kayley says slowly. "I'm sorry if this is out of line, but I just have to say... I'm so happy for you. Looks like you've found the real deal."

"What?" I repeat as I step into my office. The offices here at Zone 6 Creative look like those fancy-schmancy glass houses in the TV show *Suits*. Concrete jungle views for miles, shimmering marble floors, good-looking receptionists lining the hallways... Great for feeling like you're part of something cool and important. Horrible if you don't want people seeing you bang your head on your desk when you have a bad day.

Kayley stands next to my desk and her expression changes. Her eyes widen, jaw slackens. Two bright red spots appear on her cheeks. "Oh, you don't... Oh! Um. You haven't been online this morning, have you?"

I shake my head, a little impatiently, and Kayley stutters as

33

she rattles off my schedule. "You have brunch with Gunder and Gunder at 11 at your usual table at Crepopolis, followed by a 2pm with the LA office." She shuffles her papers, the red marks on her cheeks deepening. "Oh, and Lorna also called an impromptu meeting at 9am in the boardroom. Then, this afternoon, if you have time, we can push your interview with—"

I hold up a hand. "Wait, back up. What did you say?"

Kayley frowns apologetically. "Is it Crepopolis? I have no idea why they keep booking meetings there. The place has all the atmosphere of a five-year-old's birthday party."

"Before that."

"9am with Lorna in the boardroom?"

Oh no. Not today, of all days.

Lorna Strummings is my new boss. Flew in three months ago from the LA office. Acts like she's been here for years. And, she happens to be my only hope for the promotion I've been working towards for the past two years. The one that would give me a bigger paycheck, a bigger office, and a cross-country move to our offices on the west coast.

Not to mention a once-in-a-lifetime chance to be Zone 6's Head of Photography.

It's a career-changing opportunity. The position I've been gunning for. And, a chance to *finally* do what I love.

I've put in the time and effort, I should have it in the bag.

I was expecting her to pull me aside at some stage; I was just hoping that it wouldn't be on a Friday morning that I'm annoyed, grumpy, and smelling vaguely like chocolate cake. Although, actually, that last one could work in my favor.

Note to self: find out if Lorna has a sweet tooth.

"Any way we can reschedule that?"

Kayley shakes her head, her dark curls bouncing around her face. "Sorry, boss. She requested you..." she lowers her voice to a conspiratorial whisper, even though there's nobody else around. *"Personally."*

Not my lucky day. "Okay, Kayley. Thanks."

Kayley's almost at the office door when she pauses. "Hey, Aiden?"

I look over my shoulder. "Yeah?"

"Um..." Kayley smiles sympathetically. "You might want to take a look online before your meeting with Lorna. Maybe check your social media."

I frown. As far as I know, Lorna and I will be talking about my potential promotion and move to LA. Not social media.

Unless one of my clients posted an offbeat meme that rubbed a few people the wrong way. Nothing I can't handle. Likely just a storm in a teacup, and if I've learned anything, it's that these storms blow over. Damage control can always be done.

Kayley's fresh out of college, the generation where social media is life. Meanwhile, I'm thirty-two going on fifty. Or, that's what it sometimes feels like around here. I loathe social media, but tolerate it for my job. All so that, one day, I can be Head of Photography. Make some *real* changes at Zone 6.

I nod at Kayley, then add another "thank you" for good measure. Manners don't cost a thing.

Once the door closes, I flop down at my desk and reach for my office phone. Speed dial line one.

"Jesssssss," I moan into the phone as I swing my feet onto my desk and reach for the Rubik's Cube I keep tucked away in my top drawer.

"I was wondering when you'd call." I hear the smile in my little sister's voice. "Late night with... Brenda?"

"Breanna."

"Oh. Yeah. Wait, didn't you date a Brenda at some point? I lose track."

"Her name was Belinda. We went on one date last year."

"Ah, Belinda. With the fake, ahem..."

"Breasts," I say. Jess makes a weird fish-bubble sound, which makes me laugh. "They're called breasts, Jess. You can say the word. They're just a body part."

"I don't want to think about body parts and my brother in the same sentence, thank you very much."

"Fair." I toss my Rubik's Cube in the air and catch it one-handed. "But, for what it's worth, I didn't know they were fake."

"Oh, please, if *I* worked it out after two seconds of scrolling her Instagram, there's no way you didn't know."

Since marrying my best friend Conor after a whirlwind romance last year, Jess has certainly found her self-confidence. Which includes smack talking her big brother. And, while I love them together—they're great for each other, and they're the happiest I've ever seen them—I agree that certain things should not be discussed with your flesh and blood.

And, one thing I definitely *don't* discuss with Jess are the ins and outs of my dating life. Including the fact that I legitimately had no idea of the implant status of Belinda's chest because we went on one blind date that ended right after dinner, when I discovered that we didn't have a single thing in common.

"Soooooooooooo," Jess says, and I shift the phone to my other ear. Prop it against my shoulder so I can move my hands around the cube. Step 1: Create a daisy. Yellow square in the middle, with four white squares making a cross around it. "You seem calm. Surprisingly so. Are we gonna talk about what happened?"

"Whatever Courtney told you, I'm sure I wasn't as horrible as she makes me out to be in her skewed version of reality."

"I think Courtney's in shock, to be honest."

"What did she say?" I demand. Step 2: Create a white cross on one face, with two matched edges on each side flanking the cross. Orange, red, green, blue. Orderly and simple.

"Well, the video spoke for itself, to be honest."

I pause, hands frozen on the cube. "Video?"

As if on cue, two interns walk past, open-mouthed and staring. They frantically whisper to each other, and a cold, clammy sensation begins to creep over my skin.

"Wait... you haven't seen it?" Jess's voice is a curious tightrope walk of attempted sympathy mixed with desperately-trying-not-to-laugh.

"What video, J?" I repeat, my voice rising. I reach for my cell phone. On principle, I don't look at my phone until I get to the office, because the second I look, I'm usually sucked into work. Such is the life of brand management.

"Don't freak out," my sister begins.

"That's what people always say when the person they're talking to has every reason to freak out." I drop the Rubik's Cube and hold my thumb over my phone screen so it unlocks.

Wait...

2000 Facebook friend requests?

5000 Twitter notifications?

10,000 new Instagram followers? I don't even post on my personal Instagram. I literally only got it so my mom would shut up about not being able to tag me on "inspirational quotes."

"Before I look... Do you want to tell me what's happening?"

"It might be better for you to see for yourself."

I open Instagram gingerly. All of the notifications are related to a video I'm tagged in.

I click on it. And my stomach plummets like I'm on a rollercoaster that's hurtling towards the ground at one hundred miles per hour.

"What the flux is this?" I practically yell.

"Don't swear," Jess chides.

"I said flux."

"No, you didn't."

She's right. I didn't.

"Sorry, J." I sigh. Rub my eyes. Switch the phone to my other ear. Squint at my phone screen again, like I'm hoping I saw wrong the first time.

Sadly not. There it is, for all the world to see: Breanna screaming at me at the top of her lungs. The dessert hitting me square in the face. Diners around me exploding in uproar. Then, Courtney staring me down, locking me in the world's most intense staring contest.

Common denominator? Me.

This video makes me look like a Grade-A douchebag. Exactly like the kind of man Courtney was accusing me of being last night.

My chest suddenly feels tight. "It's just... this is unbelievable."

"If it helps, the hashtag #TeamAiden is trending?"

"It does not." Agitated, I set my phone down and pick up the cube. Focus on that, on something logical, that makes sense. Step 3: Solve the white corners. Easy. Find a corner piece with a white tile on your bottom layer and...

"Aiden?"

I snap to attention. "Huh?"

"Did you hear what I said?"

"Sorry, no."

"I said that Courtney got fired because of this."

I'm suddenly paying attention. Why didn't Jess lead with that piece of information? "What?"

"Petit Soleil said it was too much of a scandal. They let her go."

I cringe at the memory of turning up on Courtney's doorstep last night—pride mortally wounded from being publicly humiliated—and asking her to pay for my dry cleaning. Which was obviously just a move to wind her up. But still, she'd just been fired. "Is she... okay?"

"She's horrified about the video," Jess says slowly. "But, about being fired, she sounded delighted, to be honest. Said seeing your face was worth it and she's never been happier to have an excuse to get out of her job. I'm invited to her place for a Re-Fire-Ment Party tonight. Virgin pina coladas all round."

I picture Jess resting her hand tenderly on her blooming, ever-growing belly as she chuckles at her best friend's shenanigans. I don't join in. Something is bothering me. A picture I can't get out of my mind.

Courtney's eyes were red-rimmed and raw when she got out of her car last night. At the time, I thought she was just angry that I was on her doorstep—it's not like the woman is rational when it comes to me. But, was it possible that she was upset because she got fired?

Unease gathers in my stomach, but I shake it away. Surely, that can't be it—why would she lie to Jess? As far as I can tell, those two tell each other everything. If she told Jess she's fine, she's fine.

I glance at the clock, apprehension eating at my insides. "I'd better go. Meeting in a few. Have fun at your weird party tonight."

"Love you," Jess singsongs. "I'll send Conor over to your place while I'm at Courtney's."

"Works for me," I say. It'll be nice to have a distraction tonight. My place feels strangely empty since Conor, then Jess, moved out. "Love you too, J."

I hang up, pushing Courtney's teary eyes to the back of my mind. She wouldn't lie to Jess, I must've been imagining that she was upset. Trick of the light or something.

Plus, I have other things to think about.

Like the fact that I have a meeting with Lorna in a few minutes, and there's no way that she hasn't seen this video.

6

AIDEN

"Sit."

I sink into the plush chair facing Lorna Strumming's behemoth plexiglass desk, making sure to clench my hands so I don't fidget. Nobody likes a fidgeter in an important meeting.

Lorna snaps her sharp-taloned fingers and her assistant comes running with a glass bottle of water and two crystal glasses. She fixes the bespectacled kid with a look that could wither a healthily blossoming flower. "You can go now."

"Yes, ma'am." The boy legs it from the room and I wish I could follow him. I squirm in my chair, feeling less like a thirty-two-year-old man with a successful career, a four-teenth floor corner office, and a great pair of leather Prada shoes (which replaced my loafers—RIP), and more like an acne-ridden teenager who's in trouble with the school principal.

"Aiden, Aiden, Aiden." Lorna taps her fingers together as she studies me. She's a beautiful woman... in a fierce, don't-mess-with-me way. And though she terrifies me, I also admire her.

"How's your morning?" I ask, deliberately obtuse as I

study a photo of two fluffy white dogs on Lorna's wall. Anything to avoid looking directly at her. Kinda like you do with Medusa.

"Let's cut to the chase. I have precisely eleven minutes for this meeting, so no time for sweet talk."

"Okay." I reluctantly swivel my eyes to meet hers. The moment of truth.

"Here's the scoop," Lorna continues, her frosted pink lips pressed in a thin line.

The *scoop*? What is it with all these companies trying so hard to be down with the lingo? Lorna's got to be in her late fifties. Although I'll never know that for sure, because I will never, ever ask. I kind of like having all my appendages.

She sighs. "You know I love your work..."

I blink. The words sound like what I want to hear, but her expression doesn't match the good news. Not one bit. "But?"

Lorna smiles, sharklike. "You're quick, my boy. I like that about you." She crosses her arms. "There is a 'but'. You know I wanted to give you this promotion, but your little viral video has fixed me with a raging headache this morning."

My heart slams. "I'm sorry about that, it wasn't—"

"Forget 'sorry.' I don't give a hoot what you do in your personal time. Be a naked gardener or take up competitive duck herding for all I care." Lorna waves a veiny hand and her bangles jingle on her thin wrist. "But, unfortunately for you, this specific video sensation has come at precisely the wrong time."

I cock an eyebrow, my stomach twisting into a slow, painful knot.

Lorna settles back into her chair, steepling her fingers. "For months now, Zone 6 has been working on signing Ever After Resorts for a full rebrand. You know Ever After?"

Know Ever After? Of course I *know* Ever After—I've been studying their conglomeration for months. They're a big fish, a huge opportunity for our company. If I get the project—and do well with it—I'm pretty much a shoo-in for the promotion. I shift in my seat, determined to play it cool and collected. "I've done my research."

"Well, I originally recommended you to spearhead the project, and until last night, they were *this* close to signing." She pinches her thumb and forefinger together. Then, she sighs. "Their whole image is about couples in love. Honeymoons. Babymoons. Second honeymoons. And... Sex! Lots of sex. But in a clean, wholesome, couples-who-love-each-other-and-want-to-reconnect kind of way. That's their target market."

She stands and begins pacing around the room. I couldn't move even if I wanted to. I want the account, of course. Badly. But I never imagined, when Jess told me about the stupid video, that it might affect my work this way.

"Look, Aiden, can I be straight with you? Ever After's biggest demand is that they work with a representative who is *in* their target market. A man who's committed to his wife, his family. Someone like..."

Don't say it, Lorna!

"Winston."

She had to go and say it.

"Are you trying to tell me," I say, my voice a lot calmer than I feel. "That Winston Ricker might get to handle the biggest account that has ever crossed our desks because he has a WIFE?"

There's nothing wrong with Winston Ricker. He's perfectly nice. Polite guy. But... Bland, boring, flavorless. If Winston was a cereal, he'd be Raisin Bran. With room temperature milk and extra raisins. Raisins are the devil's food—why take a perfectly good grape and turn it into a withered monstrosity?

I promise I'm not being bitter. I earned this. Winston has worked here two years less than me and nowhere near as hard. Plus, the guy has a days-of-the-week calendar on his desk with facts about shrubs on it. Every day, a new shrub fact.

For 365 days.

See, Raisin Bran Man.

Lorna places her hands on the desk. "I'm saying that Winston gives off the right image."

"What's that?" I burst out incredulously. "Incredibly dull and boring?"

I know I'm being petty. But the idea that I give off the "wrong image" for a resort company bristles me. Everyone from my boss to my dinner date to my next door neighbor seems to think that I'm this playboy lothario character determined to steal women's virtue and never call again. I can't even imagine what the peanut gallery on the internet is saying.

And it all couldn't be further from the truth.

Maybe that's why Courtney's cutting comment last night stung so bad.

I've never been in love, but I gave up anything close to that playboy lifestyle awhile ago. I'm not proud of my past, and I've taken a huge step back from all of that, refrained from anything physical while casually dating.

And sure, endless first dates are unfulfilling, but it's the safest option for me. No feelings, no physical or emotional connections, no one gets hurt. The last thing I want is to hurt someone because I happen to be stunted in the ability-to-have-a-loving-relationship department.

But, how on earth do I explain that to Lorna?

"Aiden, dearest." Lorna sighs dramatically. "It's important here at Zone 6 that we make our clients feel like they're one of our own. Like family."

"I get that."

"From what I can see, you have no meaningful relationships or connections in your life right now. Nothing that can relate to..."

Lorna goes on and on about my relationship status (there's a conversation I never thought I'd be having with my boss) and it's like I'm watching my promotion, my dream job, my move to LA slip through my fingers. The dream I've worked so hard for, getting away from me.

I can't let it happen. I'll do literally anything.

"I have a girlfriend!"

The words echo around the room, loudly, and complete silence follows. That's when I realize that the words were mine.

Oh no. Where did that come from? As of last night, I have absolutely nothing even remotely close to a girlfriend.

Lorna's frosty lips pull upward. "Well. This is news to me."

News to you and me both.

"Since when?"

Think fast, Aiden. Think fast!

"It's new... And old." I scramble desperately, trying to classify Breanna. "She was my girlfriend, and will be again. Very soon. I'm going to win her back. Do everything I can to make things right."

Lorna's eyebrows just about fly off her forehead. "The girl from the video?"

"Yeah. She's, um, very family-oriented. Wants to settle down as soon as possible, yada yada yada. Domestic bliss and all that." *Oh, would you put a pin in it, Aiden! You're making it worse.* "I just... love... her."

As my mouth motors on like a reliable old Honda that

just won't quit, it occurs to me that one tiny little white lie can't hurt anyone, right? Technically, I did have a girlfriend, of sorts, until last night... And I may not have loved her, but I kind of liked her. A bit. So there's that?

"Love." Lorna sighs. "I love love. It's a great look."

Despite my internal panic, I stifle a laugh. Only Lorna Strummings would love love because it makes her more successful.

"Yup. Great to be in love. So, yeah. Winston and I have something in common, I guess."

Lorna's smile stretches and I get the sudden feeling that she'd actually *prefer* to give this account to me. Is she not totally sold on Raisin Bran Man, then?

"The internet's not wrong, you know. Your chemistry was palpable."

I lean back in my chair and tilt my head to the side so my neck cracks. "It was?"

"Sizzling, my boy. I thought it was merely a trifling attraction. But, if you say it's love, I say Godspeed. Oh, and also, dinner. Next week."

I frown. "Pardon?"

Lorna crosses her legs at the ankle, showing off her mile-high stilettos. I've never understood stilettos. Give me a girl in sneakers any day.

"Dinner, next—" Lorna squints at her computer screen, already distracted by her next order of business. "Tuesday night."

My heart races. "Does that mean you're giving me the Ever After account?"

"It *means* that we are taking Ever After's founders out for dinner. I arranged a little schmoozefest on the company dime the second your video started making the rounds. Damage control. Partners are invited, and the invitation is now extended to you and your plus one," Lorna explains impatiently, like I should have magically understood all of this without context.

Oh no. Oh no, oh no.

Breanna and me? Dinner together? My mind whirs through a mental rolodex of ways I can apologize to her.

"Oh." It's all I can say.

Lorna raises her pencilled eyebrows. "Winston and his wife have confirmed."

Dammit, Winston!

At that moment, a realization settles over me like a cartoon storm cloud swirling around my head.

Lorna didn't call me in here this morning to review the Ever After account, or to talk about the video. She called me to tell me that she'd given the account to Winston—she'd already made her decision, invited Winston to start working on the account.

And my *harmless* little white lie was the one thing that made her backtrack.

Suddenly, my lie feels more like a mountain than a molehill. What was I thinking? And how in the heck am I going to convince Breanna to go out with me again. Not only that, but convince her to pretend to be *in love* with me?

My palms sweat, and I wipe them on my suit pants. Gross. I wish I had my Rubik's Cube. Something that follows a pattern, an unbreakable order.

Step 4: Solve the middle layer by lining up three squares in a row of the same color...

"She sometimes works night shifts," I begin stupidly, a lead weight settling in the pit of my stomach.

Lorna leans forward. The look on her face is not one I want to mess with. "Well, between you and me, Aiden... I'd make sure you win her back. And have her get that Tuesday off."

I gulp. "Noted."

"Good." Lorna's smile glimmers in the morning sunshine. I offer a grimace-like smile in return.

Liar! my brain yells at me. I tell it to shut up.

I'll figure this out. It's just a blip. Nothing I can't get through.

I manage people's images as a profession. Surely, I can get my own in order for a single night.

Right?

7

COURTNEY

Liar, liar. Why have my pants not caught fire yet?!

"Cheers!" I smile broadly, clinking my oversized tiki mug with Jess's. Both cups are full of white, slushy liquid. Virgin pina colada for Jess, and a sugar-free version for me. She takes a sip and I down a big gulp for a placebo effect of courage.

She squints at me through her thick-rimmed glasses. "You sure you're okay, Courtney?"

"Never better," I say for probably the fifteenth time in the past hour. "What do I care about a stupid viral video? I'm already fired, nothing worse can happen."

Famous last words, Court.

"I've decided that this is all a sign from the universe." I wave my hand, smile wider than ever. "It's time to focus on Life is Ruff now."

Oh, who am I kidding? Any idiot could tell that I'm trying my best to convince everyone— including myself— that getting fired was a good thing. But thankfully, Jess, who is usually sharp as a tack, has wicked pregnancy brain and doesn't seem to pick up on my desperation.

"That's awesome." She grins. "I'm happy you finally get a chance to pursue your dreams."

Yup. Every little girl dreams of growing up to be thirty, single, and fired from a freaking restaurant job.

After assessing my finances last night, I solemnly came to the conclusion that, without the income from Petit Soleil, throwing my weight behind expanding Life is Ruff is too much of a risk right now. I need to keep walking dogs in the meantime, make some more money. My next big goal is to have enough saved to pay the deposit, and cover rent for a few months on a commercial space. That way, I can go all-in. No half-attempts.

"Yup, can't wait!" I chirp, then take a big gulp of pina colada. Shudder as the revolting aspartame-tinged mixture runs down my throat. I wish there was rum in it to create a nice haze around the edge of this situation.

No such luck, though. As much as I enjoy my occasional glass of sauv blanc, I usually limit myself to a glass of wine per week. I've found that it's more difficult to keep my blood sugar stable when I drink.

I need the clearest head possible, anyway. My potential client with the two bichon frises is dropping by in an hour and I have to make a solid first impression. I did some research on her, know that she's a VP of some fancy-schmancy company out of LA. If I can secure her business, that would be huge for me.

She mentioned her work schedule is insanely busy, and that she found me because one of her dogs needs extra care and meds during the day—which I can do. Her pups are her babies (I relate to this), so if we get along, maybe the sting of losing Petit Soleil won't be quite so bad.

Let's just hope that she doesn't recognize me as the insane girl from one of the internet's most viral videos of the moment. I've refused to watch the video—or read any of the comments or discussion forums—but Jess informed me that it was, indeed, posted by an influencer who happened to be dining at Petit Soleil during Puddinggate.

I don't want to think about what all the internet trolls are saying about me. I bet they've pegged me as the bad guy, and beautiful Breanna as the heroine of the story. I wonder what they're saying about Aiden.

Actually, scratch that. I don't care what they're saying about Aiden, because I don't want to think about Aiden. Or the shiver that creeps down my spine when I think of his unwavering stare.

I'm sure he'll get out of this viral video thing completely unscathed. People will swoon over him, women will DM him offering to lick pudding off him, and...

Ew. Reel it in, brain. That's the last image I want in my head, ever.

The point is, men like Aiden? They float through life taking everything they want and desire. Not caring about anyone but themselves.

I knew it from the first time I ever saw him.

It was the day I moved into my house. He strode up my driveway with a bottle of (very fine) wine, confident as could be. Meanwhile, I did a legit double take to see if I was hallucinating.

When he introduced himself, his deep, rich voice sent shivers through me. I already knew my new neighbor's name was Aiden Shaw. I had a ton of his mail.

But, I wasn't prepared for Aiden Shaw to be the best-looking specimen of a man I'd ever laid eyes on.

I couldn't help but stare. Then, I realized that he was staring at me too. I had no makeup on, my hair was a frizzy mess, and my clothes were stained and covered with enough dog hair to qualify me as a poodle.

I imagine he was staring in utter disgust. Regretted

coming over, now that he could see me up close, all my flaws on display.

So, I panicked. Shoved a box of my things in his hands. No idea why—my reflexes apparently hate me.

Then, the cherry on the crap sundae that was our awkward, embarrassing introduction came when some drop-dead-gorgeous woman showed up. She pulled up out front, wearing a sexy cut-out dress I could never wear, and I watched as a hurt, angry expression darkened her flawless face as she stared at Aiden.

Who was in my driveway. With wine.

As the gorgeous woman drove away in disgust, unseen by my new neighbor, I knew *exactly* who Aiden Shaw was. The kind of guy who hits on one woman while getting ready for a date with another.

A player. Shallow as a puddle. The type of man who dated woman after woman, leaving a trail of bleeding hearts behind that charming smile of his. So I closed my front door on him and never looked back.

Now, his serial dating ways are internet-famous. And I've been dragged into the mess. I'm fervently crossing my fingers for a celebrity cheating scandal so some of the hype around the video dies down and I can go online again.

Simple.

"Enough about me," I tell Jess. "I want to hear more frightening tales about being a Human Incubator."

Jess laughs at my nickname for her and wraps her hands lovingly around her belly. Pregnancy looks great on her, and despite my jokes, I have no doubt that she'll make the most incredible mom.

For the next thirty minutes, we sit on my snuggly old couch while I quiz her about birthing plans, raspberry leaf tea, and baby foot monitors that tell you if your newborn's heart is beating. I may have done some Googling before she got here, but the longer I keep the conversation off me and my situation, the better.

It's not that I don't trust Jess—I'd trust her with anything. It's just that I know she'd insist on helping me, insist on loaning me money for a deposit on a commercial space, or giving me paid work with her and Conor's company. And I can't accept that.

First, because she's about to become a mother—she has more important things to spend money on. Like bottle heaters and butt rash cream (for the baby, not for her). Plus, I'm used to being independent, and doing things for myself. I've never even had a proper boyfriend. It's just been my dogs and me, and I'm fine that way, thank you very much.

At one point, Cassidy lumbers over and crawls into my lap. Well, tries to. Eighty-pound lap dogs have a difficult time getting what they want in life.

Cassidy is my favorite fur baby. I know I'm not meant to have favorites, but Sundance pees on the rug, and Butch is so obsessed with food that he'd probably trade me to a pack of hungry wolves for a single piece of kibble.

Typical man.

Ding, dong!

As soon as the doorbell goes, the dogs break into a cacophony of barking and wailing.

"Conor." Jess's eyes go gooey like melted toffee as she says her husband's name. I try not to barf. They're so in love, it's disgusting.

"Don't get up," I say as Jess attempts to hoist herself off the couch. "It could also be my client. Shhh, Butch! Can it!"

I fling open the front door.

Then, I shut it again.

Ding, dong! Ding, dong!

So rude.

I sigh. Re-open the door.

"What? I told you I'm not paying your dry cleaning bill."

Aiden shifts from foot to foot. "I'm not here about that."

His cheeks are pink, his hair slightly mussed. He's dressed in another crisp, white, bicep-showing tee, athletic shorts and a pair of designer sneakers. A baseball cap sits backwards on his dark hair, and five o'clock shadow frames his jaw. There's a glow to his tanned skin like he just finished a workout. And yet, he looks fresh. The opposite of me. When I jog, I look like a swamp monster. Ugh.

"I just thought... well, I wanted to come by to—" he exhales through his teeth, exasperated, and tugs on a piece of his hair that pokes out from under the cap. "You doing okay? This whole video thing is kind of nuts."

"I'm fine," I retort coldly. We're not on the same team, and I'm not going to pretend for a second that we are. "As if you care."

"I do, actually."

Yeah, right. I'm about to tell him where to shove it when Cassidy throws himself against Aiden's legs with such force it would have knocked most people over. Aiden, annoyingly, is not most people.

Cass whimpers, then drops to the ground, exposing his belly. Traitorous little so-and-so!

Aiden shoots me the world's smuggest grin, then bends to stroke Cass's tummy. His big, tan hands move over the dog's fur confidently, like they've been best friends their whole lives.

"Good boy!" he practically coos. The dog's head rolls back in bliss, tongue lolling out of the side of his grinning mouth.

I jerk my eyes away. The two of them look like a glossy billboard for Purina Puppy Chow, and I'M NOT BUYING IT. In fact, I'm switching to no-name, generic dog food permanently.

I may also have to rethink who my favorite pet is.

Jess's husband, Conor, appears behind Aiden, jangling his truck keys. Like Aiden, he's dressed in casual athletic-wear. "Hey, Court." He steps over the Aiden and Cass love-fest and kisses my cheek. "Sorry I'm gross, we just got back from the batting cages."

"No grosser than usual," I tease as I give my best friend's hubby—who's a wonderful, teddy bear of a human —a hug, then wave him inside. "She's in the living room. May need help getting up."

"Thanks." Conor laughs richly. He shoots Aiden a look, then gives him an exaggerated wink and air-nudge. "Good luck."

"Go fall off a bridge," Aiden mutters. Conor grins, then heads inside.

Weird. What was all that about?

I turn my attention back to Aiden, purposely blocking his entrance. *You shall not pass!* "You here to see Jess, too?"

He looks up, eyes sharp. My nerves stand on end as our gazes meet. "No. I'm here to see you."

"What?" I suddenly feel super self-conscious and don't know what to do with my hands. So, I scoop up Sundance, who's trotting around in circles at our feet. The pup squirms and I cuddle him until he settles down. A smattering of auburn hairs clump on my pristine black blouse.

Oh, well. I'll just add laundry to my ever growing to-do list.

"I'm here to see you," Aiden repeats, slower and louder.

"I'm not deaf," I snap.

"Could've fooled me," he says under his breath with a

half-smile. Like I'm some kind of personal amusement that's been booked for him.

"I heard that."

"Listen, Courtney..." He stops petting Cassidy and stands, the smile leaving his face. Twists his baseball cap to face forwards. Pauses. Twists it backwards again.

I clench my fists to avoid yanking the thing off his head and flinging it into the bushes. Men shouldn't be allowed to wear backwards baseball caps. There's no reason why a ball cap and a white t-shirt should be as sexy as—if not more sexy than—a well-cut suit on a man.

Cassidy whines and leans against Aiden's legs, but Aiden keeps those midnight eyes trained on me. "I'm here because I need you to do me a favor. Um... please."

I blink, waiting for the punchline. When it doesn't come, I laugh. Hard.

Aiden does not.

"Excuse me?" I choke.

"I thought you said you weren't deaf."

"You're not making me any more eager to participate in this favor of yours."

Aiden runs a hand over the stubble on his chin, momentarily placated. "Sorry. I didn't mean to get off on the wrong foot here."

"Bit late for that."

"Court." His expression becomes pleading, and I steel myself so my resolve doesn't melt like butter on a stack of pancakes. He wants something, and he's using those ridiculous puppy dog eyes that he charms so many girls with. But, I'm not most girls, and I'm not falling for it.

"All right." I sigh. "Let's get this over with. What do you want?"

"Iwashopingyou'dtalktoBreannaforme."

I blink. Screw up my face. "Sorry? I may actually be going deaf, because I didn't get that."

"Iwashopingyou'dhaveawordwithBreanna."

"You want me to make you a smoothie with banana?" I smile, enjoying myself. "I don't have any bananas, but I do have some pina colada mix."

Aiden's eyes narrow. "I know you heard what I said." He blows out a frustrated breath. "Believe me, I wouldn't be coming to you if it wasn't important. But, this is *really* important."

I cross my arms. "Why on earth would I talk to Breanna?"

"To do the right thing and set the record straight?" Aiden swallows. "Make her realize that she made a mistake, that you and I aren't exes? She won't listen to me, won't return my calls. But, I know where she works. If you could just pop in and—"

I shift Sundance to the other side of my body and hold up a hand. "Wait. You're telling me you want me to stalk the girl who dumped you and explain to her that she should undump you?"

Aiden frowns. "Not stalk. More like... drop in on."

A thud behind me, followed by a muffled swear word and a "shhh," tells me that Conor and Jess are in the hallway, eavesdropping. Jerks.

I raise my voice. "You already got me fired, and now you want to get me arrested?"

Aiden blinks, and for a moment, his deep eyes soften a touch. "Jess told me you got fired. I'm sorry about that, Court. I could have a word with your boss and explain—"

"Woah, buddy." I scowl. "Nobody will be having words with anybody. Unlike you, I don't need your help. Ever."

"Please, Courtney." He must really like this Breanna

girl if he's willing to go to such desperate lengths to win her back. He's not even using his favorite nickname for me.

"Coo-ee!"

The shrill voice calls from the driveway, and Aiden and I jump, startled. We turn towards the voice.

"Isn't this a surprise and a half?!" A well-dressed, middle-aged lady in a Chanel suit is striding down my front walk, heels clicking on cobblestone. She has an impeccably-coiffed silver bob haircut and her eyes are lazer sharp.

But she's looking at Aiden, not me.

"Aiden, Aiden, Aiden." She air kisses him on the cheeks. "What a coincidence, I had no idea."

I set down Sundance, who scarpers into the hallway, little claws sliding on the hardwood. I smooth my blouse and stand tall.

"Hi," I say slowly. Who is this woman and why is she addressing Aiden? Surely, this can't be my new client? "I'm Courtney."

The lady extends a slim, scarlet-clawed hand. "Lorna Strummings."

The blood drains from my face. It's her. My big-wig potential client. How does she know my nemesis?

I realize I'm staring at her dumbly, and I step forward, accidentally-maybe-on-purpose elbowing Aiden in the abs (which feel inconveniently firm). I shake her hand and her skin is rough and dry, like sandpaper.

She keeps her eyes on me, though she addresses the nuisance standing close behind me. A little too close actually. I can feel the heat of his body on my back. "Well done, Aiden. That was a quick resolution. And, what are the chances? I'm so happy to hear that she's a dog lover! A beautiful one, at that."

She nods at Aiden approvingly, and I keep a big smile fixed on my face, trying to work out what on earth is happening. What resolution? Why is she happy that Aiden lives next to a dog lover?

Despite my confusion, I know that the last thing I want to do is alienate Lorna or make her feel uncomfortable. I'm relying on her business, after all. So, I turn to the only other person who might have a clue.

Unfortunately, Aiden is whiter than a freshly-bleached, laundry-load of sheets. I've never seen him look so lost.

"How do you two know each other?" I ask carefully.

Lorna laughs and slaps Aiden's arm. "You've never mentioned me?!" She gives me a conspiratorial head shake. "Men, am I right? Can't live with them, can't live without them."

I'm not usually lost for words, but this is beyond weird. I throw out a "sure?"

"Well, this meeting is going to be much shorter than I originally anticipated. Aiden, I'm sure I mentioned to you that my dogs were in need of a carer, why didn't you mention Courtney earlier? You could've saved me so much time."

"Uh..." Aiden grimaces. Is he attempting to smile right now? He looks like one of those horrid ventriloquist's puppets. Only paler. "Busy doing my job, I guess?"

Lorna slaps Aiden again, harder this time. She looks overjoyed. "That's what I like to hear. Courtney, dear, I was thrilled to find you online, and this seals the deal for me. I'd love for you to watch my babies. My assistant will be in touch tomorrow morning to work out a schedule and get your contract signed ASAP."

A huge smile spreads across my face. I did it! I don't know how I did it, but I did it. "Wonderful!"

Lorna places a hand on my shoulder, and the other on Aiden's. "And, I believe I'll have the pleasure of seeing you at dinner on Tuesday?"

At this, my smile falls off my face. "Dinner?" I ask.

Finally, Aiden—who, so far, has just been standing there like a useless puppet person—comes to life. "She'll be there." Before I can say a word in protest, he moves closer, his chest brushing my shoulder and that weird smile still on his face. "*We* will be there."

Lorna claps. "Fabulous! It's all worked out so wonderfully! Ta-ta now."

With that, Lorna is off in a cloud of perfume and heel-clicking.

Aiden stays close. "Just keep smiling, I'll explain after," he mutters under his breath.

Confused as ever, all I can do is follow his lead and wave at Lorna as she packs herself into her BMW. She zips off, and as soon as she's around the corner, Aiden drops his hand, grabs my elbow and steers me into the house. He steps in after me and closes the door.

"I never said you could come in!" I locate my pina colada on a nearby end table and pick it up, shake it in his direction. "And what in the name Taylor Swift's cats just happened?"

Aiden places a very unwanted hand on each of my arms. Very unwanted and warm and firm and... *unwanted, dammit. Focus, Courtney!*

I shake him off. "Explain yourself!"

Aiden takes a breath, his bottom lip twitching slightly. "Lorna's my boss."

That was the last thing I expected him to say. "Your *boss?*"

"Yes," he says, rather impatiently. "At Zone 6."

"I thought she was based out of LA."

Aiden's nostrils flare. "Our company has LA offices. Does this *really* matter to you right now?"

No. But, I'm not about to tell him that. I wave my hand, like he's a particularly annoying black fly.

Aiden takes a breath. Fiddles with the rim of his cap. "So, the thing is... she um..."

He trails off and my patience runs out. "What, Aiden? Spit it out! She's secretly a werewolf? She really likes cheese? She won a Nobel Prize for... bushwhacking?" *Ugh, it was all going so smoothly til that one.*

"Bushwhacking?" Aiden smiles in a way-too-pleased-with-himself way. "Really?"

My eyes narrow to slits. "Get to the point, Shaw."

The stupid grin falls off his face. "She thinks you're my girlfriend."

Behind me, Jess squeals, making Sundance howl. Conor explodes into laughter that he quickly attempts to disguise as a coughing fit.

"WHY?"

At this, Aiden shifts. Takes off his cap, runs his fingers through his hair, tugs on the ends. Bites that full lower lip. "I might've accidentally told her so."

I drop my pina colada.

8

AIDEN

"What in Kanye West's bejeweled sunglasses were you thinking?!" Courtney demands as she grabs a cloth and aggressively scrubs at a rogue piece of pineapple on the floor. "Have you lost your ever-loving mind?"

Except that she doesn't say "ever-loving."

Not even close.

In the corner, Jess and Conor both splay their hands over Jess's baby bump, as though to protect the unborn child's ears.

I sigh, grab another cloth to help her. "I wasn't thinking anything, Court. It just happened..."

Over the next several minutes, Courtney shouts at me for lying to Lorna—calls me Pinocchio, to be exact—as she tries to escort me out of her house and kick me to the curb. But, her physically trying to move me is about as effective as a five year old peewee footballer trying to tackle an NFL linebacker to the ground.

I insist on helping her clean while I explain myself, and incredibly, she lets me. I tell her about the Breanna misunderstanding, and the fact that Lorna now thinks we're an ex-

ex-couple. I also tell her that this dinner with Lorna needs to go well. I need it to be a success, which means...

"No," Courtney says as she uses her foot to, once again, shoo her dogs out of the way of the sticky drink remnants. "No way in hell or hades or valhalla or any other culture on earth's version of an eternal netherworld of fire and brimstone and mortal peril and torture am I being your fake ex-ex-girlfriend for an evening."

"So... that's a maybe, then?" I smirk as I wipe up the last morsels of fruit.

Courtney glares at me, then shoots Jess—who's been laughing uncontrollably in the corner for ten minutes—a steely look. "Quiet, you," she hisses. Turns her attention back to me. "Aiden. Even if I *did* want to help you—which I do not—why would I? There's nothing in it for me."

"Or is there?" Jess finally calms enough to pipe in. Oh so helpfully.

Courtney shoots her another glare, makes the universal sign for zipping her lips. "No. There isn't."

But, Jess has never been the greatest secret keeper and, with some gentle prodding from me—and a lot of flailing arms from Courtney that make her look like she's guiding a plane onto a runway—Jess spills the beans that Lorna isn't just *any* client.

She's Courtney's newest—and biggest—client in her dog walking side-gig.

A side-gig that she's, apparently, hoping to expand into a full-time business by opening a full-service pet care company. Jess's divulgence of this particular piece of information is met with a severely dirty look from Courtney.

I tilt my head, surprised. I had no idea that my neighbor's working on starting her own business, and from the sounds of things, it's a pretty awesome idea. She's smart,

Courtney. That much is clear. She'll probably make an excellent business owner.

If she doesn't scare away all her customers first.

"So, you're relying on Lorna's business..." I say slowly, putting things together in my mind. A real-life game of Tetris.

"Perceptive as ever, Sherlock."

I smile serenely. "And how do you think it'll look when you don't show up for a dinner you promised you'd attend?"

Courtney opens her mouth to retort. But then, she freezes, mouth half-open.

"See?" I raise an eyebrow. "You need me to be your fake ex-boyfriend, too."

"You're insane."

Shame that she doesn't appreciate my masterminding genius. "Maybe. But I'm also right."

"I doubt that greatly." She folds her arms across her chest and glares at me.

"Hear me out," I continue. "Whether you like it or not, Lorna thinks that we're exes who are back together. If either of us back out now, we'll seem unreliable, at best. We only have to pretend to be together for one dinner—I'll get our biggest account at work, and you'll get a chance to wow Lorna and secure her business." Another careful nudge. "It's just one dinner. Simple."

Courtney's nostrils flare. "Simple if you're into fraud! And... and.... Embezzlement!"

Conor pipes in. "I'm not sure that would count as embez—"

"Whose side are you on?" She cuts him off with a death glare. "What kind of clinically insane moron pretends to have an ex-girlfriend they're desperate to win back when they are, in fact, the world's biggest serial dater?"

I grin, unable to help myself. "You really do keep close track of my personal life, Corny."

Courtney turns a brilliant new shade of red. "UGHH-HHH! This is exactly why I can't pretend to be your girlfriend for a single second, never mind an entire dinner!"

"Why?" I inquire, sweet as pie. No, sweet as Devil's Food Cake. Extra frosting.

"Because you drive me crazy!" Courtney looks so frazzled, I almost feel bad. But then, I don't, because I remember my suit. And my loafers. And the fact that if she hadn't wound Breanna up at the restaurant, the viral video wouldn't exist, and my promotion would be safely in the bag.

"Women usually love it when I drive them crazy," I joke.

"Don't be a douchebag," Jess tells me.

Conor laughs and I narrow my eyes at my supposed best buddy. "My little sister has developed quite the potty mouth since getting hitched to you."

"Fantastic, isn't it?" Conor beams, slinging an arm around Jess.

"Hellooooooooooo!" Courtney windmills her arms. "Sorry to break up this little family love-fest, but can we get back to the point, please? Even if I *could* make it through dinner, how could it just be one night? She'll see both of us after Tuesday."

"The woman has a point." Conor crosses his arms and leans against the door jamb. He looks to me for a rebuttal, like this is the most entertaining TV courtroom drama he's ever watched.

"We can break up." I pick up the bucket of dirty water, make my way to the kitchen, and pour it in the sink. Courtney's eyes follow me every step of the way. "Once Lorna hands me the Ever After account and I sign the contract, we'll say we broke up. Lorna will be none the wiser."

While Conor, Jess and Courtney consider my plan, I pick up a washing brush in the shape of a pig and wave it.

"Nice pig." I bite my lip to hide a smile. Since I got inside, I'll admit that I've been sneaking glances to check out Courtney's place. It's exactly like I thought it would be, yet, somehow, different. It's smaller than my place, and neater than I imagined. The walls are painted sunshine yellow, and photographs and line art I'm dying to examine cover the walls.

The other decor consists mainly of houseplants, knit blankets, and a riot of fluffy throw pillows. The kitchen has those vintage black and white checkered floor tiles, and there's a huge shelf loaded with vinyls, books and trinkets. I have a strange urge to look at every book, every record, just to know what she fills her senses with.

"Leave Piggie Smalls out of this!" Courtney's demand cuts through my thoughts. Obediently, I set down the brush.

"I think you should do it," Jess says eagerly, all bright-eyed and bushy-tailed. Ever the optimist, Jess is clearly off in dreamland, where she has her best friend and big brother married off and living in wedded bliss. I love her dearly, but sometimes she's nuttier than a squirrel eating a jar of peanut butter.

"Shhh," Courtney tells her before facing me. Her tongue runs along her lower lip, and she seems to seriously consider my proposition.

Then, she smiles, and I think I've got her.

"No," she says instead. That smile of hers turns wicked.

I frown. "Why not?"

She shrugs. Flips her hair over her shoulder. "This is *your* mess. You got yourself into this situation, you can dig yourself out of it. My answer is no."

I'm confused. Despite our differences, this actually makes sense for the both of us. We could each stand to gain so much with this one simple move... I stare at her, and that's when I see it—the glint of challenge in her eyes, the smug pull of her smile that causes a dimple to pop in her left cheek.

She knows this makes sense. She's just going to make me work for it. Beg for her "yes."

Not happening, Courtney. Two can play at this game.

I appraise her coolly, letting my eyes linger on her face until her confident smirk falters.

"Fine." I shrug. "I'll find another way."

Courtney blinks and her lips press together. I weirdly miss her dimple. "Fine by me."

And there we have it: the first moves have been made. Game on.

9

AIDEN

We're playing chess. Each move is calculated, plotted...

And unbelievably slow.

It's been three days, and Courtney hasn't made a single move in my direction. Hasn't even given me the slightest hint that she may fold.

On Saturday morning, I saw her in her yard with the dogs. So, I strategically placed myself in my own backyard, watering my wilting flower beds (I think they're flowerbeds. I could have been watering a bunch of weeds, for all I know). I made sure to stare at her, and I waited for her to get all mad and red and flustered.

She didn't.

Sunday morning, I was walking back to my house from the coffee shop on the corner, and she was out front with her little underbite dog. When she saw me, she led the dog straight to my front lawn, where he lifted a leg and took a pee on my mailbox.

"Hey," I yelled.

Courtney smiled, patted the dog's head. "Good boy."

Then, she kept walking. No mention of the date.

Now, it's Monday evening. Less than twenty-four hours

until the big dinner with Lorna and Ever After. And instead of looking for a possible solution to this glaring problem of mine, I'm having the most useless phone conversation of all time.

"Did you really believe she'd say yes?" The question is followed by a bout of incredulous laughter. Rich, indulgent laughter. At my expense.

I know I deserve it, but still. What happened to brotherhood? "I called you for some solidarity, bro."

"Solidarity?" Pete, my oldest friend, gasps, his high-pitched question crackling over the speakerphone. "My boss has never falsely believed I'm dating a woman who hates me." Pete pauses. "You *do* know she hates you, right?"

I glower at the road as I loosen my tie and pop the top button of my shirt. Pete, with his blissfully happy marriage to Mia—Conor's sister—and his two gorgeous children, was obviously the wrong person to call in this situation. But between him and Conor, Pete was the better choice. No meddling little sister lurking in the background.

"Of course I know she hates me," I say flippantly. Like it doesn't bother me. "But, that doesn't change the facts."

I flip on my blinker and turn onto the main boulevard that leads to my neighborhood. The traffic is light by now, rush-hour long over, and I'm glad to finally almost be home. It's been a long day. I just want to destress and relax. Lift some weights, watch football, order UberEats. Solitary self-care 101.

"Only you, Aiden. Only you." Pete breaks into another wheezing fit of laughter, and I debate hanging up.

As the only single guy in my friend group, I can appreciate how funny this situation might look to an outside eye. I'm usually pretty easy going, but right now, I'm starting to feel the weight of the humiliation that comes with being caked in dessert and scorned on the internet as a womanizing bastard, then having to convince a woman who despises me to pretend to be my girlfriend.

The sad thing is, ever since that damn video went viral and the internet roasted me for supposedly taking one woman on a date to make another jealous, my DMs have filled up with propositions—each woman wanting to be the one to change my philandering ways.

Hah. Imagine if any of them knew the truth. I just have to remind myself that it's all for a reason—it's everything I've been working towards. In LA, this will all be a distant memory.

"Yup, only me."

At that moment, a flash of black and blond zips into my eyeline. The blur pops out onto the road ahead of me and I step on the brake.

What the?!

"Pete, I have to call you back." I end the call and slam the brakes.

Come to a screeching halt just as Courtney Turner throws herself on the hood of my car.

I roll down my window. Stare at my neighbor. Who has now removed her person from my vehicle and is standing in the middle of the street, arms outstretched like she's about to catch... something.

"Courtney, what do you think you're doing?" I ask incredulously. "Get off the road!"

"Oh!" She glances around, like she's just realizing where she is. She skips onto the sidewalk, and I pull over. Get out of the vehicle.

"Hi, Aiden!" she says peppily. "Didn't see you there."

I slam my car door shut and point a finger at her. "What were you thinking?" I'm not usually a yeller, but she could've gotten herself killed. "I almost hit you!"

"Oh, yes. Thank goodness you didn't. Very quick, um, reflexes."

She bounces from foot to foot, and I look at her properly. Take in her black lycra running outfit, bobbing ponytail and... sneakers.

My kryptonite.

For a moment, I can't even think as I look at her.

She seems to register my eyes traveling over her, and her face turns bright red, mouth twisting in a scowl. I look away, embarrassed by the flush clinging to my neck.

Why does she have to be so—for lack of a better word—hot? A hotness that's only accentuated by her current, fresh-faced, sweaty-from-a-run state. She's usually so put together, but she looks even better like this. More herself.

"Who are you and what have you done with Courtney Turner?" I snap. More aggressively than I mean to. But seriously, she ran onto the road like a lunatic. And since when does she give me compliments? Strange as that compliment may have been.

"I'm just being friendly, Aiden." Courtney crosses her lean arms and fixes me with a glare. Then, she seems to realize that what she said is at odds with her actions, and drops her arms. Smiles.

I narrow my eyes, immediately suspicious. "Why?"

"Because yes."

"Yes, what?"

"I'll do it."

I blink. Is she caving? She'll go on the fake date?

My lips curl in a smile. I want to hear her say it. "You'll do what?" I ask, playing dumb.

"This dinner thingy. Your crazy plan. I'll do it."

"Really?"

Courtney gives me a big, fake smile. "You're welcome."

"What made you change your mind?"

Her grin falters, and she momentarily looks so lost that I almost forget that the woman in front of me drives me round the bend, and all I want to do is hug her. But then, the smile comes back, wider than ever.

"T-H-A-N-K-Y-O-U."

"Why are you spelling 'thank you?'"

"You looked like you needed the help." Courtney shrugs with an angelic smile. "And just so you know, I prefer flowers to chocolates. Cash to gift cards. But, all tokens of your appreciation are welcome."

"Are you high?" I straighten my suit jacket lapels. "You do know that this arrangement helps you as much as it does me?"

"I'm pretty confident that Lorna would still want me as her dog walker if I didn't show up at the dinner, Aiden."

"So why are you here, Corny?"

"Because I can't take that risk right now." She tilts her head up and juts her jaw defiantly, but I don't miss the tremble of her bottom lip.

Guilt washes over me. Sometimes, it's difficult to know where the line is with our little verbal sparring sessions, and now, I feel like I've crossed one. I don't like it. "I'm sorry—"

"I don't want your sympathy, k? What I want is a free dinner and to secure a dog walking contract with Lorna. In return, you'll get a *loving* girlfriend for one night only."

She flutters her eyelashes dramatically, then her expression turns horrified.

"Dinner!" she squeaks. "One DINNER only."

I stifle a laugh, and because Courtney Turner seems infinitely more comfortable sparring in the street than having me show her any warmth, I smirk. "Which is it, then? Dinner or the night?"

She emits such a huge shiver of disgust, it's almost comical. I can only imagine what must be at stake if she's willing to hurl herself into oncoming traffic just to tell her sworn enemy that she'll go on a date with him.

Once again, the memory of her red, raw eyes the other night pinpricks me. I wonder if she's okay. I hope so.

"You'll only ever get me for the night in your dreams, Aiden Shaw. Understand?"

"Loud and clear." I have to bite my lip to stop from smiling. She looks so darn cute with her cheeks all pink.

"What time is dinner?"

"8."

"Pick me up at 6.50."

"6.50?"

"Yes. I like to get to restaurants early so I can read the menu."

"Why? Are you that slow of a reader?"

"Might want to keep comments like that to yourself, Aiden. Or who knows what kind of girlfriend I'll turn out to be tomorrow night." With that, she winks, spins on her heel and jogs off at lightning speed, blond hair streaming behind her.

I shiver as I watch her retreating, yoga-pant clad figure.

But, it's not with disgust. Not at all.

What have I just gotten myself into?

10

COURTNEY

Mortification seeps through my skin, clogging every pore and suffocating me as I jog down the road. Head down, one foot in front of the other. A steady rhythm that won't betray the fact that I'm currently dying inside.

I know that Aiden's watching me run away. Probably laughing at me. Or shaking his head in amazement at just how insane I am.

Want to know how to get a guy to go on a date with you? The answer is simple—do the opposite of everything I just did. I.e. don't throw yourself on someone's windshield like a splattering bug. Especially when you're all gross and sweaty from a run.

What was I thinking? For four years, I've carefully and strategically made sure that nobody—especially not my neighbor from hell—sees me without my protective armor of foundation, bronzer, mascara and lipgloss. Shiny as possible, at all times.

Maybe not quite beautiful, but presentable. Flaws covered.

But, I saw Aiden's car and didn't stop to consider the fact that he was on his way home, and I could've stopped by later. Once I was showered and dressed and freshly made-up.

Nope. That would have been way too logical.

Instead, panic took over.

Last week, I thought that I'd get the upper hand by holding out on saying "yes" to Aiden's ridiculous fake date request. I would've done anything if it meant ingratiating myself to Lorna and getting in her good graces. But, that didn't mean I wanted Aiden to know he was right. Didn't want him to smile that stupid smug smile of his. I wanted to make him wait, keep my "yes" just out of reach.

In reality, though, my genius plan backfired royally. What actually came out of me trying to wind Aiden up was that I couldn't get him off my mind all freaking weekend.

I couldn't stop thinking about how arrogant he was the other night, moving around my house all too comfortably, perfectly at ease. Though, I have to admit that it was somewhat nice to see a big, hulking man in my kitchen with a mop bucket. I've never had a relationship serious enough to let a guy into my house, or my private life. I stick to romance books, live vicariously through the heroines on my Kindle.

It wasn't just that Aiden looked at home in my kitchen, though. My stupid mind also kept recalling the way his forearms tensed as he cleaned. How, when he asked me to do him a favor, his eyes burned with the special kind of intensity some men get when they're on a mission. Though I know his mission was entirely selfish, the look in those eyes set my body alight. Completely against my will.

Like he was engaging in some masterful guerilla warfare, sneaking in through the crevices of my subconscious to taunt me.

So, when I set out for my evening run tonight, I was, once again, thinking about Aiden. And a realization hit me with all the force of a rocket ship launching into space...

It was Monday evening. Twenty-four hours until lift-off.

What if I'd left it too late? What if Aiden told Lorna that I was crazy, and she shouldn't leave her dogs in my care any more than I should be invited to their company dinner?

It was something he *would* do, after all.

My blood began to boil and simmer at the Aiden of my subconscious dissing me to the most important client lead I've ever had. And that's when the real flesh-and-blood-Aiden's stupid flashy Audi appeared around the corner as if my rage had summoned it.

Accio, Audi!

With Voldemort himself at the wheel.

My body acted before I could think, before I could consider the consequences of what I was doing. Which, in retrospect, included potentially being flung over the hood of a very expensive car. I leapt into the road without a second thought, determined to secure that date—and therefore, Lorna.

By some miracle, it worked—Aiden still needs me to join him tomorrow night. Which means that I have leverage.

"Courtney, wait!"

My self-satisfied, slightly smug smile disappears right off my face at the sound of Aiden's voice. I suddenly register that he's driving alongside me.

Of course he is.

His window's down and he's craned his head out. Like a dog. "Can I give you a ride?"

I roll my eyes. I'm about twenty minutes from home if I keep up this unforgiving pace (sprinting like a startled gazelle). But, there's no way on earth that I'm getting in that car under any circumstances.

"You cannot." I wave my arms like I'm directing planes on a runway. "Move along, now."

Aiden smiles. Slows even more. There's a line of traffic forming behind him now, but he doesn't seem to care. "We might need to talk about some stuff before tomorrow night."

"Like what? How to survive being suffocated by your toxic masculinity?"

I pick up my pace and Aiden accelerates ever so slightly, so he's driving exactly beside me. I slow, and he follows suit. Speed up again, and he matches me. The most infuriating display ever. His grin grows wider as we engage in this dance of wills.

"I'm a proud feminist, actually," he says conversationally. The driver behind him honks, annoyed, and he ignores it. "And what I meant is that our stories need to match."

"What stories? It's one date."

One fake date, I silently add.

Aiden raises his eyebrows. "Like, for example, why did we break up the first time?"

"Because you're an insufferable fool who harasses women when they're out jogging," I snap. "I watched a 20/20 episode about this, you know. I didn't know you were the culprit."

Aiden bursts into laughter. It's a lovely sound, low and throaty and sexy and... *Oi! Pipe down, brain! Now is not the time for your ridiculous escapades.*

I stop moving forward and jog on the spot, waiting to see what he'll do. He pauses, idling the car in the middle of the street without a care in the world. The car behind him honks again. And again. Then, the driver zips around while waving a very rude hand gesture.

Aiden doesn't seem to notice, nor care. He's still grinning. "So, we broke up because I'm a serial harasser of women. And you decided to get back together with me because...?"

I shrug. Pick up my pace again. "Maybe Stockholm Syndrome? Temporary insanity? A light brain hemorrhage? You spiked my drinking water and I had no idea what I was agreeing to?"

"Okay, so we'll need to work on our stories." Aiden chuckles. "How about I pick you up at 6.30 so we can smooth things out before dinner?"

"6.50," I insist stubbornly.

"6.30, it is," Aiden says cheerfully. "Sure I can't give you a ride home?"

"I'd rather take a bath in acid," I say haughtily. He smirks again, and I shake my fist at him. "Don't you dare think about me in the bath! Stop that!"

"You started it." He's enjoying himself way too much, and I want to grab him and physically squash that stupid look right off his face.

"And now, I'm ending it. Goodbye." I extend the same hand gesture as the angry motorist, and sprint off as fast as my legs can carry me.

"Miss you already, my sweet girlfriend!" he calls. My feet hit the pavement to the beat of his laughter growing more distant and faint.

When I'm finally out of sight of him, I stop. Double over. Clutch my knees as I gasp for breath and my heart pounds out a dizzying drum solo Led Zeppelin would be proud of.

Girlfriend.

Yeah, right.

This date is going to be one and done. Over before I know it.

And after tomorrow night, I'll never say "yes" to Aiden Shaw ever again.

11

COURTNEY

I take a deep breath.

Then another.

Then a third, puffing out my cheeks like I'm a blowfish.

In one quick, rip-the-band-aid-off motion, I hit the Play button, wincing like I'm preparing for physical impact.

My eyes are glued to the phone screen as I finally watch the video.

I take in the flickering candlelight. French piano music. Breanna wailing like a banshee. Then, chaos. And, in the middle of it all, my neighbor and me, silently staring at each other with laser focus. Tension crackles almost visibly around us, a veritable halo of energy buzzing like a force field. One that we're sucked into. At the mercy of. No escape.

Whew.

The video rolls to a close and I let out a breath I didn't realize I was holding. It's the closest I've ever come to feeling like I'm in a romance book. Book heroines are always letting out breaths they have no idea they originally inhaled.

Under the video is a flashing, click-baity poll: *Do these*

two want to rip each other's heads off, or rip each other's clothes off? Vote now!

Exsqueeze me? This has to be some sort of violation of my privacy. Of my rights to happily hate someone in the comfort of my own home without the internet weighing in.

And obviously, the answer is A. Duhh.

Even one of those weird moles with no eyes and gross tentacle-y noses who live in underground caves would be able to see that.

Right?

I don't want to engage with this. At all. I don't have a personal Instagram account—just one for my dogs—and my Facebook privacy settings are cranked to 1000. As far as the Internet knows, I'm a mystery. And I want to keep it that way.

But, more than that, a part of me wants to know that everyone else sees what I see between Aiden and me: Hate. Disgust. Rivalry. Bitter civil war. We're the militant separatist groups in Northern Ireland, chucking petrol bombs over the fence to the enemy's side. No surrender!

My thumb hovers over my screen, and then I take the bait. Hit A.

The results page loads.

I just about throw my phone across the room.

96% of the 111,475 votes have been cast in favor of "Rip each other's clothes off"?!

NO.

NO FREAKING WAY.

I frantically try to tap option A again, and get an error message: *Sorry, you have already voted.*

Don't they understand that mine is the only vote that counts?!

Alarm bells ring in my ears and all I can think is—*has Aiden seen this?* And if so, what does he think? Is he laughing at how ridiculous this misinterpretation of our tension is? Is he wishing that the Internet was shipping him with Beautiful Breanna instead?

I grit my teeth. Remind myself that I don't care what Aiden thinks or what his wishes are. I'm going on one, single fake date with him, and then he can go back to chasing skirts without us ever having to interact again.

To prove that I don't care in the least, I text Jess.

Courtney: How ya doing, Ragu?

It's my latest nickname for her. You know, because of the Prego spaghetti sauce? I Googled "funniest names for pregnant women" and now have a whole list of options. This week, it was between "Ragu" and "Boobzilla", but the latter might make me sound like I'm just jealous of my bestie's ample assets. Which I obviously am.

Jess: Feeling somewhere between a garden shed and beached whale at this point.

Courtney: Sexy.

Jess: How're you?

Courtney: I'm hanging out. Catching up on some knitting.

Jess: You've never knitted a thing in your entire life, you big fibber.

Courtney: Not true. I knitted a scarf once.

In third grade. But, Jess doesn't need to know that.

Jess: What are you really texting about?

Courtney: Knitting patterns. I'm thinking of making a matching hat for my scarf.

Jess: I know your date with Aiden is tonight, Court.

Courtney: Oh, is it?

Courtney: I totally forgot.

Jess: If you're not careful, your nose is going to be Pinocchio-sized by the time you get to the restaurant.

Courtney: Jiminy Cricket, is that the time? Better dash, knitting calls.

Jess: I'll be texting you *both* later for a recap, so you won't be able to get away with lying then ;)

Courtney: Get real, Pregasaurus. We both know you'll be fast asleep with your body pillow by 8.

Jess: One more word out of you and I'm calling the baby Caiden. After my two fave people.

Courtney: YOU WOULDN'T DARE.

Jess: Try me, see what happens.

Courtney: I'm rescinding your best friendship. Effective immediately.

Jess: Tell my brother I say hi ;)

I send her a gif of David Rose from Schitt's Creek telling her to eat glass, and throw my phone on the bed.

"You're only doing this because you need the money," I mutter. "I repeat, you're only doing this because you need the money..."

Wait! If I'm in this for money, does that make me an escort?

I cringe in horror, especially as I recall the unfortunate "one night only" comment I made to Aiden yesterday. If there's ever been a time that I wished the ground would open up and swallow me whole, that was it. The feeling only escalated when I got home, looked in the mirror, and confirmed that yes, I was gross, sweaty, and sporting a wispy, wild flyaway ponytail.

The dream date material of precisely... nobody. Which is why I need to make sure I look extra good tonight.

I stand and check my reflection in the long mirror in my bedroom. Smooth my silky cream wrap dress, knotted at my waist, with shaky hands. Watching that video right before the dreaded date (from here on out, known as "D-Date") was not good for my nerves.

I try to focus on my appearance and not my gut-wrenching anticipation. I've paired my dress with a cropped black jacket and low, block-heeled sandals. The outfit draws emphasis away from my flat chest, bony elbows and broad shoulders. Shows off my long legs. I'm tall, and I always make a conscious choice to embrace my lengthy limbs. I'll never be one of those Thumbelina, pint-sized pixie-girls who are button-nosed and button-cute.

But you know what? I'm over it. Height happens.

Plus—bonus!—my entire ensemble cost less than twenty bucks. Yay for careful thrift shopping!

"You can do this, Courtney," I mumble. Then, I fix my reflection with a critical stare—my hair's looking thin tonight. Thinner than usual.

Stress always makes it worse, I know that. I've been keeping a consistent exercise routine in an attempt to balance my anxiety around being fired and having my dream teeter on a rocky, unsteady precipice, but it's clearly not enough.

I mutter a string of creative, colorful words as I run my hand through my wispy tresses. Then, I scramble in my top dresser drawer for a clip-in hair extension. Sundance bounces in and I wrap my hands around his fluffy little head.

"Cover those innocent ears, baby. Bad Mommy." Sundance's tongue lolls from the side of his mouth and I scratch him under the chin before sliding my thumb pads gently over his eyelids and easing them upwards. "Looking a little cloudy there, boy."

Sundance whimpers and lays his head in my lap like he understands English. Which I'm pretty sure he might. He's such a sweet little guy, and totally beautiful if you're willing to look past his odd, lopsided mouth. I saw him at the animal shelter I sometimes volunteer at, and my heart cracked in two. He was only four months old, unloved and unwanted. There was no way he was getting put down, not on my watch.

I stroke his sweet, warm fur, nuzzling my nose against him to counteract the sinking feeling in my chest. Cloudy eyes equals more medication. Time for a trip to the vet.

"I love you, Sundance," I murmur. "You're perfect to me."

After a couple moments snuggling him, I gently set him down and he proceeds to bound out of the room again. Sighing, I pick up the clip-in extension and slide it along the base of my hair, combing the whole lot into a neat bun at the nape of my neck.

Sleek, professional, polished.

Just like I'll be tonight.

My lips are red, my cheeks bronzed, and my eyes are sporting a particularly tricky-to-pull-off winged liner. I take a deep breath, then sling my trusty black backpack over one shoulder. It clashes horrendously with my outfit, but I rarely leave the house without it.

Everyone thinks it's just one of my quirks. Offbeat. Cutesy. Individualistic.

But I know otherwise.

Ding Dong!

Showtime.

12

COURTNEY

"Comfortable?" Aiden looks at me with this warm, sexy half-smile that I've never had directed at me before.

For a moment, I almost smile back. Then, I remember who I'm sitting next to, and the fact that he's my nemesis.

Our latest battle has already begun.

"Never been more comfortable in my life," I say coolly, shifting entirely uncomfortably in the passenger seat so my bare legs don't suction themselves to the leather. It might be fall, but it's still pretty balmy outside.

Aiden and I have been driving in a slightly tense silence for a few minutes now. I've never been in his vehicle before, and I feel hyper aware of absolutely everything. The car smells like crisply-starched linen and soft, buttery leather, punctuated with this warm, woody scent that's so smooth, so sensual, it's like the man bathes in pure freaking pheromones.

Which, if he does, I feel gives him an unfair advantage in this little power struggle of a "date". Inverted commas necessary.

Serial-dating-neighbor-from-hell Aiden is bad enough,

but fake-boyfriend Aiden might be worse, if that's even possible.

The man can't help himself—flirting is like oxygen for him. And Aiden's using every weapon in his arsenal, trying to make me nervous, get me off my game. Tonight, he's taking full advantage of his position as "fake boyfriend" to up the ante. He's pulling out all the stops to mess with me, and he's already at advantage number four of the evening.

Four! And we're not even at the restaurant yet.

Advantage one came when he arrived on my doorstep dressed in a dark navy suit jacket the exact color of his eyes, worn over a white dress shirt. The top button was popped, exposing a triangle of tanned, olive skin. He looked like one of those custom cakes that exists to be admired—you know, the type that must taste delicious but looks too special to actually eat.

Sadly, he ruined the whole effect by smirking when he caught me ogling at his too-good-to-eat appearance like a starving Dickensian orphan.

The second advantage came when he complimented how I looked, with minimal smirking and maximal smoldering. I was lucky I didn't burst into flames. But, I grabbed my mental fire extinguisher and hosed myself down. Reminded myself that this is Aiden in charmer mode—this is the Aiden that all women he dates get at their front door.

And then, of course, he had to give me a bouquet of daffodils. The least first-date-ish flowers on earth, that also happen to be my favorites in the whole wide world. I always loved that the cheerful spring bloomers symbolize rebirth. New beginnings.

Which this is not. Obviously.

I asked him why he chose daffodils, and he shrugged—a little bashfully, actually—and I knew Jess must've advised him on that particular purchase. Which was kind of sweet.

Or, more likely, just another smooth move.

Now, I sneak a sideways glance at him. He's driving lazily, his posture perfectly relaxed, a small, playful smile on his lips.

Curiosity gets the best of me. "What?"

His midnight gaze lingers on my face, then on my legs. He faces the road again. "What do you mean, what?"

"What are you doing?"

"Driving. What are you doing?"

"Asking you what you're doing."

"We should have more conversations like this. They're so stimulating."

A little snort escapes me, but I reel myself back in. He's being sassy and patronizing, not trying to make me laugh. And I'm definitely not looking at how the muscles in his arm tense when he shifts gears. I can't drive a stick shift, but I can tell you how hot attractive men look driving them.

Not that I think Aiden's hot. I can't... I mean, I don't.

"I think we should have as few conversations as necessary, actually." I look at him with wide, innocent doe eyes and Aiden gives me this silly little smile that makes my silly little heart flip flop like a dying fish. Starved of that delicious underwater oxygen it needs to breathe.

Do these two want to rip each other's heads off, or rip each other's clothes off? Vote now! The poll jumps into my mind like an annoying infomercial yelling at me for no good reason. "Billy Mays here with Courtney's sanity!"

Clearly Billy Mays must have my sanity, and I need to call the toll-free number immediately to buy it back (along with some OxiClean and a Grater Plater). Because I do not appear to be in possession of any sanity whatsoever at this moment. Because I have to keep reminding myself the answer is A. Heads. Heads heads heads.

All clothing will stay on at all times.

"Suits me." Aiden runs his teeth over his bottom lip, like he's physically trying to bite back a laugh. Nothing I say seems to bug him or ruffle his feathers. He's a perfectly preened parrot—pretty and unruffleable and my least favorite animal (birds are terrifying and anyone who thinks otherwise is insane).

"Fine by me."

"Good."

There's a long, heavy pause and I shift in my seat again.

Of course, I crack first. "The only reason I agreed to meet with you so early is to get our stories straight. So, how long were we dating the first time?"

Aiden smirks, and when he speaks, he mimics me, all high-pitched and indignant. "*What?*"

"Please don't start."

He laughs, smooth and rich as freshly-brewed espresso. "Three months?"

"Two."

"Two and a half."

"Fine. You asked me out, obviously."

"What do you mean, 'obviously?'"

"You were so hot for me that you couldn't help yourself." I sound much more confident than I feel.

"Okay, fine. But if we're going for that storyline, you said 'I love you' first."

"I did not!"

"You totally did. You were waiting on my doorstep when I came home one night. I'd barely gotten out of my car when you launched yourself into my arms, unable to spend another moment without me. Yelled your love for me at the top of your lungs. It was so cute."

"Was not!" I'm way too worked up about this fabricated situation. "It was romantic as all heck and you responded by telling me you'd never felt this way about anyone in your life. Told me you couldn't live without me and—"

Aiden grins like a devil. "Whisked you off to my bedroom for a passionate night of—"

"Ew, ew, ew!" I clap my hands over my ears. "Absolutely not. No nights of..." Aiden's eyes glint, laughing, and my blood pressure skyrockets. "HEY, STOP THINKING ABOUT THAT!"

"I can't. It's in my head now, Court. It's all I'm going to be thinking about all evening. That's how us guys function —you put an idea in our heads and we roll with it."

"That was *your* idea! I said nothing of the sort!"

But, it's too late, and a series of *very* unwelcome thoughts start dancing through my brain. I squeeze my eyes closed and think about needlepoint embroidery and Disney cartoons and nursing homes.

Yes! Nursing homes. Full of old people and antiseptic smell and overcooked oatmeal. The least sexy places on earth. The perfect decoy to force myself not to think about Aiden like... that.

Aiden's still smiling. "That's no way to talk about your loving *boyfriend's* lovema—"

"AIDEN!"

He's still attempting to hold back a laugh. Still failing.

My heart bangs in my ribcage and clammy precipitation gathers at my temples and under my arms (thank goodness I wore a jacket). I don't think I've ever been this frazzled in my life. I may as well have shoved a finger or two in a socket because the effects would've been similar.

"Never, ever say anything of that sort in my presence again," I grumble. "Ever. Okay?"

He cups a hand over his ear, leans towards me. "What?"

I roll my eyes. If he wants to play it that way, I'm not backing down either. I'm coming out, all guns blazing.

89

Aiden, Aiden, Aiden. You don't know what you've just started.

13

AIDEN

You know that old saying, "revenge is a dish best served cold"?

Yeah, it's wrong. So, so wrong.

Courtney Turner serves revenge piping hot. With an extra sprinkle of salt and spite for garnish. And, the worst part is I've only got myself to blame for this one.

But, I couldn't help it. On the drive over, I took the opportunity to get her back for my ruined loafers, and I wound her up like a Jack-in-the-Box. Now, she's sprung out of that box with a vengeance.

Lorna asked us Zone 6ers to meet at the elegant sushi restaurant so we could get our ducks in a row before the Ever After clients showed up. As expected, Courtney and I arrived first. Almost an hour early. And, as she said she would, Courtney ignored me while she studied the menu carefully, intently, like she was reading a bomb disposal manual or something.

The only time she looked up was when the waitress came to our table and squealed in recognition.

"Aiden and Courtney! It's really you!" She clapped her

hands. "I knew you two would get back together when I saw the video."

Courtney shot her a sly smile. "Oh, no. We're here to make another video. Got any throwable dessert on your menu?"

The waitress laughed for about a year before asking for a selfie with us. Which was bizarre, to say the least. But Courtney took it in her stride. So I did, too.

Thankfully, we were spared from doing any more photo opps by the arrival of Lorna and her husband, followed by Winston and his wife.

And it was like someone flipped a Courtney switch.

She snapped the menu shut, looked at me with dreamy, moony eyes, and began playing the part of girlfriend-in-love like she'd been born for the role. Within minutes, she'd absolutely charmed the pants off everyone I work with.

"Babe." Courtney flutters those baby blues at me now, running a finger along my shoulders. "I can't believe you never mentioned that you have a colleague with all the same hobbies you do!" She turns her shining eyes at Winston and his wife, Rochelle, who are both entirely under her spell. "Aiden has tons of free time on weekends. Especially Friday and Saturday nights. You guys should totally go trainspotting together."

"Sweetheart," I say through gritted teeth. "Those are our date nights."

Courtney laughs gaily. "Nonsense. Surely, you're all dated out by now! I'll happily share you with Winston for a few nights. You know how much I support your hobbies. That midnight train three hours away sounds like an absolute must-see." She beams. "Aiden doesn't mind driving, either. He loves late night road trips, don't you honey?"

Frick.

"Aiden, your girlfriend is so kind." Lorna is the worst of

the bunch. Lorna—who has never warmed to any of her employees—has taken to Courtney like a match to a gasoline-soaked bonfire.

Courtney's side of this agreement is clearly well taken care of. At this point, it wouldn't surprise me to hear Lorna giving Courtney shared custody of her pups.

"I'm so glad that you two are together, and giving your relationship a second chance." Lorna takes a sip of wine. "But Aiden, why didn't you tell us that you suffered so badly with Irritable Bowel Syndrome?"

Because I don't.

Just keep smiling, Aiden. "It's not so bad."

Courtney lays a hand on my arm. "Don't downplay it, honeybunch. These people spend over forty hours a week with you, you should be honest about your flare-ups." She looks at Winston and Lorna, winks, then stage-whispers. "They're dreadful. Can't be in the same room as him."

"You're being a tad dramatic, *dear*."

"Aiden, I thought you said you were a feminist. Wanted me to passionately speak my mind."

Lorna frowns at me.

"I'm totally a feminist," I insist quickly.

"I'm prone to ingrown toenails, if that helps," Winston says somberly.

No, Winston. It does not.

Courtney practically gags. "Lovely."

I grin. Seize my opportunity.

"Courtney's really into pedicures. You should show her sometime," I interject. Throw a casual arm around Courtney. "Has a thing for feet, my girl does. I often find her curled up, watching that show about the doctor who operates on those oozing foot afflictions."

"Oh yes, Rochelle and I hugely enjoy that one." Winston leans in and I smirk at Courtney.

"That's disgusting," Lorna's husband says. He's a quiet soul with round glasses and a shiny bald head.

I nod sagely. "It is, but nobody's perfect. Right, Corny?"

"Watch it." She smiles, all sugar and sunshine. But there's a look in her eyes that could make the Caribbean Sea freeze over.

"Courtney, you have to tell me where you got that jacket." Lorna changes the topic without missing a beat. She catches my eye and taps her nose none-too-discreetly.

I look at her in bafflement. She legitimately thinks that Courtney and I are the embodiment of a second chance romance. That we're madly in love and fighting for our relationship because we belong together. She's rooting for us.

Just like all those people who left comments on the video.

I finally cracked and scrolled through them this afternoon. There were some claiming that Breanna set the whole thing up for attention. Others lectured me about how men should stop playing games with women. I wrote back to those ones saying that I agreed, that people should never play mind games when dating. For some reason, nobody believed it was really me.

For the most part though, there was page after page of comments about how Courtney and I have insane chemistry. How we should "just get back together already."

Also, Jess was wrong. #TeamAiden is not trending.

#TeamCourtneyandAiden, however, is.

I have a distinct feeling that my darling sister missed that tiny, oh-so-important detail entirely on purpose.

"It's vintage," Courtney says with a slight twinge to her voice, like something in her response bothers her. It's subtle enough that I'm the only one who picks up on it, and I wonder what she's thinking. She looks at her jacket, and when she raises her eyes again, her face and voice are smooth and calm. "I just love vintage. Almost as much as I love those earrings, Lorna."

I furrow my brow, eyes trained on her. Interesting how she deflected the conversation away from herself.

Suddenly, there's an abrupt change in Courtney's expression. Her angelic, satisfied smile drops and her spine stiffens. She jerks towards me and, when she speaks, her voice is low and urgent. "Aiden, could I, um, have a quick word with you? In private?" She smiles at Lorna. "Please excuse us for a moment."

Before I can say anything, she tightens a vice-like hold on my arm and frog-marches me across the restaurant to a dark corner.

"Hi!" she says brightly to a couple of diners as she drops down at a table next to them. She drags me down with her. "Don't mind us, we'll only be here for a sec."

The diners—a loved-up couple who are clearly too busy murmuring sweet words over their chocolate fondue to pay much attention to anything else—don't seem too bothered. Courtney faces me. Moves closer. So close I can smell her perfume—light and sweet, like a midsummer evening.

"What's going on, Court?" I ask, frowning in confusion. "The foot thing was a joke, no need to freak out."

"Forget the freaking foot thing!" she whisper-shouts, holding up a menu to shield her face. "Who are the clients we're meeting tonight?"

I narrow my eyes. What's she playing at? "Ever After Resorts."

"Only resorts?"

"Well, the resorts make up one of the biggest departments of Andersen Hospitality. Why?"

"Hospitality?" Courtney presses her lips together. "What other kinds of 'hospitality' do they offer?"

"They're a family-run business... They own mostly

hotels and restaurants," I explain slowly. What's her deal right now?

Courtney's face goes an unnatural shade of pale. "Restaurants?" she squeaks.

I nod. Mentally flip through their file. "The father is the CEO, runs the business with his wife. But, he plans to hand over control to his sons soon. Hence the new branding strategy. They seem really nice, don't worry—"

"What are the sons' names?" Courtney cuts me off swiftly. Anxious energy radiates off of her as she drums her fingernails on the table. Well, her fingertips. The nails themselves are bitten to the quick. They're ragged, stumpy and super-short—a stark contrast to her otherwise pristine appearance. She's clearly a chronic nailbiter. How have I not noticed that before?

"Can you relax? You're being weird." Why does she care who our potential client's kids are? Still, she's clearly agitated, so I try to recall the names. "I think they're Jean Marc and, uh—"

"Courtney?" A deep voice speaks from behind me.

Courtney freezes, staring blankly at a spot above my head. Her face turns white as porcelain.

I turn in my seat to see a large man in a pristine suit peering down at us.

"Hi, Philippe!" Courtney squeaks.

That's right. Philippe.

That was the other son's name.

The man shoots a confused glance at me, then looks at Courtney, who's scrambling to her feet. He moves towards her and kisses her cheeks. I don't miss how he places his hand on her hip, letting it linger as he steps back. The gesture is overly-familiar, and a little flare ignites within me.

One I immediately squash. Why would I care who touches Courtney on the hip? Or anywhere, for that matter?

Philippe looks at me again. Narrows his eyes a touch, like he recognizes me. *Please, please, let him not have seen the video.*

My manners kick into gear and I smile, extending a hand towards the well-groomed guy. "I'm Aiden Shaw. Senior Brand Manager for Zone 6. We're so looking forward to working with you."

"Philippe Andersen. How do you know Courtney?" He says it like he already knows the answer.

"She's my, um, girlfriend." *Wow, that sounds weird.*

"Is that so?" A slow, knowing smile crosses Philippe's face. "New relationship or have you been together a while?"

I frown. His tone is... odd. Tinged with a knowing, laughing quality I can't decipher.

I look at Courtney and she's fire-engine red. She tilts her head up, and the candlelight catches the sharp line of her cheekbones, highlighted with some kind of sparkly powder she absolutely doesn't need.

It's funny. In my profession, I've learned that women seem to wear makeup for one of two reasons—they enjoy wearing it and it makes them feel beautiful, or they wear it with the goal of covering up something they believe isn't beautiful.

Something tells me that Courtney falls in the latter camp. I'm not sure why, but this thought bothers me. More than it should.

"I'm sure you've seen the video, Philippe," Courtney says.

"How could I have missed it?"

Courtney rolls her eyes but I see the flash of upset on her face. "So, you know the answer is both new and old. We just got back together. Didn't we, Aiden?"

"We did." Strangely bothered, I turn to Philippe. "How do *you* know Courtney?"

He smiles placidly. "I am—*was*—her boss."

The penny drops.

This guy runs Petit Soleil.

I barely paid attention to the staff the other night. My focus was solely trained on Courtney and the creme caramel being flung into my face.

This is the guy who fired Courtney.

A surprisingly strong protective instinct surges in me and, before I can think about it, I put an arm around Courtney's shoulder and pull her close. Unfortunately, it's (understandably) the last thing she expects me to do, so she ends up practically toppling into me, her body colliding with my chest. Warmth spreads through me where we're touching.

"Whoops," I say with what I hope is a doting boyfriend smile. Then, I shoot this Philippe character a cool look. I don't like the way he's looking at her, like she's beneath him. "I'm sorry to hear you lost your best employee."

Courtney blinks up at me like a startled meerkat.

"Me too," Philippe says, then he winks at Courtney. "But, by the looks of things, *la charmante dame ne regrette rien*. So all's well that ends well, right, *ma cherie*?"

Courtney glowers at him, and he smiles wider. Huh?

"Should we join the others?" Philippe asks. "I am afraid we are on the verge of appearing extremely rude."

Rude.

Our table! Our clients!

I swear under my breath. I was so focused on what was going on with Philippe and Courtney, I forgot why we were here in the first place.

How did I miss that Petit Soleil was managed by John Andersen's son?! I pride myself on knowing everything there is to know about my clients, but clearly, I was so distracted by this freaking date that I missed this one, glaring, key detail.

My mind starts to spiral. Hard.

If Philippe fired Courtney over what went down the other night, what would stop Ever After from firing us, too? Surely, when they realize who I am—that I'm the catalyst for the debacle that brought shame on one of their fanciest restaurants—they'll kick Zone 6 to the curb.

A lead pit collects in my stomach, sour and metallic.

I turn towards our table, expecting to see Lorna looking at me like she's ready to string me up and stick pins in me. But she's... smiling. A slash of scarlet lipstick stretched wide across her cheeks.

Winston, meanwhile, looks downtrodden. Someone must've told him Raisin Bran was being discontinued.

As we walk over, Lorna turns to a steel-haired man in a steel-colored suit.

John Andersen. Our biggest client ever.

He holds up a glass like he's making a toast. "To the happy couple living Happily Ever After."

My eyebrows just about shoot off my face. Beside me, Philippe stifles a chuckle and Courtney's eyes widen to roughly the size of the restaurant's dinner plates.

She leans towards me and whisper-hisses through her teeth. "What in the name of Oprah Winfrey's pajamas is going on here?"

14

COURTNEY

We have officially entered *The Twilight Zone*.

Cue the creepy *do do do do, do do do do* music. Because, just like the Disney ride themed for the old TV show, the bottom has dropped out of tonight and I am plummeting to my almost-certain demise.

My only reassurance is that Aiden looks just as lost as I feel. His hands are curled in his lap, his spine is poker-straight, and he's staring at the Ever After clients with an expression I've never seen on his face: fear, apprehension, and uncertainty.

If I wasn't in the same boat right now, this would probably bring me an unhealthy amount of *schadenfreude*. But, unfortunately for me, we're sharing the leaky little dinghy that's been set unceremoniously adrift.

From what I can deduce from the excited chatter around the table, ever since the video went viral, the phone at Petit Soleil has been ringing off the hook. There's now a two month waitlist to get a table.

And the craziest part? They literally think the entire thing was a set up. That the angry little stare-off between

Aiden and me was actually "very cleverly staged to draw social media attention to their restaurant brand."

They believe that it was all a publicity stunt designed to get their attention, and demonstrate, in real time, that Zone 6 is the best in the business when it comes to reviving tired brands with a splash.

Winston looks perplexed. John looks delighted. Philippe looks bothered.

And Lorna, of course, is rolling with it. Like any professional with her reputation on the line would do.

"Oh yes," she tells John eagerly. "Aiden is extremely inventive. Loves to think outside the box. When he realized his ex-girlfriend worked at one of your restaurants, he seized the opportunity to show you what he could do. And, if he can bring so much attention to one of your restaurants, imagine what he can do with your resort brand!"

One look at Aiden tells me that Lorna is full of crap.

But, I guess these people *are* branding professionals. Their job is to spin things.

I shift awkwardly in my chair. Take a sip of water. All I have to do is keep quiet, keep my head down, and this night will be over before I know it. Whatever they think about the video, it sounds like they'll be signing a contract with Zone 6.

Aiden will get Ever After as a client. I'll get Lorna's dog-walking business. And we can both get out of here as soon as possible and agree to never do something as stupid as pretend to be exes, ever again.

It's a plan.

Or, it's a plan until John Andersen turns his steely eyes —that match both his suit and his hair—to me. "So, Courtney, you and Aiden actually got back together after he staged this video?"

Oh boy.

I shoot a sideways glance at Aiden, but he's staring straight ahead.

I have no choice but to bob my head up and down like one of those stupid nodding dogs. "I guess so?"

My words come out like a question, but thankfully, nobody seems to notice.

Aiden gives me a relieved, thankful look, and I give him a sassy little smirk in return. Sooner we're done here, the sooner this little charade is over and we both get what we need. That's the only reason I covered for him.

Selfish reasons. Yes.

I look around the table, and my eyes land on Philippe. He's staring back at me with a gleam in his green eyes. A gleam I don't like one bit. He doesn't believe a word of this story.

This is the man who passed me up for a promotion time and time again, then fired me after one wrong move. The man who, despite dating *plenty* of waitresses, clearly thought he was too good for me.

And now, he doesn't believe that I could be with Aiden.

He catches my eye and smiles. "Here I was, under the impression that you had a little crush on me," he says lightly, silkily.

Then, he winks at Aiden. Slippery as could be.

"Oh!" I blink. "Oh, no. No no no... That's *funny*. Hahahahahahah." And, completely against my will, this fake little laugh comes out of me, all tinkly and high-pitched.

Luckily, the rest of the table has already consumed a serious amount of wine, and they join in my laughter. Philippe smirks at me, and I redden. Try and quell the sudden, desperate urge to throw a salmon skin roll at him.

But, the night gets even weirder.

On my left, Aiden Shaw reaches for his napkin. Wipes his fingers, slow and deliberate. Puts his palms on the table, and leans towards Philippe. "I think she *did* have a little crush on you. Once upon a time. But, it only took a few minutes with me for her to forget all about you."

Oh, my gosh.

He just went and got all sexy Alpha-male on Philippe. For me.

I stare at Aiden, dumbfounded, but he keeps his eyes trained on Philippe.

There's one uncomfortable, silent beat. Two.

Then, Aiden goes in for the kill. Slaps Philippe on the arm—pretty hard, by the looks of things—and laughs jovially. Slings an arm around me and pulls me close to his chest. I hold my breath so I don't have to breathe in his confusingly sexy smell. "So, I guess I have you to thank for not asking her out first. Cheers, buddy."

He says "buddy" like he's spitting a cuss, all the while smiling pleasantly, like this is all one big happy joke-around.

Philippe gives a tense smile, while John—oblivious to the brouhaha his son just lost—smacks the table. "Brilliant! You two are a hoot!"

I'm reeling in shock.

But, Philippe's not done. A slow, predatory smile spreads across his face. "They are. Just such a *cute* couple. So cute, I have an idea..."

"Well." I pull into a vacant spot in front of my house, right behind Courtney's old Jeep. I turn to her. "That was..."

"Bizarre?" she supplies, quirking an eyebrow. It's the first time we've spoken since we got in the car.

"Bizarre," I agree, killing the engine and pulling the keys out so I have something to fiddle with. There are three keys on my keychain—car, house, and office—plus a gym membership fob and a grocery store loyalty card. I turn each item around the loop of the keychain, one by one. "Are you really okay with it all?"

She takes a long moment to consider this. Finally, she nods. "I think so. It makes sense. Which is weird, because nothing about this situation makes sense."

"I'll say," I mutter in agreement.

Tonight, John Andersen and Ever After Resorts signed a contract with Zone 6 Creative. Champagne was ordered and popped ceremoniously. Backs were patted, congratulations were cheered.

Somewhere in the mix, *Philippe*—Courtney's ex-boss and the man who, I can confirm, should win the award of "world's douchiest restaurant manager"—made a derisive comment about her that I couldn't ignore. I rose to the bait, gave him a hard time. And, I initially thought I'd put him in his place.

But then, he tossed out an idea. A harebrained, insane, crazy idea—that we should double down on the success of the video. Because what better way to ride the tails of free publicity than to help the internet's favorite pair of exes fall in love all over again...

At one of Ever After Resorts' couples retreats.

That's right. His idea is to send us to a couple's retreat. In the Caribbean.

Together. Courtney and me. To rekindle our love for the world to see.

It would mark the beginning of Ever After's master rebrand: A Second Chance at Happily Ever After.

How could I say no? They clearly thought that Zone 6 had strategized the most brilliant pitch with the viral video. A pitch none of us had actually made or intended. So much for us Zone 6ers being a bunch of competent brand managers.

We were cornered. Ducks in a barrel. I stood there, palms clenched, waiting for Courtney to light a stick of dynamite and blow the entire thing. Lay the truth on the table. I mean, why on earth would she agree to a couples' retreat with her lifetime nemesis?

Instead, she smiled. Looked into my eyes like she truly loved me. And, as that look rocked me to my core, she uttered three little words that rendered me speechless: "We'd love to."

I still have no idea why on earth she agreed, but I wasn't protesting. I'd just landed a career-changing account that would put my promotion—and my move to LA—in the bag.

We spent the rest of dinner—officially the longest dinner of my life—hashing out the details: three nights in the Caribbean at one of Ever After's luxury resorts. They're looking to attract a younger, more social-media savvy, millennial crowd, and they want a fresh perspective. Which means beautiful scenery photos and a non-stigmatized, self-improvement spin on couple's counselling.

As John Andersen himself said, "who better to handle a rebrand about second chances than a man who's living his own second chance romance?"

Lies upon lies. Upon lies.

"So... see you Friday?" Courtney asks, jolting me back to the present.

"Cool," I reply. Although it's obviously not. Insanity is what it is.

She opens her door and swings her long legs out of the car.

"Hey, Courtney?" I say.

"Hmm?"

"Thanks. For tonight and for... going along with this."

She shoots me a strange look, steeped with uncertainty. Then, she tosses her hair. Laughs scornfully. "You're so full of yourself, Shaw. I didn't do it for you."

"I'll bet you didn't." I smile. "But, thank you, anyway."

Courtney frowns for a moment, then smiles back. Her smiles have rarely, if ever, been directed at me before, and this one is so slow and sweet and honeyed, it dazzles me. "We'll just say you owe me one."

I turn my gaze away from her mouth, her curved lips. "Deal."

She slides out of the car, then pokes her head back in. "Oh, and Aiden?"

"Yeah?"

"Hope your IBS doesn't flare up after all that sushi." She shimmies triumphantly, then slams the car door with a flourish. I watch her walk down the sidewalk, across her driveway and into her house.

Point, Turner.

With a laugh, I make my way up my own driveway, shaking my head. What a crazy night it's been.

"Honey, I'm home," I mutter as I walk into my house.

The silence laughs back at me. I slip off my shoes, set them on the shoe rack in the hall closet. Then, I stand in the shower for an eternity, letting the water scald my skin. Tonight took more twists and turns than a Formula 1 racetrack.

A weekend away with Courtney. On a couple's retreat, of all things. We've never spent any time alone together, save for bickering over the garden fence. Which hardly counts. Now, we'll be alone together for three whole days, pretending to reignite our love story for the ages.

As if that would ever happen.

She was great tonight—my colleagues loved her, John Andersen loved her. And Philippe? Well, he's clearly a scummy guy who doesn't treat his staff right. I was impressed by how strong and sure of herself Courtney seemed in his presence, though I could imagine that, underneath it all, she was ridiculously uncomfortable.

All in all, I saw yet another side of my crazy neighbor. A side that I actually like.

As long as she doesn't murder me in my sleep at the resort, this might actually be fun.

Though we've been neighbors for years, this time last week, I'd never been inside Courtney's house. She'd never been in my car. We'd never gone anywhere together, or done anything together. Why would we? She could barely stand to look at me when we swapped our mail.

If only Last Week Aiden could see what was about to unfold. If I went back in time and tried to tell myself of what was to come, Last Week Aiden would get me committed to an asylum.

When my skin is so shrivelled, it practically gets prune status, I reluctantly turn off the shower. I change into sweat-pants, then pad barefoot and shirtless into the kitchen where I flip on a light, take a pitcher of orange juice from the fridge, and lean against the island as I drain one glass. Two.

My phone buzzes on the counter, the vibration cutting through the silence. I'm surprised to see "Mom" flash across the screen.

My parents have been on a world tour for a few years, moving around Southeast Asia and having the time of their lives. It's the first time I've heard from Mom since they briefly came home for Jess's wedding. At that point, their next stop was jungle-trekking in Northern Thailand, and they were looking forward to sampling the local delicacy of barbecued wild rat.

Mom: Aiden, honey, just back in service after a marvelous Kushti training camp. You should have seen your father out there!

Kushti? I do a quick Google search. Discover that Kushti is, in fact, Indian mud wrestling. In Speedos. There's a mental image I never wanted.

The picture that follows in Mom's next text is an actual image I never wanted. Gross.

Aiden: Dad looks... shapely. Guess you're in India now?

Mom: India today, then going where the wind takes us tomorrow. Maybe Bangladesh. Or Lombok. I'll email you as soon as we know, sweetie.

I press my lips together. I know she means well, but I'd be surprised to hear from her before Christmas.

Mom: How's the love life? My third eye tells me there's love on the horizon for you.

Ever since my mother "opened her third eye chakra" at a meditation retreat in Cambodia, she's predicted that Jess would marry Johnny (her very much *ex* boyfriend), and that she and my father would have another baby (even though there's no way that ship hasn't sailed). For me, she keeps predicting that my one true love will be along at any moment.

A little third eye blind, if you ask me. But, what do I know about the mystical ways of being a seer?

Aiden: Glad you're having a good time, Mom.

Mom: Thanks, honey. We are so grateful.

I set my phone down and sigh. I love my parents, but sometimes, it feels like I'm the parent. Which is a frightening thought. Though I'm probably way more responsible than they ever were when Jess and I were growing up.

I look around my house and a pleasant, familiar calm settles over me. I can't deny the fact that my house serves as a bit of a security blanket—the thing that tells me I don't want for anything. I love my parents, and know they love me, but I can't say I was anywhere near this lucky growing up. The memories still sometimes crop up at the most unexpected moments, and I'm thankful for everything I have now.

I force myself to think of something else. Like, where I'll live in LA when I move. Perhaps an apartment? Near the beach, maybe.

As much as I love this house, I'm ready for change. Conor and Jess have long moved out and moved on, together. Pete and his wife, Mia, are super busy with their two kids. Even my friend Luke—the eternal playboy who very much *did* deserve his reputation—is planning to propose to his girlfriend, Mindy.

Everyone's grown up, has their own lives. We all used to go out every Friday night to bars. Now, it's baby showers and Little League games and sticky pink cupcakes and games of tag.

I love my friends, and their families. But when it comes down to it, there's nothing keeping me here anymore.

Case in point: it feels way too quiet in my house right now. So perfectly tidy and organized, thanks to Teresa, who comes twice a week. I'm thankful for her and everything she does, but at the same time, I hate how clean it is. It's so startlingly, glaringly obvious that nobody lives here. Nobody except one man who comes and goes in a revolving door of work trips and social gatherings and aloneness.

I dip my finger in my glass and run it across the white marble countertop, leaving a sticky orange trail in my wake. Signs of life.

I lick my finger clean, and move to the sink to get a cloth.

My kitchen window—a large picture pane of glass with an antique frame—looks right into Courtney's kitchen. My house is a little higher than hers, meaning I have a better view into her house than she does into mine. But, despite it offering a perfect opportunity to gather ammunition for our war, I don't look. Invading her privacy just feels a tad... dirty.

Okay, I don't look often.

Fine. I look once in a while. But, only when she's not home.

Tonight, the lights are off and her window is wide open. Dishes are stacked in the sink, and boxes of dog food and an array of potted plants line every inch of counter space. The soft sounds of music carry from the old record player I saw propped on her kitchen shelf the other night, next to a haphazard, colorful stack of vinyl sleeves and a weepy, over-sized English ivy.

An old song is playing—a guy with a deep, gravelly voice. Maybe Tom Waits or Leonard Cohen? Singing about how he hopes he doesn't fall in love.

In the dim glow of a distant streetlight, Courtney twirls into view.

She leans forward, holds out a hand like she's the smooth guy in a fifties movie asking a girl to dance. Then, she begins to move. Swaying slowly, spinning in circles, holding her hands above her head and closing her eyes as she gets lost in the music.

I unashamedly stare. Gone is the dress and the makeup, replaced by pajamas covered in daisies and barefaced beauty. She unpins her hair and shakes it out as she moves, and I imagine the fragrant breeze swirling around her as she pirouettes across the kitchen tiles. She picks up the puppy, cradles him to her chest, and strokes his fur as she continues to waltz.

She's never been so captivating. So... Courtney.

I've never seen her like this. This picture in front of me feels like a snapshot of who she *really* is.

What happened tonight to make her feel like dancing? Surely not our upcoming vacation? My heart picks up speed, and I reject that notion.

She's probably just plotting her next battle move with glee.

Right?

As much as I don't want to look away, never lose sight of this, I step back. Shut my blinds. This is too much. She thinks of me as the enemy, and she would never let her guard down like that in front of me voluntarily. This is a side of her I've never seen before, one that she doesn't want me to see.

I've just witnessed something intimate, something personal that wasn't meant for me.

But, I can't say I'm not glad I did.

16

COURTNEY

Here's a list of the top three things I never thought I'd spend this weekend doing:

1. Cage diving with great white sharks while wearing a lei made of tuna steaks
2. Flaming tequila shots at a frat party with Her Majesty the Queen Elizabeth II of England
3. Pretending to fall in love with Aiden Shaw at a five-star couples resort on a remote Caribbean island

Honestly, if I had a choice, I'd take my chances with the toothy predators. I've seen Finding Nemo. Many times, actually. And, if it taught me anything, it was that fish are friends, not food. Maybe I'd meet a chummy great white who didn't want to turn *me* into chum.

Alas, my choices have been stripped from me like Lance Armstrong's Tour de France medals. When Philippe proposed his "grand idea" at dinner the other night, there was a malicious gleam in his eyes. Like he expected me to crack on the spot. Admit that this was all a ruse.

Piggie Smalls would come to life, *Toy Story* style, and fly past my window before that happened. I might have a healthy amount of hate for Aiden Shaw, but at that moment, Aiden was actually the lesser of two evils.

So, I stood my ground and said yes to Philippe's ridiculous "Caribbean retreat with my ex" plan. Figured I'd find a way out of it later.

But, after dinner, when I thought I was finally free and trying to hightail it out of the restaurant, Philippe cornered me. Said he'd underestimated me. Apologized. Those gleaming green eyes sparkled as he told me that he was glad I was so happy with Aiden.

Then, the magic words: I could come back to work at Petit Soleil if everything went well at the resort.

And I wouldn't have my old job, but the promotion I'd been wanting for months.

With the pay raise, Life is Ruff—and renting the space for it—would be well within my reach again.

When I finally—finally—made it home after the Tower of Terror ride of a dinner, I chose to focus on that positive. I forgot Aiden, forgot Philippe's smug arrogance, and danced around my kitchen, choosing to celebrate my one win: I was back on track to financing my business with my own money. *And* I was getting a free vacation to the Caribbean!

With my nemesis. But no pain, no gain, am I right?

That is why I'm sitting in Lorna Strummings' glass menagerie of an office this fine Friday morning. With Aiden Shaw himself at my side.

"Tickets? Passports? Cute outfits for photos?" Lorna shoots questions at us, one by one.

"Yes ma'am." Aiden gestures at what must be his holiday-casual-to-a-fancy-destination attire: dark, fitted jeans, designer sneakers, perfectly-pressed navy t-shirt. It's weird

—he's wearing the simplest outfit, yet makes it look like a statement. A good statement, sadly.

If I'm being honest, though, Aiden is one of those guys who could make a fanny pack, socks and sandals, and a neon anorak look good. People would Regina George the moment and copy it, thinking "Nineties German Tourist" is suddenly having its haute couture moment.

Ugh, the life of the naturally beautiful and confident.

I'm so lost in thought that I don't realize I'm staring. Aiden catches me and smirks before turning back to Lorna. "Packed all my cutest looks."

"Zip it, Zippy," Lorna responds mildly.

Aiden zips it. And I love her even more. Seriously. The woman is all power suits and power moves and great taste in office decor. I kind of want to be her.

"Courtney, dear? Nice outfits packed for your tropical vacay?"

"Yes, indeedy." I beam, suddenly excited. Because even though I don't have a clue about where I'm going or what I'm in for, I can't remember the last time I had any kind of "vacay." And I've never had a tropical one.

Unless you count Daytona Beach. Which I don't, for obvious reasons.

My bags are packed, and Zone 6 is graciously paying for a special—and astronomically expensive—pet sitter, who I had to train specifically for my dogs' medical needs. Best part is, I managed to arrange this with Lorna without Aiden having to know a thing.

I'm now ready for some sand, sea and sunshine. Until I remember who I'm going on said vacation with, and I reel back my smile a couple notches.

Maybe I can chuck him overboard a catamaran.

"Okay." Lorna straightens in her chair and consults her notes. "So, there will be three days of activities that focus on teamwork as a couple, a counseling session to improve communication, a couple of romantic candlelit dinners. Oh, and a spa day to focus on connection. You will both need to be present for all of them to fulfill the contract obligations."

"Counseling?" Aiden says, at the same time as I say, "spa day?"

My heart bangs against my ribs, which suddenly feel hollow. We look at each other, then back at Lorna, expectant.

She sets her papers on the desk. "Counseling is great for healing past hurts, making a plan for the future... I know you two must have a lot to talk about."

She's looking at me like she expects an answer, so I choke out a non-committal "nggggggh" sound. Which seems to please her enough to continue.

"And yes, a fabulous spa day complete with all the treatments, you lucky things!"

I suddenly feel that I may have grossly underestimated the gravity of this situation. When I said yes to this whole plan, I never considered the fact that I'd actually have to spend three days, alone, with Aiden Shaw. On a beach.

He will see me in a spa robe. Worse... in a bathing suit.

No way am I letting that happen. He'll probably laugh, then try to trade me in for a swimwear model.

"And, um," I squeak. "Every activity is mandatory?"

"Correct." Lorna nods. "You will both need to participate. The resort staff will be observing you for the duration of the stay and they will produce a full report to send back to Ever After headquarters on your progress as a couple."

"We're getting *graded*?" I blurt.

Lorna nods once. "And Aiden, this is your chance to shine. To capture photos that are worthy of the beauty and magic of the experience. We're counting on you."

"I won't let you down, ma'am," Aiden says seriously.

His joking little salute, though, brings a wry, almost frighteningly confident smile to Lorna's face.

I must see if I can practice that same smile in the mirror.

A rap at Lorna's door startles me.

"Mrs. Strummings?" A nervous, twitchy boy of about twenty with a bad case of cystic acne cranes his neck around the door.

"What, Kenneth?" Lorna snaps, practically baring her teeth at the boy. I shoot him a sympathetic smile.

"I have Mr. Van Heusten for you. Line one. Says it's urgent."

"Lawyers," she explains with a sigh, then turns to the unfortunate Kenneth. "Patch them through."

"Yes, ma'am."

"I won't be a minute." Lorna holds up a finger and answers the phone.

I shift in my seat, trying to steady my breath. Aiden is watching me closely.

"It's not too late to back out, Courtney," he says quietly, sincerely. "If you're uncomfortable, we can end this."

I almost smile. That's uncharacteristically thoughtful of him. Like the other night, when he told off Philippe, acted like I was the most incredible prize. It was almost like he was being nice. Actually nice. As if...

Wait a second. Is he baiting me? Does he want me to back out? Call the whole thing off now that his precious contract is signed and he got what he wanted out of our fake date?

I'm sure he's looked it over and figured out another angle to take. One that doesn't involve having to pretend to date me. Maybe Breanna's on her way now and he's trying to shake me off. Convince the internet that the rising model and social star was the right choice for his Second Chance at Happily Ever After.

I grit my teeth. Yeah, I get it. Nice try, Shaw, I'm not about to lose this battle.

"I'm no quitter," I retort, smiling sweetly. Nobody will make me crack. Not Philippe, not Aiden. Not anybody. "But you're welcome to throw in the towel."

Aiden frowns, like he's considering my suggestion. Then, he shoots me a lopsided smile which makes me feel a little jittery. "Nah... kinda want to see how this thing plays out."

I roll my eyes. "I bet you say that to all the girls."

He laughs. Then, he pauses. Looks at me, his eyes giving nothing away. "You'd be surprised."

17

COURTNEY

Every Atlantan knows there are two universal facts about the Hartsfield Jackson International Airport.

First off, it's the busiest airport on earth. Has been for, like, twenty years in a row. It's an honor that the airport takes very seriously. It's announced over the tannoy, written across the posters, and on the welcome screen for the free airport Wifi. You can't forget for a second.

Secondly, there's a Plane Train in the airport. That's right, the place is so big, they built a train to lug passengers to their concourse. An actual, real-life train like we're commuting on the New York Subway.

As I play these facts in my mind, I decide to take advantage of being in an insanely huge airport, packed full of people.

Plot "getting lost" as soon as possible.

Aiden and I are standing at the airline counter, checking in. The smiling lady wearing an alarming amount of electric-blue eyeshadow is smiling bigger and brighter since Aiden started talking to her. I've already handed over my suitcase, which was so heavy, it garnered a bright orange

"Warning!" label so the ground crew don't throw their backs out or something.

I made a very funny joke about how I'm transporting livestock but Smiley wasn't a fan. At all.

Now, I'm standing a few paces off, not listening, mind focused on the plan at hand. I'm James Bond, sans martini and tuxedo. And, you know, male whatsits and what-have-yous.

Maybe I'm more of a Bond Girl—a Halle Berry, perhaps... But, I digress.

Smiley McSmilerson hands our passports back to Aiden, a boarding pass tucked safely inside each. I don't miss her odd, almost jealous look in my direction.

Hmm. Did I do my hair extra nicely today? It's not like she's jealous that Aiden and I are flying together. At first glance, I probably look like his gawky assistant or something.

But, never mind that now. Bond, remember? I am on a top secret mission.

I stuff my passport and ticket in my backpack without looking at it, and turn to Aiden, whose expression is quite pleasant, for once. There's something about airports—the thrum and buzz of people coming and going, the tangible hum of excitement and anticipation in the air—that brings out either the best, or the worst, in people.

Aiden appears to be in the first category. For now.

I feel a glimmer of guilt, but soldier on. It's an emergency.

"Shall we get a coffee?" he asks.

This is my opportunity!

"Sure," I say, all casual. "Coffee sounds nice. I'm just going to run to the restroom first to, uh, freshen up." (Nice save! Don't let him think about you peeing, that's just weird.)

"Want me to wait for you here?"

"Nah." I wave a hand. "Why don't I meet you at Starbucks?"

"Sounds good." Aiden slings his carry-on bag—a nice, masculine leather duffel—on his shoulder. "What can I get for you?"

Oh. Shoot.

"Um, nothing for me, thanks."

He raises a brow. "You sure?"

"Yeah. Not, um, sure what I want yet. Maybe a latte, or a mochaccino, or one of those frappy thingies."

I have no idea what they're called. I can never drink that much sugar in one sitting so I'm just guessing. Weirdly, Aiden nods like I'm actually making sense. "Sounds good, see you in a bit."

He lopes off towards a cafeteria-looking place in the landside area, like I hoped. I watch him walk off, and notice I'm not the only one doing so. Every woman within a hundred yard radius seems to have a magnetic, head-swivelling pull towards tall, dark, and annoyingly handsome Aiden.

Which makes *me* annoyed that I'm among those staring women. Could people actually believe we're a couple?

Once Aiden is safely tucked into a moving throng of people, I adjust my backpack and run for security.

Want to know another fun fact about Hartsfield Jackson International Airport?

It boasts no less than six Starbucks.

18

COURTNEY

My best guess is that it'll take Aiden ten minutes—fifteen, tops—to start looking for me.

My plan's simple. I'll shrug. Smile stupidly. Simper "ohhhh, you thought I meant *that* Starbucks."

What I didn't count on was security taking twenty-five million years, or Aiden having superhuman tracking skills. You know, like the bad vampire in *Twilight*.

I'm only halfway through the line for the bag and body scanners when my phone starts ringing. And keeps ringing. Again and again. To the point where people start shooting me dirty looks and saying "she should probably get that" while nodding at each other like those nodding dogs.

I join in the act, craning my head like I'm looking for the antisocial phone culprit myself.

"Please, for the love of all that is holy, answer that phone before I have to cut someone." The woman who mutters this stands a couple rows back and, with her scowling expression, hooded sweatshirt, black lipstick and thrice-pierced nose, she actually looks like she would cut someone. For fun, even.

Le sigh. I pull my phone out of my pocket.

"Hello?" I answer sweetly, mouthing "sorry, sorry" at the tutting, shaking heads.

"Courtney, where are you?" Aiden's voice is sharp as the imaginary knife goth-girl was expecting to shank me with.

"I'm on my way to Starbucks," I say, wrapping my cardigan around me like a security blanket.

"From where? Antarctica? The Taj Mahal? The other side of the Milky Way?"

"From the bathroom, Aiden." I am cool as a cucumber. Although I never got that saying. Lots of things are cooler than cucumbers, both temperature- and fashion-wise.

"So, you've left the bathroom and are on your way to Starbucks?"

"Umm, I'm pretty sure that's what I said."

"What were you doing in there, rewriting the Magna Carta?"

"What I do in the bathroom is of no concern to you, so shove that in your you-know-what-a."

Aiden snorts. With laughter? Or derision?

Don't know, don't care.

"So, you're almost at Starbucks?"

"Yahuh." Why does he keep repeating himself like a parrot? I refrain from asking as I am, technically, only telling a half truth. No need to ruffle any more feathers than necessary.

"Good. See you soon."

"See you soon!" I chirp back. This should stall him for a few minutes so I can slide safely through security and then pull my shrug-and-smile act.

"Oh, and Courtney?" Aiden says casually. Too casually.

"Yeah?" I dart a furtive glance to my right, but my eyes lock with goth girl's for a frightening moment so I pretend to be really interested in my shoes.

"That girl, halfway up the security line?"

Oh, no. Is goth girl coming for me?! "Which girl?"

"Hmmm... how do I describe her?" Aiden says. "Let's see. The one who looks exactly like you, who's wearing the same white sundress and carrying the same black backpack. Any guesses on who she is?"

Shoot!

The blood drains from my face. Furtive glance left, then right. No sign of Goldfinger.

"Um, a very well-dressed and good-looking stranger to us both?" I crane my neck at an unnatural angle. Still can't see him. Where is he hiding?

I am a truly crap Bond Girl, it turns out.

"Try again." His voice is low, and a shiver skims down my spine. Like he's running his thumb along my bare skin, physically eliciting a reaction.

"HahahahahahahahIthoughtyoumeant*that*Starbucks!" I blurt.

Nooo, that's not how I was meant to say it.

Aiden sighs. A loud, long-suffering kind of sigh, the kind that's usually reserved for weary parents with toddlers who won't eat their vegetables for the tenth night in a row. "Why don't I meet you at the gate, Courtney?"

"Sounds good to me." I pause. Look around again.

And, in the distance, at the back of the security hall, I finally spot Aiden. His phone is propped between ear and shoulder, and I watch as he tosses two large Starbucks cups in the trash and makes his way to the back of the line.

The glimmer of guilt in my chest has been stoked, producing a single flame that's currently licking at my insides. "I'm... sorry."

"Okay." The line goes dead.

Fiddlesticks and fudge brownies and... funky chickens.

Now, I *feel* bad.

At that moment, I'm waved forward by a woman who could double as an NFL linebacker. "Ticket and ID," she grunts.

I hand them over, guilt still eating at me. For the first time, my eyes skim the ticket and... WOWZERS, we're traveling in First Class?!

Score! I can't believe Ever After paid for that. Wouldn't have bothered standing in this insane line if I'd known. Don't fancy first classers get their own private little screening area?

No idea, I've never flown anything other than coach. On a discount airline.

The lady squints at me, then hands back my passport and ticket with one meaty paw. A flicker of something passes through her eyes. "Wait... aren't you the girl from that—"

Oh, no. I'm being recognized.

"Me?" I cut her off, my voice rising about an octave. "No. Nooooo, no siree. Not me. Have a nice day and thank you for your service."

I give her a salute, which stuns her into baffled silence. Likely because she works for the TSA, not the US Army. Then, I leg it to the closest scanning area.

I grab a gray tray and begin unpacking my backpack.

Needles. Lancets. Glucagon and Insulin with their little pharmaceutical labels neatly pointed upward. Emergency supplies, just in case.

I wave over an agent and hand her my little red and blue card. The one that declares "I am wearing a required medical device prescribed by my physician." Smile apologetically.

The agent nods and calls for a female colleague, who smiles back a touch pityingly. "Okie dokie. Come with me, Ms. Turner."

I quickly look around. No sign of Aiden. Good. Maybe he doesn't know that we're flying first class either, and he's still way back in the line.

I walk around the body scanners and into a side area, where the agent pats me down like her life depends on it.

As if I could ever be a Bond Girl, unzipping my catsuit and showing off my bikini for all the world to see.

As if anyone would want to see *that*.

In school, I was always the "weird" girl.

Not an outcast, exactly. But the girl that usually said the wrong thing, or acted the wrong way, was never considered cool. I didn't get swirlies or shoved against lockers, but I wasn't chosen first for group projects or dodgeball teams either. Never got invited to those super-selective, cliquey sleepovers that all the most popular girls attended on Saturday nights.

Oh, how I wanted to go to one of those sleepovers. I would've killed to be invited to Lisa or Bethany or Amy K's house. To turn up with a smile on my face and a sleeping bag tucked under my arm.

Then, in ninth grade, by some miracle, I finally scored an invite—*Marina Cicero's 14th birthday bash! Bring snacks and nail polish!*

For an entire month, I was excited for that sleepover. It was all I could talk about, all I could think about.

When the big night finally came, my Gramma delivered me to the Ciceros' front door, armed with a salon's worth of nail polish bottles, a jumbo bag of chips, and a pair of pink flannel pajamas.

It was wonderful. Fantastic. Everything I dreamed it could be.

Until I woke up in the middle of the night, soaking wet and freezing cold.

I'd wet the bed. Or, the pull-out futon, to be exact.

You can imagine how that went down with a group of teenage girls. Yup, like a lead balloon.

Marina's mom was very nice about it. She gave me a spare pair of her daughter's pajamas, loaded my sleeping bag and soaked PJs into the washer, and called my Gramma to come get me. At my insistence. Even though it was 3am.

I was never invited to another sleepover after that. And Marina suddenly became one of the most interesting girls at school.

The bedwetting happened twice more, at home, before Gramma took me to the doctor.

Diabetes Type 1. Autoimmune. Incurable. Lifelong treatment required.

At the time of diagnosis, I was almost relieved. Glad to have an explanation for the humiliating event that had caused me to become the sudden subject of name-calling chants, whispered rumors and sidelong glances at school.

I went home from the doctor that day and learned how to give injections by stabbing an orange a million times. I went on with my life with a stout resolution: never again was I going to aspire to be popular, or well-liked.

I didn't fit in with my classmates. Never would.

Wanting to fit in had been my mistake. And I, Courtney Turner, learn from my mistakes.

I made a decision that day—I'd always be myself, even if that meant keeping to myself. But, I wasn't about to be the butt of everyone's jokes, either. So, I clothed myself in armor that kept people at a safe distance. If I looked the part, people wouldn't take any interest in me. Wouldn't single me out. I could blend.

That way, I wouldn't be defined by anybody else's opinion of me, and I wouldn't be defined by my illness.

I still live by this decision. I'm fiercely independent, and do everything I can to be fully self-sufficient. It's the reason I got set up with my medical devices—an insulin pump implanted near my belly and a CGM monitor that make my disease infinitely more manageable. I also carry my backpack everywhere, stacked with emergency supplies and snacks.

As much as I appreciate the pump for giving me, well, life, it is part of the reason I've never had a serious boyfriend. Or *any* type of boyfriend. I've been on dates over the years, but never let anyone get close. Not that anyone seems to want to, anyway. Philippe sure didn't. Despite my long and drawn out, unrequited crush, I'm mostly okay with my lack of love life—I have my friends and my dogs. That's enough.

The less people know about my diabetes, the better. Not because I'm ashamed, but because I don't want anybody's pity or sympathy.

Especially not Aiden Shaw's.

Which is why I'm now standing in line at one of the airport's many nondescript Starbucks, calling Jess to ask what her brother takes in his coffee.

On the other end of the line, she's laughing at me.

Laughing, I tell you. Like a drunken hyena.

"Let me get this straight." Jess howls. "You ditched Aiden in the airport, but now you feel bad, so you want to buy him apology coffee?"

"Let's go with that." I step forward in line, adjusting my backpack. The thing is, I don't actually *want* to feel bad, but somehow, I do. As terrible a human as Aiden is, it was a rude move on my part to run off with no explanation.

Plus, maybe it wasn't the *nicest* thing in the world for

me to tell his boss that he has IBS. Though it was pretty funny at the time.

I guess that darn humanity of mine ain't dead yet. All I need to do is buy Aiden one teeny little coffee, and we'll be even. Then, I won't have to feel bad anymore.

Simple pimple.

"He drinks Americanos. Black. Just like you do."

"Really?" I say skeptically. Aiden Shaw and I have yet *another* thing in common? Ew.

"Really, really. And lucky for you, he's the forgiving type." In the background, I hear Conor holler something indecipherable. I smirk to myself, imagining Jess splayed across the couch while Conor yells at her to hurry up. "Listen, I have to go. Conor and I are going to a birthing class."

"Gross."

Jess laughs. "I'll see you the day after you get back? At Ollie's party?"

"Sure." Our mutual friends' little boy, Oliver, is turning four next week. Pete and Mia, the doting parents, have rented out an entire arcade. Which is an odd venue choice for a four year old, but we're not complaining. Pete likely chose it more for the adults than the kids. "If I make it back alive."

"Don't kill my brother, k? Be good." I hear the wicked smile in my best friend's voice. "Or not."

The exact words I said to her the first night she made out with Conor.

What a brat.

The line goes dead before I can tell her A.

Option A.

19

AIDEN

What are we doing?

Or, more to the point, what am *I* doing?

I sling my bag over my shoulder and walk out of security, towards the Plane Train. I've garnered more than a few interested stares and whispers—clearly a result of that bothersome video—so I keep my head down as I walk. The fluorescent lights are oh-so-bright, and the place smells like heady, thick perfumes, fast food, coffee and body odor combined. I suddenly feel a bit sick.

What kind of moron upgrades his fake girlfriend to first class right before she, quite literally, runs away from him?

In my mind, it was a nice touch. An olive branch. A signifier that we can get along for this weekend and whatever it brings.

Because the Courtney living rent-free in my head hasn't left the building all week. In fact, ever since that dinner, she's built a massive extension on her residence, occupying more room than ever.

Obviously, I can't tell her this. But I thought, at the very least, that I could show her that I'm not as bad as she might think. If we're going to be forced together for the next few days, I'd like us both to feel somewhat okay with the setup. I even told her, this morning, that we could back out if she wasn't comfortable. But, she was adamant.

Stupidly, I took this to be a good sign.

WRONG.

Instead, I had to go and get ahead of myself. Clearly, the flight upgrade was too much. Freaked Courtney out so that she ran for the hills before I could explain that I fly so often for work, I have more than enough points to cover this.

"Idiot," I mutter to myself as I board the train. The woman behind me gasps, and I quickly add, "Not you, ma'am."

She catches sight of my face and her horrified expression is replaced by one of wonder. "Oh my. You're the guy from..."

I hurry away before she can finish her sentence.

When I get to the correct concourse, I stall, dragging my feet past shops full of souvenirs, tacky chain restaurants and shoe shine kiosks (seriously, people still use those?) I hate to admit it, but I'm embarrassed. Courtney hates me, and I need to face that fact. She has no interest in being anything remotely close to friends. Maybe it's best if we try to avoid each other on this trip.

When I get to my gate, though, I'm greeted by the opposite of what I'm expecting.

Courtney's standing off to one side, looking so indescribably enticing in that floaty white sundress. Her eyes are wide, her lips are curved in a small, slightly apologetic smile.

In her hands, she has two large Starbucks cups.

"Got you a replacement coffee," she says as I approach. "To apologize for the mix-up."

In my heart of hearts, I know that there was no mix-up. I have no idea what she's playing at, but seeing as she looks

131

decidedly calmer now than she did earlier, I let it go. Frankly, for now, I'm glad to have the peace of mind that she's still getting on the plane with me.

I shoot her a tentative smile back, then chew on my lip. "I'm sorry, too. I didn't mean anything by it, it wasn't a come-on or anything."

She looks at me for a moment like she's not sure what I mean. Then, she nods.

I breathe a sigh of relief. "Thanks for the coffee."

I take a sip, and it's exactly what I always order: Grand Americano, extra shot. Black. How did she know? I'd put ten bucks on Jess. Always the well-meaning but ill-advised meddler, our Jess.

"Didn't want to owe you one," Courtney explains.

"There's a shocker," I murmur. Everything is always a game with her, another battle to win.

Courtney takes a long sip of her drink, then frowns, shooting a little glance around. "Random question, but do people keep recognizing you from the video?"

I look at her, and take in the glint of seaglass green in her pale blue eyes when they catch the light, the deep bow of her full, dark pink lips, and the smattering of golden freckles that only appear when you're close enough to see through her carefully-applied makeup.

"Yeah. Sucks, doesn't it?"

She nods. Tilts her head to the side. "There's someone staring right now, as a matter of fact."

I groan.

"Shall we get out of the public eye and load up on free oysters and caviar in the first class lounge, like the celebrities we are?" Courtney twinkles.

Both her clear derision for her internet fame, and her unbridled optimism about airport lounges make me laugh.

"Might be more realistic to expect lukewarm pre-made paninis and fruit cups."

"Perfect. Way more practical for smuggling out in my backpack. Who likes oysters, anyway?"

⚓

True to her word, Courtney leaves the SkyLounge and boards the plane with a backpack full of chicken melts and berry parfaits. Didn't matter how many times I told her there would be plenty of food on the plane—and that the resort is full-board, all meals included—she kept saying "you can't be too prepared." Like she was Miss Frizzle about to board *The Magic School Bus*.

Is she one of those food hoarders? I'm sure I watched a TLC show about that once. And I'm also sure I'll never admit to watching said show, should anyone ask.

Now in her seat, Courtney's squirming and looking around with childlike wonder, checking out her entertainment system and how far her seat reclines. She's already kicked off her sandals and tried on the complimentary fluffy slippers. It's kind of endearing, and I can't look away. She may be wearing white linen and fancy makeup, but she's acting like a kid who got a puppy on Christmas morning.

Her behavior—the excitement, the food smuggling, the glee of flying first class—is somehow hilariously unexpected, yet unsurprising.

I'm beginning to think that, beneath the hard exterior, Courtney is a very different person than I thought she was. Her poised, cool appearance seems so at odds with how wildly unpredictable her behavior is. She's a rainbow—a blaze of strong, individual colors that shine together as an unexpected, but beautiful whole.

Every time I think I have her figured out, she pulls the

rug out from under me. Keeps me on my toes, keeps me guessing. She's unlike anyone I've ever met.

The TVs flicker to life and the safety demonstrations play as the plane moves toward the runway. Courtney eyes the screen, where a mother is placing an oxygen mask over her face before assisting her child. Then, she turns away, looks out the window, and sucks in a sharp breath like she's gasping for oxygen herself. She closes her eyes for a moment.

"Not a fan of flying?"

She shakes her head. "Just take off and landing."

Statistically, the most dangerous parts of the journey. Probably not a good thing to say aloud, though. Instead, I simply ask, "what helps?"

"Flight attendants prepare for takeoff," the pilot says over the intercom. The plane accelerates, and the rumble of the engine and the wheels bouncing over the tarmac get louder.

"Distractions," she mutters, eyes still screwed up tight. "Distractions help."

"Am I a distraction?" The words tumble out of my mouth. There's a flirtatious edge to my voice, which I recognize easily, and a genuinely curious tinge, which I don't.

I want to know what she thinks.

Courtney's eyes snap open. "You drive me to distraction, if that's what you're getting at."

She sounds all tough and sassy, but I don't miss that telltale tremor in her voice. The way she picks at her thumbnail. Fear of the flight, or is this something else?

"Well then, I'm the perfect man for the job, aren't I?" I joke. "Tell me about a time you wanted to punch me in the face."

"Right now?" Courtney asks with a small smile.

"I dare you to." I wiggle my eyebrows. "There's an older

lady over there who looks like she'd love to see a good brawl break out in first class."

"Huh?" Courtney peers around me at an ancient, shrivelled woman with immaculately coiffed hair and huge glasses that make her look like a startled tortoise. She's dripping in diamonds and wears a crisp pantsuit along with her sour, puckered expression.

"She looks like a regular UFC-goer, right?" I ask.

Courtney breaks into laughter.

"Suffers terribly from roid rage." I shake my head sadly.

The plane lifts off and Courtney's laugh cuts off short.

Her face screws up again as her hand darts out and finds mine. The touch is sudden, electric. Sunshine after a rainy day. Her hand is small and soft, her fingers slim and deft. I can barely breathe. Every one of my senses is dialed in on this one, small point of contact. A lifeline.

The plane shudders, and Courtney squeezes. Hard. I gently rub my thumb across her knuckles, the rough pad skimming over her cool, silky skin. Just to let her know I'm here, I've got her.

We don't speak for a few minutes, but our hands stay connected. A paradigm shift from our usual way of existing together.

We sit like that, straight-backed and staring ahead, linked at the hand, until a flight attendant peeks in at us. "Good afternoon, sir. Ma'am."

"Agh!" Courtney yelps, dropping my hand like a hot potato. She smiles up at the flight attendant, eyes skimming across her name badge. "Sorry, Miranda. You startled me."

I run my hands over my thighs. I can't remember the last time I held hands with a woman. For a strange moment, I imagine what it would be like to go on vacation with a real girlfriend—a woman who loved me for real.

I shake myself off. Psychology dictates that, statistically, we get more emotional on planes due to the recycled oxygen. That must be it.

"I apologize, ma'am." The flight attendant smiles at Courtney. "Can I offer you a beverage? Tea or coffee, juice, champagne?"

I raise an eyebrow at Court. "Champagne? To celebrate?"

"Our vacation, or making it through takeoff?"

"Both."

Courtney frowns. Bites her lip. Then, nods. "Okay."

Miranda laughs. "Aren't y'all the cutest?"

"Cutest thing you've ever seen," Courtney says. "Aiden here is the cutest little guy out there. Cuter than a fluffy little bunny rabbit in a bonnet."

"I love how strong and masculine you make me feel, darlin'," I drawl with an exaggerated, honey and molasses Southern accent.

Courtney snorts with laughter.

Miranda pours our glasses and moves to the next row. As she fades from earshot, I narrow my eyes at Courtney jokingly. "Little? Really?"

"Tiny."

"I must have, like, six inches on you." I sit up straight, as if to illustrate my height advantage while we're seated.

"I prefer men to be over seven feet tall, actually." Courtney shifts to the side, dramatically plastering herself to the window, eyes comically big.

I bark out a laugh. "Oh yeah? What else do you look for in a man?"

Courtney takes a sip of her drink, sets it down. Smiles like the devil. "Someone who knows when to stop talking."

I grin. Mime zipping my lips.

She grabs a plushy sleep mask from the seat-back

136

pocket, pulls it over her face. "Hey, do I look like a Kardashian?"

Better.

"Yup." I stretch in my seat. "All you need now is a seven foot tall NBA player at your side. Sorry I can't oblige."

Courtney looks me up and down. "You'll do. For now."

"I'll hold you to that."

Courtney turns both pink and white at once. Then, she seems to remember who she's talking to. She looks at her hands, then reaches for her headphones. "I'm gonna watch a movie."

"Okay."

"Don't bother me while I'm watching. That's right up there with not knowing when to stop talking on my pet peeves list."

I give her an army salute. "Yes, sergeant."

She glares daggers at me. It's almost laughable.

But, for a few minutes there, we both seemed to forget that we were at war. Managed to have a bit of a laugh, relax. And right on cue, Courtney pulled the shutters down, threw out a jab. Back to our normal.

It puts a funny feeling in my chest. How on earth are we going to spend the next three days pretending to be a couple in love when we can't even sit next to each other for ten minutes without squabbling like we belong in a schoolyard?

And, a little voice pipes up like a taunting onlooker, *how much longer are you going to ignore the fact that you've thought about her more than you'd like to admit this week?*

To be honest, I'm not sure what to say to that. I'm all too aware that, this morning, I noticed how Courtney bites the tip of her tongue when she's thinking. That her fingernails are tangerine orange, the polish not hiding the fact that they're more bitten down and ragged than before. That her eyes shifted when I got to the gate, her voice cracking in that telltale way. Like she's hiding something.

I look at my TV, and Courtney turns to her own screen. She folds those hands tight on her lap. Keeps them there for the rest of the flight.

Including the landing.

20

COURTNEY

Haven Resort should be renamed Heaven Resort. Stat.

That's the first point on my list for Ever After's brand overhaul.

I mean... Wow, it's a literal paradise. Right in front of me. Real as could be, but I keep blinking like I'm about to wake up from a particularly bizarre and vivid dream.

First, we had to take a float plane to get here. Yup, you heard that right. After we landed at the main airport, we were driven to a dock to board one of those weird little half-plane-half-boat things that land on water. The type you always see in those luxury Instagrammers' videos about jetting off to the Maldives (Kardashians, eat your heart out!)

I was so overwhelmed by the warm sunshine, tropical palm trees swaying in the salt-tinged breeze, and vast expanse of aquamarine water that I forgot to be scared for takeoff and landing. A good thing, too. Because, this time, I managed to keep my hands to myself.

Score one for Courtney. I blame the altitude for that embarrassing little mishap. What was I thinking, letting Aiden Shaw hold my hand and order champagne and make me forget for a moment that he's the worst?

Thank goodness I managed to snap out of it and remember that, while this trip is pretty much heaven, the person I'm on vacation with is decidedly NOT an angel. Of any sort.

The float plane landed in the middle of a perfect stretch of turquoise ocean bordered by white sand beach. An idyllic setting I don't even think I have the words to describe, and so far, I've just disembarked the plane.

Aiden's already taken out his fancy camera for work and is *click-clicking* around the beach. I saw him trying to sneak an unflattering photo or two of me, so I have strategically been holding my hand in front of my face for the past ten minutes, like I'm giving myself a "talk to the hand." Probably makes me look mildly insane, but what can you do?

While I unashamedly and oh-so-attractively assess the scenery from behind my hand, open mouth flapping in the wind, a tall, rangy man materializes as if out of thin air. He wears an unbuttoned linen shirt, baggy pajama-type pants, and a serene smile beneath his bushy beard.

He presses his palms together in a "Namaste" gesture and dips his head in our direction. "Welcome, Mr. and Mrs. Shaw."

I choke on a mouthful of my (very delicious) welcome drink—a freshly-squeezed tropical juice concoction. Aiden taps me on the back and I gasp in a big "hurgghhhh" of breath, spraying juice pulp all over the place.

"Turner. MISS Turner," I wheeze and splutter.

"Doing okay there, *Miss Turner?*" I hear the smirk in Aiden's voice.

The Russell Brand wannabe looks perplexed. "Please accept my deepest apologies, Miss Turner, as I extend you and Mr. Shaw a warm welcome to Haven Healing Couples

Resort. I am Blaze Crescent Moon, your liaison for the duration of the retreat."

I assess Blaze Moon skeptically. *This* hippie-dippie character will be writing a report on Aiden and me? This should be easy-peasy, lemon-squeezy. If Aiden and I ever slip—show ourselves to be the true nemeses we are—I'll just distract Blaze with some witty banter about past lives or Mercury retrograde or something.

While my mind scrounges for any possible astrological fact it may know, Blaze continues. "Would you like me to lead you in a breathing exercise?"

"Maybe lead us to our rooms, instead?" I mutter. A tad grumpily. Embarrassment tends to bring out the worst in me.

"Right this way." Blaze grabs a tiki torch and the cuff of his shirt slips down to reveal an Ohm tattoo on his wrist. He sets the torch alight and smiles at us. "To light our path through the darkness."

I raise an eyebrow. It's currently 3pm. The mid-afternoon sun is literally beaming down in a blanket of heat and light

"Blaze is an interesting name. Unique," Aiden says pleasantly as we walk. "What's the origin?"

"The druids, mainly." Blaze's mystical accent slips slightly, and Aiden catches my eye. Winks. I hold back a snort and attempt to arrange my face into a placid smile. I'll bet anything this guy's real name is Bobby Jones, and he's originally a plumber from Cleveland.

We follow Bobby Blaze onto a grand, white dock and my jaw drops.

Oh my gosh. I have actually died and gone to heaven.

The resort is made up of a network of overwater bunga-lows. All dotted along the dock, which snakes through the pristine ocean.

I wasn't joking when I said that my most exotic vacation was Daytona Beach. Gramma's favorite place was Daytona Beach. It's a great place for college spring breakers and seniors looking to "get their grooves on", but not as much fun for a slightly odd teenager left to her own devices.

Since I've been old enough to travel alone, between my illness and my dogs, it's never been easy.

Aiden stops every few feet to snap photos of the bungalows and sparkling water, and I use the opportunity to peer off the edge of the dock, taking in the darting schools of pink and orange fish. A catamaran lazily cruises by, topped by a flock of beautiful people sunning themselves.

We arrive at one of the palapa-style bungalows, tucked away in a frighteningly secluded corner. It's all teak trim and whitewashed walls and shining hanging baskets of tropical flowers.

Blaze presents us with keycards. "I will leave you to get settled. Your bags are already inside and you can call on the intercom for anything you need."

My heart picks up speed. Bungalow. Singular.

One little house to hold both Aiden and me.

"This is for the... two of us?" I croak stupidly.

Blaze looks a little dumbfounded. "Um, yes."

"Like, we're *both* staying in this bungalow?"

"That was the plan, Miss Turner. Unless you would prefer to be moved to a different accommodation?" Blaze's chill-guy facade looks a little stretched at this point. Like he's incredibly tired of picky guests, and I am the pickiest of the bunch.

"Oh, no, um—"

"Perfect. I hope it's to your liking." Blaze gives a little bow and goes on his merry way.

But, I feel frozen to the spot. I've dipped my legs in imaginary concrete that has already set in immovable blocks. I thought I went over every possible scenario for this vacation in my mind. Countless times. How did I miss THIS glaring, wooly-mammoth-sized elephant in the room?

We're on a COUPLE'S RETREAT, for goodness sake. Of course we're staying together. Am I that dense? That sheltered?

Likely both.

My stomach parachutes to my toes. What on earth was I thinking, coming here with the biggest player on the planet? My only solace is he's very unlikely to put his Lothario moves on me. Maybe he'll find himself a nice bartender or waitress. But then, where will I go? Will I have to sleep outside?

My mind whirs with a million ridiculous scenarios, but I'm slightly gratified to see that Aiden's face is pale as he turns to me.

"I can try and book a second bungalow..." he trails off, and I don't blame him. These surely cost thousands of dollars. Per night.

I purse my lips. We both made the decision to come here, so it's hardly fair that I bankrupt the guy. Much as I'd like to.

"Let's go inside and see how it's set up. Maybe there are two bedrooms?" The note of hope in my voice is undeniable.

We just can't share a room. Ever.

1. Because of all the obvious reasons. You know—I hate him, and he's exceedingly good-looking, and there is no way he's ever seeing me in my pajamas.
2. Because what if my CGM alarm goes off in the middle of the night? I guess I could always claim that it was a fire alarm and the bungalow

is going up in flames, but that seems implausible given the vast stretches of water all around.

"Maybe." Aiden nods skeptically. The breeze has ruffled his hair and he's wearing those ridiculously sexy sunglasses you always see on male models and handsome celebrities—the type that make the guy look like he's about to don expensive leather driving gloves and cruise off into the English countryside in his Aston Martin.

Or, am I just thinking about James Bond again?

I put on a brave face as I grasp the doorknob to the bungalow, but my stomach clenches as I step inside.

My troubles immediately melt like lemon drops. I'm in a huge living room with a glass wall of accordion doors looking over panoramic ocean views. The floor is also made of glass. I kid you not. Literal glass, so you can see the marine life swimming below.

"Whoaaaa," I breathe.

"It's something, isn't it." Aiden is suddenly right beside me and his smooth voice makes me jump like a grasshopper, springing inelegantly sideways with my arms flailing and legs pogo-ing.

"Mmmmm," I say in this high-pitched tone that is nothing like my regular voice.

He chuckles. "Come on."

I turn to him, about to say that he can't tell me what to do and insist I won't be going anywhere with him. But then, he smiles. A real, wide, white-toothed, cheek-dimpled smile that knocks the breath out of me.

He's breathtaking, lit up and grinning like a kid on Christmas morning. His enthusiasm is contagious.

So, I snap my mouth shut. Swallow all my force-of-habit retorts. As much as I dislike the guy, his oh-so-brilliant plan *is* the reason I'm here right now.

We tour the bungalow slowly, discovering the palatial bathroom next. It has a soaker tub that could fit an entire soccer team, and a shower as big as my bedroom back home. Outside is even better—the bungalow's expansive deck stretches over the shimmering ocean, offering a plunge pool, loungers, hammock, a dining area and even a hot tub.

My chest tingles. I'm dizzy from the adrenaline, the Caribbean sunshine, and the salty ocean scent. This can't be real.

"Pinch me," I murmur.

Aiden obliges.

"Ow!" I squawk.

I reach out and pinch him back. Mistake. My fingers connect with his forearm and his solid, firm muscles. I pinch a little (okay, a lot) harder than necessary. He barely flinches.

I pinch harder still.

"Enough of that." He smiles again, playfully this time, and easily pries my hand off his person before he darts back inside.

Together, we discover the last piece of uncharted territory: the bedroom.

As we walk in, my entire body feels like it's being pinched.

There's just one bed.

Of course there's just one bed. I'm a romance reader, I know this.

I *should* have known this.

It's an expansive, oversized king, made up with bright white sheets, and perfectly positioned in front of glass double doors that open onto the ocean. The doors are currently ajar, and the white linen drapes billow softly. Champagne rests on ice in a silver bucket, and there's a platter of chocolate-covered strawberries on the side table.

This room was made for romance. Designed for it.

And, as if to taunt us, our suitcases sit neatly at the end of the bed. Side by side.

"There's no way we're both sleeping here!" I blurt.

"Don't worry, Court, I'll sleep on the couch." Aiden's face is almost... kind. It stirs something unfamiliar inside me. Is he serious? Is he really, genuinely, putting my comfort before his own?

Surely not.

I put a hand on my hip and stare him down. He stares right back, impassive.

"Are you just offering to sleep on the couch because I'm a woman?"

Aiden looks bemused for a moment, but then smiles. "If you'd rather I take the bed..." He takes a threatening step forward.

"No, no!" I say quickly, then swallow. "Um, no, thank you. Uh, I mean thank you. For the bed. You're sure the couch is okay for you?"

He laughs. "The couch is huge, I'll be good there. That is, if you're comfortable with me being in the next room?"

I'm not comfortable with Aiden being *anywhere* near me, smelling all clean and cedar-y, and sparkling like sunshine. It's too intoxicating, too confusing. But, I find myself nodding. "Never been more comfortable in my life."

Now, where have I heard that before?

I take off my backpack. Set it on the bed.

Slip off my shoes. Look down. Underfoot, a lone ray swims by.

Aiden's watching me. Not even trying to hide it.

For the second time in a few minutes, no sarcastic

verbal clap leaves my mouth like it usually would. I'm feeling more ruffled by his intent, focused attention than I am annoyed.

"We're going to have a good time this weekend, Courtney," he says simply, like it's an obvious fact: the sky is blue, the grass is green, Aiden and Courtney will have fun on their bizarre couple's vacation.

Only, we're not a real couple. Never will be.

"We'll stay out of each other's way as much as possible." I nod firmly.

"Orrrrr," Aiden says, drawing out the syllable. "What if we do this?"

"Do what?"

He moves like a flash of lightning. Darts across the bedroom, grabs my hand. And for some reason—probably misplaced that pesky sanity of mine again—I let him. His grip is firm and warm, solid and stable. Just like in the plane.

He kicks off his shoes and, the next thing I know, we're running. I let him drag me along—not that I could've stopped him even if I tried. We run through the doors, across the deck. Running and running...

And then, nothing.

Weightless. Suspended in freefall for just a single stitch in time.

SPLASH!

We plummet into the warm, salty ocean together. Side by side. Fully clothed.

Underwater is calm, peaceful. Serene. The seconds that tick by feel like hours as we float back to the surface. When we pop our heads up, I'm ready to be mad as a scalded cat. Yell at him for tricking me into taking a fully-clothed swim.

"You sneaky little as—"

"You loved it," Aiden interrupts my outburst. The sun glints on his hair, and his lips stretch into a wide smile.

147

The curse dies on my tongue.

"Come on," he tells me again, making for the ladder.

It's only then that I realize our hands are still intertwined.

I stare at them in horror, mentally purchase new sanity, and shake his hand away like it's a rogue piece of seaweed that I accidentally got tangled in.

Problem solved.

For now.

21

AIDEN

Welcome to the Neighbor War, Caribbean edition.

It's season two, and the stakes are raised. New territories are mapped out. And Courtney and I now share a single, flimsy wall that separates my residence in the living room from her luxury master bedroom.

We've laid down our weapons and entered an even deadlier battle: a game of strategy.

To be honest, it's making me a little crazy.

After discovering that we'd be sharing one bungalow, Courtney was quiet. Totally different from the way she usually is with me. No matter how spacious our bungalow might be, sharing a house with me was *not* on Courtney's list of things that should ever happen.

So, what brilliant strategic move did I come up with? Yup, I took her hand and tugged her into the ocean, fully clothed. Figured if I gave her something to get mad at, everything would feel normal. She'd be back in her comfort zone. We'd get wet, then have a verbal sparring match.

But, my plan backfired. Instead, I found myself thinking crazy thoughts about how her hand felt in mine. How the sun grazed her skin and the light shone in her eyes as we broke the surface. She looked happy. Truly happy. For a moment, I forgot that the entire point of my plan was to make her annoyed with me.

After we hauled ourselves out of the ocean, though, Courtney wrapped her arms around herself, glared, and I knew we were back to our usual equilibrium. She even proceeded to call me a "douchenoggin." Which I thought was pretty creative, actually.

She disappeared before I could tell her that.

I got cleaned up and spent the afternoon exploring the resort. Alone. Of course, Courtney made herself as scarce as could be when "trapped" with your nemesis on a secluded tropical island resort. Which, it turns out, is very scarce.

As I explored, I took photos—of the beach, the Turkish spa, the gourmet restaurants, the huge swimming pool and network of lazy rivers that run through the grounds.

When I got back to the bungalow, I went for another swim—this time, dressed for it.

Courtney returned at some point while I was in the ocean, and proceeded to go straight to the bedroom without saying a word.

I tried not to feel disappointed. Because I wasn't.

We're here to publicly act like a fake couple falling back in love. When we're alone together, all bets are off.

The first event in our "couple's programming" starts in T-30 minutes now. Tonight is a beach party with dinner and dancing, according to the brochure. With Courtney as my date.

My heart beats fast as I lean forward over the bathroom counter, splash water on my face, then add a touch of after-shave. I'm dressed in a crisp, clean, white button-down shirt, and khaki-color slacks. The fancy-dinner-at-the-beach uniform of men everywhere.

I stare at myself in the mirror. I look tanned and relaxed

already. If I was here with any other woman, I'd give myself a pep talk, tell myself to just be me and act normal tonight.

But, I'm here with Courtney, and I know how she feels about my normal—it ain't pretty. And I'm beginning to question if I even *want* our normal.

With a sigh, I step out of the steamy bathroom and onto the deck.

It's twilight and the sun dips low on the horizon, setting the surface of the ocean ablaze in pinks and reds. Fairy lights, strung in rows along the dock, twinkle overhead. The tide laps gently, cicadas chirp in the distance, and the humid breeze smells like salt and citrus and campfires.

In the middle of it all stands Courtney, glowing in the halo of light from the setting sun. She wears a butter-yellow halter sundress with a cinched waist and short, flared skirt. On her feet are simple gold flip-flops. Her hair is in wild waves, her face fresh and cheeks sun-kissed from an afternoon outside.

I finger the buttons on my camera, wishing I could take a photo of her, capture this moment. No matter how frustrating and hot-and-cold and hell-bent on hating me Courtney may be, there is no denying the universal, inextricable, unequivocal (thank you, Words With Friends) fact that she's downright stunning.

As well as a little crazy.

I suck in a breath. "You look—"

"Don't say it." Her voice is strong, but her index finger finds her thumbnail, picking at that same spot she always does when she's uncomfortable. She looks down at herself before her next words tumble out. "I know I'm a mess. My straightener wouldn't work, and I can't find my makeup bag, and my feet are swollen from the heat so my heels won't fit, and—"

"I was going to say you look great," I say with a shrug.

151

Her head snaps up, eyes shrewd, lips pressed in a line. She looks at me for a long moment, like she's waiting for a punchline. When none comes, she raises a brow. "Getting into fake falling-in-love mode or something?"

"Sure," I lie smoothly. No need for her to know how truly beautiful I think she looks right now. She'd probably find a way to use that as ammunition against me. I take a step towards her, into her personal space. Her eyes widen, which makes my pulse jump. "You look great, *girlfriend*."

"Better keep those loving boyfriend comments coming or I might run off with Blaze Full Moon."

"You would make a striking Mrs. Moon Cycle."

"Thanks for being so understanding about my impending fake infidelity." Courtney presses her lips together, and the hint of a genuine smile crosses her features. Then, she shuffles awkwardly, gestures towards me. "You look, um... uh...."

"That good, huh?" I tease. Her cheeks redden, and I run a hand over my chin. "To think I shaved for you."

I wait for her to offer up some withering comment about how I look like a naked mole rat or something. "I didn't mind the scruff," she says instead. Her blush deepens. "I mean... if you're into that kinda thing. I'm, um, a beard girl myself. Huge beards. Bigger and bushier, the better."

"Oh yeah?" I chuckle as we leave the bungalow and walk down the beautifully-lit dock.

"Totally. Love me a beard or two." Courtney frowns. "Wait, no. That sounded wrong. One at a time, I mean."

I throw my head back and laugh. "Easy there, Cleopatra. So, are we talking, like, Duck Dynasty or Hagrid in the beard department?"

"Santa Claus, actually."

"Well, as your boyfriend for the weekend, I'd better get

to work on growing mine out." I grin. "That, and gaining eight inches of height."

At that moment, her flip-flop catches on an uneven piece of dock and she stumbles. I reach out to steady her, and she grasps my forearm, her thumb pressing lightly into my pulse point. "Oops. Clumsy." She laughs a breathy laugh. "But, do yourself a favor and never grow out your beard. You wouldn't look like Santa, you'd look more like a pirate."

"Arr," I agree.

"Blackbeard. You'd be Blackbeard. He was killed in action, you know. Multiple stab wounds."

"Remind me to keep you away from sharp utensils this evening."

"Aiden," Courtney chides with a wicked smile. "This is a five-star resort. I'm sure there'll be about six knives at every place setting."

"I'd better be on my best behavior, then."

22

COURTNEY

Thirty is a strange age.

For one, you're technically a full-grown adult in the eyes of the world. You can't get away with excuses about being "immature for your age" or "just enjoying your twenties".

Secondly, it's an age where you can look in the mirror and simultaneously discover a brand new zit and a wrinkle.

Fabulous.

I was the lucky recipient of all of the above when I dared look in the mirror earlier this evening. A lovely little eye wrinkle and a shiny pink pimple on my chin. To make things abundantly worse, my makeup bag apparently didn't make the trip with us, and is likely hanging out in a gray security scanner bin at ATL. *Merde.* My straightener, also, is sadly sitting forgotten in my bathroom at home.

Talk about fresh out of luck.

After these terrifying discoveries, I seriously considered popping outside and swimming back to Atlanta (can't be that far, right?). Or, finding a couple friendly dolphins to hitch a ride with.

Having Aiden see me all frizzy, pimply, and wrinkly

was just about the worst thing I could imagine. And now, in the span of a week, he's seen me gross, sweaty and sans makeup *twice*.

Sacré freaking bleu.

I talked myself out of my little spiral of despair and pep talked myself into not caring what Aiden might think.

When we met for dinner, he actually had the audacity to say that I looked great.

Great.

With no trace of sarcasm. What's his angle?

Since we got here a few hours ago, things have been... confusing, to say the least. He's been, in turn, hot and cold and flirty and maddening and nice. Plus, somehow, in this island paradise setting, he looks more handsome than ever. Which I can't say I'm a fan of.

After he rudely tricked me into holding his hand for the second time today—then proceeded to pull me into the ocean as his idea of a brilliant prank—I fled the bungalow. Spent the afternoon on the beach, reading my book and getting lost in a real love story.

But now, evening has come and I'm back to living my fake one. With a fake boyfriend I can't stand.

One who I may or may not have just told that I have a thing for Santa Claus beards. I don't know why I said that, it was the first thing that came to mind. Which, to be honest, should have been my warning signal to not open my mouth.

Silly me.

Now, after our fantastically stimulating and witty (not) conversation about my (completely made up) love of bushy beards, we arrive at the beach to find a welcome committee.

"Miss Shaw, Mr. Turner!" Blaze booms.

"Other way around," I tell him. "It's Mr. Shaw and Miss Turner."

He frowns at me like he has no idea what I'm talking about. "That's what I said."

Beside me, Aiden chuckles. Jerk.

Instead of bothering to correct Blaze—who's probably in the throes of some magic mushroom trip or something—I elbow Aiden in the ribs. Which is very satisfying for a moment. Until he responds by daring to put an arm around me and pull me close to his side, effectively tucking me under the crook of his arm. Like I'm a rolled up newspaper!

My immediate reaction is to squirm away from him and his ideally bicepy biceps and his intoxicating scent of cedar and suntan lotion and spring rain. But, he just holds me closer.

Then, he ruffles my hair.

RUFFLES MY HAIR.

"My girlfriend's a little tired from all the traveling," Aiden explains to Blaze, while beaming down at me with a doting smile that clashes with his teasing, gleaming eyes. Double jerk.

Blaze nods like this explains my stiff and disjointed position under Aiden's arm. "Best to nourish your bodies with vitamin-rich food, and then rejuvenate your minds with a good night's sleep."

"So, we eat dinner then go to bed?" Aiden asks, and I have to stifle a highly unattractive snort.

Blaze gives us an odd look. "Yes, isn't that what I said?"

Aiden shrugs, his shoulders shaking as he bites back laughter. "Um, maybe a table for two, then?"

"Coming right up."

Blaze seats us along the beachfront and Aiden wanders for a few minutes, taking photos of the stunning, romantic, candle-lit setting. Well, it would be romantic if I was here with any other man than Aiden Shaw.

While Aiden walks around, I stare towards the ocean

with my lips slightly pursed, feigning a sexy, faraway kind of look. Like I'm Marilyn Monroe on vacation. Or, Audrey Hepburn. You know, one of those blasé, confident, glamorous leading ladies. The height of sophistication. The epitome of—

"What's wrong with your mouth?" Aiden asks as he plops down in his chair next to me.

I un-purse my lips and seal them in a thin line so an accidental four-letter word or six don't fall out. Aiden clasps his hands on the table, his camera next to him, and we sit there for a moment, looking at each other in silence.

"Well. This is weird," Aiden eventually says.

"You're weird," I retort stupidly. I can't think of anything else to say.

Because he's right. This is the weirdest thing ever— Aiden Shaw and me on a dinner date, at the beach.

And seeing as we suddenly don't know how to act or what to say, we each grab a plate and stock up on freshly grilled seafood, veggies and bread. Neither of us saying a word.

All the while, I feel the eyes of the resort staff trained on us. Watching our every move. Prepping their stories for their reports to Ever After HQ, perhaps? Between this report business and the viral video, I'm starting to feel pretty sick of being in the public eye. Maybe I'm okay not being Marilyn Monroe or Audrey Hepburn.

When we get back to the table, Aiden clears his throat.

"What?" I look up from the crab leg I'm currently attempting to crack. Nothing sexier on a fake date than smushed up bits of crustacean shell everywhere (i.e. in my hair).

"I don't think anyone's buying this." Aiden gestures vaguely. "Us."

"I wonder why on earth that is?"

He doesn't laugh. Shifts in his chair. "What if... Um, what if we called a truce? Just so that we can get through the weekend without raising suspicion."

A worry line forms on his forehead as he squints at me. Almost like he's nervous. But, he's not, he couldn't be. He just needs me to cooperate so he can get his promotion.

And I need my job back.

I consider all of this as I chew on a (delicious) piece of pineapple.

As much as I hate to admit it, Aiden's right. We're meant to be a couple. People are watching. And if that darned report doesn't look good for us, who knows how "promotion giving" Philippe might feel?

Which means that, even though we each have a different goal to achieve while we're here, we need the other person to help. We do, effectively, need to team up. As long as I can remember that—remember that he's the enemy... Well, there's no harm in keeping my enemies close for a few short days. Right?

Besides, I want to enjoy myself. Want to make the most of being on a once-in-a-lifetime (probably) vacation.

Aiden's leaning towards me, face filled with something that looks remarkably like hope. "So, truce?" he asks again.

I nod once. "Okay."

He grins that beautiful, confident, not-a-care-in-the-world, chill-inducing grin that makes my stomach flip. "Good decision."

"Famous last words, Shaw," I retort, pressing down on my crab cracker. Hard. Splinters of shell explode in a shower all over my plate.

"I think you should call me 'Aiden' if anyone's going to believe that we're an item."

"Fine. As long as you never call me 'Corny' again as long as you live."

"You drive a hard bargain." Laughter lines crease his eyes. "But I can do that. *Courtney*."

With that, we eat. And, for some reason, the truce seems to shift something between us. As we devour our food, we manage to have an entire conversation without wanting to kill each other. Which is new. Very new.

To any passerby, we must look like a starry-eyed couple whispering sweet nothings.

Hah. If only they knew.

After we finish our meal, a band begins to play. Caribbean music, warm and soulful.

Dancing. The part of the evening I've been dreading.

Couples stand from their tables and I swallow. Wipe my crab-spattered hands on a napkin. Wish I hadn't picked the messiest, smelliest menu item.

Aiden looks from the watchful staff, to the dancing couples, to our empty plates. He holds out a hand. "Shall we?"

"Guess we have to," I say. But, I shoot him a small smile to tell him I'm not as grumpy as I sound.

I reach for his outstretched hand and feel a thrill of unexpected pleasure as he envelopes mine in his. Weird.

And, just like that, for the third time in one day, we are holding hands. I remind myself that I'm simply playing the role of dutiful girlfriend, and let Aiden lead me to the area of sand doubling as a dance floor. Try not to think about how small my hand feels in his.

We face each other, and I suddenly feel like an awkward, gawky tweenager going to her first school dance.

"Okay," I boss in my best "take charge" voice. "Let's lay down some ground rules for this dancing malarkey."

"Malarkey?" Aiden's lips curl upwards.

I ignore him, press on. "Keep your hands where I can see them and no funny business."

"What sort of funny business could you possibly mean?" He takes a step towards me, and I feel my chest rise and fall as my breathing speeds up. Wonder if his does, too.

"How about you put your hands on my shoulders and I'll put mine on yours?" I look everywhere but at him as I hold my arms straight in front of me. Stiff as a board, like an Egyptian Mummy.

"When I asked you to dance, I didn't mean Russian Folk Dancing, Court."

"What did you mean, then?" I demand, oddly embarrassed.

"How about this?" Aiden takes another step so there's just a few inches between our bodies. Then, he takes my hands and guides them to his shoulders. Sets his own hands in a surprisingly chaste, PG position on my mid-back.

Great. Just keep those things far, far away from my stomach. It would be very surprising if he grabbed my stomach for slow-dancing purposes, but you can never be too careful.

"This okay?" he asks quietly.

I nod, speechless, as his eyes lock on mine. We begin to move slowly, swaying back and forth while I do my best to keep a couple bible lengths between us, just like I learned at Sunday School.

But, alas, his hands tighten on my back, drawing me closer and I don't resist it. I feel the pulse in his wrist, beating irregularly fast. Just like mine.

"Don't get cocky and start thinking I don't still hate you," I say, strangely breathless.

Aiden smiles. "Wouldn't dream of it."

23

COURTNEY

"Jessica Isabel Doris Shaw Brady, you shut your mouth!" I whisper-yell into my cupped hand so Aiden doesn't overhear.

I'm in our (our!) bungalow. In bed. Under the covers. Trying to have a serious conversation with my apparent best friend while keeping her brother, who's asleep in the next room, from hearing.

"Hey! I told you the Doris thing in confidence."

"And I told *you* that NOTHING IS GOING TO HAPPEN!" My whisper-yell becomes more of a repressed screech with every word. "Temporary truces do not lead to... *things* happening!"

"Mmmmmhmmmmmmm," she says in this smug, know-it-all tone that self-satisfied, happily-married women use on their single friends.

"It's too early for so much smugness," I huff, regretting telling her about the truce. "You're going to give yourself morning sickness."

Jess laughs. I do not.

I'm tired because I didn't sleep well last night. For two reasons.

First, when we got back from dinner and dancing (dancing! Together!) Aiden and I sat on the deck and talked for a while. Like two normal, adult human beings. Nothing deep or personal, nothing inflammatory or argumentative. He asked me about Life is Ruff, and I found myself telling him my plan. Just for something to talk about, of course.

He seemed genuinely interested, listening attentively to everything I said. I was even more shocked when he said he thought it was an excellent idea. Looked like he meant it, too.

It was... nice. But, obviously not that nice. We were simply jetlagged, I assume. If jetlag is a thing with a one-hour time difference.

Secondly, when I did go to bed, Aiden being in the next room made it unbelievably difficult to relax. I was keyed up, like a wind-up toy that had been wound too tight.

As a result, I woke up on the wrong side of the (very soft, plush, comfy—sorry, Aiden) bed this morning. Without a scrap of makeup—save for strawberry lip gloss—to cover the bags under my eyes.

"I'm not being smug," Jess insists. "It's just... interesting that you guys are getting to know each other without bickering like toddlers, and you're not hating it."

"I never said that! I *said* that I don't hate the five-star luxury resort where everything is free," I protest indignantly. "Your brother, I do hate. Always have, always will."

But, here's the thing I don't tell her, because she'd get all haughty and insist that she's right. I don't know if it's the humidity, or a touch of heatstroke, but we've been here for one night, and suddenly—while I obviously (duhh) still hate Aiden—I am finding that I don't hate being *around* him. Like, at all.

I can't work out what his angle is: if he's just being nice and sweet because I'm the only female for him to talk to. Or, if he's in character full-time—the perfect, doting boyfriend seeking a second chance.

For as long as I can remember, my skin has chilled and my heart has thudded when Aiden came near me. Here at Haven Resort, it's no exception. The only thing is that, since we called that (possibly very dangerous) truce, the chills kind of feel like the good kind, and my accelerated heartbeat flutters more with anticipation than anger.

He was a true gentleman when we danced, going out of his way to make me comfortable. And, to my surprise, despite the singer of the band being one of the most drop-dead-gorgeous women I've ever seen, he didn't even give her a second glance.

Instead, he looked at me like I was the only woman on the beach, like he only had eyes for me. Frizzy hair, bare face, lack of footwear and all.

He's good at this fake boyfriend thing. So good that, during the dance, his ocean eyes suddenly looked like a body of water I might consider taking a little boat out on. Just for a few minutes, just to try. No swimming, of course. But I could stay dry and still go for a little sail, couldn't I?

I didn't get enough travel insurance to cover capsizing a sailboat, though. And I have to remember that this is Aiden Shaw whose sea I'm sailing on. Womanizing, heartbreaking Aiden Shaw. The man with a constant revolving-door of women he dates, beds and leaves.

Although, now that I think about it, I've never actually seen any women leaving his house in the wee hours of the morning.

He probably makes them leave via the back door. Being the gentleman that he is.

Aiden's casual dating habits aside, I have to admit that this trip has been a strange and surprising journey. I'm probably ready to audition for the next season of *Bachelor in*

Paradise. At this point, I've got the "very confused about what is happening to me, but choosing to live in the moment because I'm on a beach, so real life doesn't matter" thing down pat. Also mastered the "hiding in the bedroom so I don't have to see Aiden go swimming without a shirt on" thing.

Bonus! Because who knows how my stupid body would react to that? Even though my brain knows much, much better. Better to be "recluse" woman than "weak at the knees for the womanizer" woman.

Fact.

Just two more days of this, and things can go back to their uncomplicated normal. Right?

"Come on, Courtney. Tell the truth," Jess coaxes.

Ugh. My best friend and her optimistic, meddlesome ways will be the death of me.

"Stop projecting!" I tell her. "You're living in Lalaland. A temporary truce does not exactly set the scene for the world's next great love story."

"Um, tell that to Elizabeth Bennet."

"Don't even think about using the greatest romance novel of all time against me!" I grab a pillow and squeeze it. "Plus, if you'd actually read *Pride & Prejudice*, you'd know that at no time in the book did they call a temporary truce."

"Exactly." I hear the smirk in Jess's voice. "They did more than that—they realized they'd misjudged each other, and fell madly in love. Madly. Plus, Darcy really wanted Lizzy to get along with his sister."

"You're delusional. And blind. Delusionally blind, I tell you! Crazy as a—"

There's movement in the living room. The bathroom door closes and I hear the rush of the shower. Aiden's in there, just beyond the door... getting naked. To shower. His body.

Sacré freaking bleu. Think other thoughts, Courtney. Any other thoughts. Think about... chickens. Or, or broccoli salad. Why do they always put sugar in that? It's weird.

"Courtneyyyy?" Jess sings. "Have I lost you?"

I blow out a huge breath, flushed and flustered and suddenly exceedingly warm. The air conditioning must be on the fritz.

"Still here," I say, mouth dry.

"Good. So, you going to give it up already?"

I sigh, squeeze my eyes shut. And then, because Jessica Brady is nothing if not relentless, I allow a little crack in my armor.

"Okay, okay!" I cup the receiver and hiss into it. "Maybe 'hate' is a strong word..."

⚔

"No." I cross my arms across my chest and fix Blaze Whatsit Moon with what I hope is a fierce stare. "Absofreakinglutely not."

After a small eternity on the phone with my *former* best friend, Jessica, I spent another eternity trying on bathing suits before settling on a bikini in a thick neoprene-style material with super high-waisted bottoms. I'd specifically shopped for cute yet high-coverage bikinis for this trip. Just in case I was forced to spend time with Aiden in a beach or water setting. And thank goodness I did.

I added a sarong over the top for good measure. Safety in layers.

I didn't stop to dwell on why I so badly wanted to look good today. I was rather afraid of the answer.

So, I convinced myself that it has nothing to do with an intense pair of midnight blue eyes, and the way a certain someone's two big, manly hands felt on my lower back not twelve hours ago.

Now, Aiden and I are seated at the open-air breakfast restaurant by the beach, being interrogated by a middle-aged hippie who is apparently dead-set on torturing me. Aiden, darn him, is shaking with silent laughter in the most infuriating way possible. I immediately regret both my agreement to a truce and my concession on the phone to Jess earlier, because right now, I really want to hate him.

And, I would. If he A) didn't look so heartbreakingly handsome, with his instant holiday tan popping against his white t-shirt. And, B) hadn't been so thoughtful this morning by bringing me coffee while I was getting ready. Americano, too. The man's got a good memory.

I settle for shooting him a withering look, and he grins at me. Takes a casual sip of his fresh pineapple juice like we hadn't just been informed that we're to spend the next two hours of our lives in a "hands on couples yoga session." Together.

I liked the plan I had in my head for this morning—where Aiden went snorkeling, and I went as far away from him as possible while waiting for updates on whether he'd run into a shark.

I didn't expect the whole "couples programming" thing to start right at breakfast. Or that we'd begin with handsy yoga.

"Please. Is there anything else we can do?" I plead, breaking my muffin in two more roughly than necessary. "Maybe horseback riding? Or, or... axe throwing?"

"Axe throwing?" Aiden grimaces. "Not after your comments about the knives last night."

I kick him under the table and he smirks. No fair. Why does Aiden get to be so cool, calm and collected about this miserable endeavor?

I guess this is all par-for-the-course for him. Maybe he does this with all his real girlfriends.

"Child," Blaze soothes, stretching his hands out. What happened to "Miss Turner"? How have I been downgraded to "child"?! "It is an essential part of the program. We connect couples on three levels: body, mind and soul. We begin with the body."

I would rather stick my head in a pot of boiling oil than "connect" my body with Aiden's. Just the feeling of his hands on my back last night was enough to stir up so much confusing, sizzling heat that I could barely breathe. Couples yoga—having Aiden's body so close to mine—would probably make me pass out.

But, I can't exactly tell Blaze that.

So, I opt for the old, whiny, clichéd, "oh, but I have such a bad knee. Flares up from time to time." For good measure, I wince and rub the non-existent injury. It's an Oscar-worthy performance. Way better than anything Leo's ever done.

Blaze smiles serenely. "Yoga is good for the joints, child. Your partner can rub aromatherapy oil in the areas providing grievance. We will see you both in forty minutes, in the yoga sanctuary."

He floats away, long silk scarves billowing behind him. And I mean scarves (plural)—he's wearing about six of them.

I whirl around to Aiden and point a breadstick at him. Unfortunately, he uses this opportunity to take a photo of me. Breadstick wielding and all. "Stop that! And there will be *no* rubbing of oil anywhere. Under any circumstances. *Comprende?*"

I expect Aiden to fire back some ridiculously flirtatious comment to make me blush, as per usual. Instead, he lowers his camera and rolls his eyes. "Relax, Court. We'll go in there, mess around with some yoga poses and leave. What's the big deal?"

I open my mouth. Shut it again. Reopen it, and stuff my breadstick into it so it appears like I opened my mouth to eat, and not to gape like a stunned salmon.

What *is* the big deal? Surely, couple's yoga can't be that bad? I've done yoga before. Once. I used a coupon for a free class. It was held in a school gym that smelled like cheese and feet, and now that I think about it, probably wasn't very authentic, as far as yoga classes go.

"Look," Aiden continues, splaying his hands. "It's part of the deal. We have to do all the activities, remember? It's going to be in the report. You don't want to piss off Blaze Half Moon already, do you?"

This is true. I don't want to get sent home early in disgrace. Or have Philippe change his mind about giving me my job back. Imagine he figured out that I was lying and laughed at me for pretending to have a boyfriend (because, how pathetic).

Plus, I really do want to go snorkeling.

"Okay," I grouch. "Just make sure your hands nama-stay away from my butt, okay?"

Aiden laughs. "I think I can manage that."

As soon as we finish breakfast, I run back to the bungalow at breakneck speed and change out of my sundress and bikini. Instead, I rifle through my bag and throw on the baggiest tank top I can find along with a pair of leggings. I scrape my humidity-puffed hair into a tight bun and take a glance in the mirror.

Makeup free, frizzy hair, bag-lady clothes. I barely recognize myself.

The universe must be getting a real kick out of this crazy, cosmic joke that is my current life situation.

But, there's nothing I can do. The hair and makeup has

been decided for me (I checked at the front desk—they have free hairdryers available, but no straighteners. And, no guest makeup, which surely must downgrade them half a star, don't you think?)

The clothes, though, are for my own protection. Definitely don't need Aiden to identify the lump near my belly button.

We may have called a truce for now, but this is still war. And you never give away your secrets to the enemy.

24

AIDEN

I regret laughing.

Because yoga? Yeah, way harder than it looks.

I'm ashamed to admit that all those times I saw people lining up at the gym in their Lululemons with their glittery mats and designer water bottles, I made a terribly unfair assumption. A judgment I would now like to formally and officially retract.

My stomach muscles ache, there's a river of sweat trickling down my spine, and freaking Blaze—who's wearing tie-dye leggings and a cropped belly shirt—keeps telling me to "just *breathe* into it."

Whatever the heck that means.

We haven't even gotten to the "couples" portion of the workout yet. According to Blaze, "for a healthy relationship to flourish, you must first focus on being healthy and whole yourself, on being the best version of yourself. Then, you can truly invest in your partner."

It's surprisingly good advice, coming from a middle-aged guy with feather earrings and a blue streak in his hair. I just wish that the warm, candlelit, mirror-walled studio space—which smells like a soothing combination of lemon-

170

grass and sage—had given me an indication of how difficult the workout would be. Or, that I'd been aware of how embarrassingly inflexible I am.

Glancing around the room, I'm slightly gratified to see that none of the other men seem to be faring any better.

Courtney, meanwhile, looks perfectly poised and zen, the picture of yin-yang in a slouchy, but cute, white tank top and black leggings. Her skin glows, and her hair is pulled back to show off the elegant angles of her neck and shoulders.

We're in the middle of a merciful five minute break, and I've used the break as an excuse to get out of my pretzel position and take pictures for the rebranding. I've captured the room, the couples, Blaze helping a lady while her man looks on.

And, I've got plenty of photos of Courtney. So many photos of Courtney, it's almost embarrassing. I have her laughing, her face twisted in concentration mid-pose, her meditating with her eyes closed.

Eventually, I lower my camera and join her on our mats. She's leaning forward, delicately stretching. She seems unaware of the attention she's getting, the stolen glances she's attracting from everyone, myself included.

A guy across the room keeps looking at her like his eyes have been stuck with superglue. I can't say I'm a fan. He's here with his partner, and all his attention is on *my* partner.

Back off, Bozo! I give the guy a stern warning look before fixing my gaze back on Court. A flutter kicks in my stomach at the still-strange thought that I'm here with Courtney Turner.

Her hands move down her leg and wrap around her foot as she pulls her body forward, arcing over her long limbs. Heat gathers in my stomach, and as she gives me a side-eyed smile, I studiously guzzle my water.

"Doing okay there, Shaw?"

"Never better." I wipe the sweat from my brow with a towel. I work out four days a week—why am I suffering so badly?

"You can tap out, you know. Quit. No one will judge you." She tugs on her toes, deepening her stretch, and my fingers tighten on my water bottle. "Well, almost no one. I'll judge you. Harshly."

"Nothing new, then. I'm sure I can handle it."

"Oh no. This will be a whole new level of scorn." Her tongue darts along her lower lip. "I thought you were in good shape."

I can't help but smirk. "Thanks for noticing."

I'm happy to see that mesmerizing flush bloom on her cheeks, across her neck and collarbones.

Bonggggg!

Blaze, who has already taken us through an hour of pretzel contortions, bangs the gong twice more. "Okay, lovers. Now, we'll enter the 'couples' part of the class."

Courtney's blush deepens.

"Looking a little overheated, Turner." I grin. "Maybe you're the one who wants to tap out?"

"In your dreams," she practically snarls.

"Yogis, we begin this practice by coming to a seat. Cross-legged and facing your lover." Blaze waves his hands like he's performing a complicated magic ritual.

I shoot Courtney a smile and pat my mat. "Let's go, *lover*."

"Call me that one more time and I'll *accidentally* downward dog you in the danglies."

I burst into laughter. "Has anyone ever told you that you have a way with words?"

"Constantly." Courtney pats her own mat. "And you can come next to me. I'm not moving."

"Okay." Then, while she still seems surprised that I agreed with her, I move to sit in front of her. Cross-legged. And way closer than necessary.

My knees skim hers, and I swear she inhales a quick breath.

"Comfortable?" I inquire innocently, my voice perfectly masking my pulse, which is throbbing like a strobe light at a 90's rave. This close, I can smell her scent—a combination of sweet and salt and heat. Warm salted caramel swirls in cool vanilla ice cream.

"Never better," she shoots my own words back at me without missing a beat. Smiles broadly. "So comfortable I could do this all day."

Challenge accepted.

I smirk. Inch forward a little so her knees slot under mine. She's wearing pants, so our skin doesn't actually touch, but heat simmers where our legs are pressed together. She looks at our limbs intently, and her teeth press on her bottom lip. Then, she lifts her head to meet my gaze.

The look in her eyes makes me suck in a breath. There's still a challenge in her expression, but behind that, there's something else. Something that looks nervous, yet wanting, all at once. Like, touching has sparked a brand new sensation that we're both trying to pretend doesn't affect us in the least. Because admitting the truth would mean losing the battle.

"Still comfortable?" I ask, my voice thicker than expected.

She shakes her head slightly, eyes never leaving mine. "No."

The word sends my insides into freefall.

"Perfect, Mr. Shaw, Miss Turner," Blaze booms suddenly, making us spring apart. The movement is so sudden, I lose my balance and do a weird Humpty-Dumpty roll backwards, windmilling my arms to right myself.

Courtney looks thrilled. Hides a smile behind her hand.

"Perfect," she echoes Blaze in a voice just quiet enough for only me to hear. She's smiling like she won the lottery. "That was literally perfect. You looked like a boiled egg."

"A boiled egg?"

"Yeah. You're lucky. If you were a raw egg, you would have cracked clean in two."

"Bet you would have loved that."

She ignores me. "You know, if you sit forward a little, straighten your back and tense your stomach muscles, you'll have better balance when cross-legged."

"Is that what you're doing?" My voice is low and rough as sandpaper. I try not to imagine her abs contracting under her tank top as she sits before me.

Courtney visibly tenses at my words, making my imagination go haywire.

At that moment, Blaze materializes next to us once again. "I'll use you two to demonstrate."

I blink out of my tense-muscle-trance. "Huh?"

"Oh no, that won't be necessary—" Courtney starts.

But, Blaze is already kneeling in front of us. "Everyone, please turn your attention here."

Ten pairs of curious eyes fall on us. Courtney winces, and I feel a bit bad for getting her into this situation. She seems to hate attention. Not what I expected from my loud-mouthed neighbor. But this is becoming quite a regular thing with Courtney—always expect the unexpected.

Blaze has us resume our cross-legged-knees-touching position, then asks us to stretch our arms, palms up, in a "gesture of vulnerability and openness."

I take Courtney's suggestion—straight spine, weight

forward. My abs tense, and my center of gravity immediately feels more stable. More grounded.

"Thanks for the tip," I mutter while Blaze continues addressing the class.

Courtney chuckles, and her sweet breath washes over me. "Didn't want to bring in all the king's horses and men for repairs."

I snort with laughter and Courtney smirks. Our eyes catch and hold. Just like they did the night of the viral video. But, this time, the stakes feel higher.

"Yes, yes," Blaze coaxes. "Maintain that eye contact. Now, I want you to touch each other using your eyes."

I'm on the verge of *rolling* my eyes at that statement. Which sounds as ludicrous as "breathe into that yoga pose."

Then, Blaze adds, "communicate your feelings for each other without using words."

It's a pretty insane notion. But, I'm here and I've already suffered through yoga, so why not do another un-Aiden-like thing today?

I focus my attention on my eye contact with Courtney. We've done this before. But, as I stare at her, something I've never, ever experienced happens. My pulse quickens, my breath goes shallow, and then, I see her pupils dilate.

It's like a flare goes off in my body. Heat springs to the surface of my skin, which simultaneously chills with goosebumps. I take in Courtney's wide eyes, her parted lips, and my mind goes hazy with static. Just like in the restaurant over a week ago, the background fades away. The candles, the incense, the windchimes, the staring couples melt into oblivion.

This time, though, there's no tension, no icicle daggers, no battle being fought. And, with all those distractions stripped away, I simply stare into the transparent, crystal blue of her irises, and I see her.

Really see her.

I want to dig deeper, learn more.

It occurs to me that I'm feeling something that isn't logical, hasn't been thought out in advance. None of what I'm feeling makes any sense whatsoever... and yet, I want to keep on feeling it.

As I gaze into Courtney's eyes, I can't help but wonder: does this have to be war?

And, if not, am I willing to wave my white flag for good?

25

COURTNEY

"This is ridiculous," I mutter—more to myself than to Aiden —as I put my bushwhacking skills to the test and karate-chop a shrubby thing out of my way. The stubborn bush stays in place, not budging an inch, and my hand throbs in pain. "Owww!"

Spoiler: If there really *were* such an insane thing as a Nobel prize in bushwhacking, I would not be receiving it any time this century.

I give up on bushwhacking for a moment so I can swat a pesky mosquito on my arm, and I'm rewarded with a wet *squelch* as the blood-filled critter explodes under my palm. Gross.

My hair is a cloud of humidity frizz, there's bug bites over every inch of my exposed flesh, and I need to pee. Badly. But, the nearest bathroom is miles away, and I will literally lie down and sacrifice myself to the killer mosquitoes for lunch before I squat behind a tree and pee out here in the jungle with Aiden Shaw.

I grit my teeth. Adjust my backpack. Take another step forward. And trip over a tree root.

"Whoa, you okay there?"

Two paces ahead of me, Aiden has morphed into Indiana Jones, moving through the jungle with agility and grace. His hair is tousled, his smile is wide, and the ropes of muscle in his tanned arms ripple as he makes a path for us. All the while not tripping over a single thing or breaking out in red welts. Not fair.

"Just dandy," I mutter darkly as Aiden holds out a strong hand to steady me. "Thanks."

Surprisingly, Aiden is the least annoying thing about the current situation—aside from his apparent ability to repel mosquitoes so successfully that they attack me instead.

He's finally put away that freaking camera of his—at my repeated insistence after one too many in-my-face *click-clicks*. No one should have the misfortune of seeing me in this state, and if I wasn't using all of my mental energy to survive, I would happily launch the thing over the nearest bug-infested waterfall.

We've been hiking for about half an hour, but it only took me five minutes to work out that I am not cut out for wilderness life. After we make it out of this jungle, I'm going to take a long, hot bubble bath. Then, I'm going to craft a strongly-worded complaint letter about Blaze freaking Crescent Moon and his intolerable cruelty to resort guests under the guise of an activity called a "survival simulation."

This is what is supposed to constitute the "mind" section of our body, mind and soul revamp as a couple. As beautiful as the lush jungle is—with the startlingly green vegetation, tropical-scented flowers, and sunlight streaming through the canopy of trees—I'd prefer to be here for a pleasant walk of my own accord. Instead of being stuck on a forced mission to foil the resort staff into thinking Aiden and I are falling back in love with each other.

Hah.

Today's task is to follow a cryptic map, which we have to navigate to the finish line. As if we didn't have enough excitement for one day at couples' yoga earlier.

A dangerous thrill runs through my body as I remember that dark, incensed yoga studio. How close I was to Aiden. His Pacific eyes bored into mine, wild and untamed as a crashing California tide.

This time, I'll admit that I grabbed a surfboard. Paddled out a little. Before riding to shore clinging onto my fibreglass liferaft for dear life.

I didn't hate it. In fact, it gave me a rush. And I let myself relish the feeling of being slightly out of my depths, slightly out of control of the situation.

Now, here we are again, a few short hours later, and I've voluntarily handed over the reins. The Courtney from just two days ago would have yanked the map out of Aiden's hands and insisted on doing it her way (never mind the fact that she is directionally-challenged). Then, she would've argued with Aiden every step of the way. Just because she didn't want to give over any power, let him get one up on her.

And okay, fine. I admit that I may have done just that for the first few minutes of our expedition. I may have taken the map and commandeered the lead. And that may be the reason we're lost.

But, at least I'm able to admit that? Well, Aiden made me admit it as I handed over the map with my tail between my legs (his exact words were "Repeat after me: My name is Courtney Turner and I am not always right.")

As it turns out, Aiden is a much better navigator than I am. As in, when he looks at the map, he actually seems to understand it. So, against all my natural instincts, I am following him.

Though I still draw the line at peeing anywhere in his vicinity.

I'm so lost in thought, I don't notice when Aiden comes to a sudden stop.

I run into his brick wall of a body, solid and muscular, and the air leaves my lungs. "Oof!"

He reaches out to steady me, but before I can speak, he puts a finger to his lips. "Shhh."

He wraps one arm around my shoulders protectively, pulling my body close. His large fingers splay over my clavicle, sending a million tiny daggers of sensation to concentrate in the area. He tilts his head to one side, indicating what he sees.

"Stay still," he murmurs into my hair, his voice a little *too* calm. "Make no sudden movements."

I, of course, practically swivel my head right off my neck to look.

All the blood drains from my face.

Monkeys. Everywhere.

And not cute, cuddly monkeys a la Marcel from *Friends* or Abu from *Aladdin*.

I'm talking nightmare monkeys. Teeth-baring monkeys.

Hundreds, maybe thousands, of them.

Closing in.

Their beady eyes are locked on us. Looking at us like we're the Capulets gatecrashing a Montague family reunion —I.e. We are not welcome. At all.

Sweat pricks my forehead and my hands go clammy.

"Aiden?" My whisper comes out all pitchy and strange.

Aiden tightens his grip, holds me close. He puts his lips to my ear. "I've got you, you're safe. On my count, we'll back away slowly, okay?"

"Okay," I wheeze, because all the oxygen has left my body.

"And whatever you do, don't run."

I nod once.

Then, I run.

∿

"Agggggggh!"

I sprint through the trees, feeling like I've been running forever. In reality, it's been about eighteen seconds. But, time slows down when you're about to die.

Fact.

There are heavy footsteps behind me, hot on my heels, but no way am I slowing down to find out if it's Aiden or King Kong.

I thought monkeys were meant to be cute, fluffy and adorable? Wrong wrong wrong. I'm suing Curious George for wrongful impersonation when—*if*—I get home.

I stumble forward blindly. Then, something grabs me, wraps around my body, and I let out another blood-curdling shriek.

"Trying to deafen me, Court? Keep it down!"

"Aiden?" I gasp hoarsely, relief flooding my body. There is apparently a first time for everything, and right now, I am exceedingly glad that Aiden Shaw has graced me with his presence.

"Don't worry, I've got you." Aiden's mouth is so close, his minty breath tickles my cheek. His hands settle on my hips, and I'm not too terrified to notice the sparks flying through me when his skin touches mine. My adrenaline spikes further. Which is precisely the last thing I need.

At that moment, Aiden jerks my body left, off the path and into a wall of trees.

"What are you doing?" I hiss. "Aren't there a thousand monkeys chasing us?"

"There were, like, five of them, Court. I don't know if they're coming after us, but we need to get out of here, just in case."

His hands slide from my hips, coaxing a shiver from me, and he takes my hand. He pulls me forward and I trip along, letting him guide me once again. Not that I have much of a choice at this point. The last thing I want is for my obituary to read "death by monkey."

We trudge through the forest, stumbling over tree roots and vines, a cloud of silence surrounding us, until finally, a few very long minutes later, Aiden visibly relaxes. "I think we're good, they aren't coming after us."

I still can't speak, so I nod. Right as we pop out into a lush, green clearing.

It's a stunning sight, and I instantly feel more relaxed. We might as well have just come across an oasis. The air is calm and floral-scented, and the warm sun beats down. There's a waterfall at the far end of a stretch of green grass, sputtering over jutting rocks and into a small, sapphire-hued pool.

I slow to a stop, mesmerized, and Aiden slows too.

"Wow," he breathes.

Satisfied that we've shaken off our predators (for now), I walk towards the pool and Aiden follows close behind me. I'm dripping with sweat, my heart still lurching frantically, and I want nothing more than to catch my breath.

We settle on a large boulder overlooking the pond, and Aiden pulls off his sneakers. He dangles his feet into the water, and I copy him. The water is blessedly cool as it slides over my feet and up my calves, and I sigh in relief.

My pounding heart starts to settle to a rhythm less like a galloping showpony. As my head clears from its fear fog, I realize what I've done.

"I never should've taken off like that, Aiden. I'm sorry. I

panicked..." I trail off, my mouth dry as I recall that terrifying moment.

But, instead of seeming angry or frustrated (as he probably should), Aiden flashes that smug grin that, not two days ago, made me want to rip his head off. "I thought you were an animal lover."

"I am. I adore animals. All of them. Except birds." I frown. "And monkeys, as it turns out."

"Birds?"

"Are the living incarnations of evil."

Aiden laughs, the sound a comforting rumble. "Don't worry about it, we weren't in any real danger." A pause. "At least, I don't think we were."

"We definitely were," I insist, moving my feet back and forth in the water to create ripples on the surface. "Grave danger. Only reason I ran away, pinky swear."

This comment earns me a smile. "And here I was, thinking that this morning's yoga class would be the most eventful thing to happen today."

"Blaze has so much to answer for," I grumble.

"Maybe I'll lock him in the steam room at the spa tomorrow so he can't bother us for the rest of the trip."

"Deal."

Aiden chuckles again and we lapse into silence. A calm, comfortable silence. Almost a... friendly silence. Which is big of him, if I'm honest. I pretty much sacrificed the man to a gang of monkeys.

I bite my lip as I swirl my feet through the pool, noticing how close my toes get to Aiden's without actually touching him.

"I should send my parents here," Aiden says. "They'd think Blaze was a kindred spirit."

I scoop my hair over one shoulder to let the sun hit my back. Aiden's eyes follow my hands, and despite the warmth, his attention pulls another shiver out of me. Ridiculous. I am a shiver-free zone, usually. Must be delirious from my near-death experience.

"Jess keeps me vaguely updated on their whereabouts," I say. "Last I heard, they were in Kathmandu?"

"Mud wrestling in India." Aiden offers me a wry smile and a shrug of his shoulders. "They're batty, but I love them. You have insane parents, too?"

A lump forms in my throat, and I shake my head as if trying to dislodge it. "No."

The pressure of today feels a bit much at this moment—Aiden, so close to me. Aiden, saving me. Aiden, Aiden, Aiden.

"My Gramma raised me. She passed away a few years back."

Aiden presses his lips together. "Sorry, Court. Not my place to ask."

"Don't be. I never knew my dad, and my mom... Well, I guess I wasn't the daughter she hoped for." I hold my hands up in a "meh, what can you do?" motion.

"How so?"

A painful throb moves through my temples, and my eyes get teary. "She left when I was little."

Aiden moves his hand closer to mine on the boulder. I don't move away, for some reason. Not even when his thumb grazes over the edge of my hand, tracing it. "I'm so sorry, Courtney."

Somehow, the sensation of his thumb moving along my skin soothes the ache in my heart. The hollow pain I feel when I think about how, since my Gramma died, I've been alone in the world. "It's okay. It made me stronger, helped me stand on my own two feet."

Aiden nods, like he understands. "That doesn't make it any less difficult, though."

"I guess not. But I'm fine," I insist, cringing at the thought of his sympathy. "More than fine, in fact. I've got everything under control."

Except these confusing new feelings for you.

"I know you do, Court. You're incredibly strong."

"Thanks. I usually don't like to talk about my family."

"I get that."

"I sometimes wonder what it would've been like to grow up in a family with two parents. With a brother or sister. You and Jess are so close, it's nice." Jess is my best friend in the world, but I know that our friendship will never replace blood. Replace that bond that she has with Aiden.

"I'd do anything for Jess," Aiden says. "I know I'm lucky to have my family, but sometimes..." He stops. Startles. Nods at a point just in front of us. "Hey, check it out."

I put my hands over my eyes, stomach twisting. "Please don't tell me the rogue primates have found us."

"I promise, it's not. Just look."

I press my lips together then decide to believe him. I peek through scrunched-up piggie eyes, like squinting will protect me from any impending wildlife attacks. When I see what he sees, I clap a hand over my mouth. "Oh!"

On the extended limb of a tree in front of us sprawls a huge, steel-gray lizard, sunning himself. He has a spiny tail, a horned nose, and a hideously ugly, wrinkled hide.

"He's so cute!" I coo softly. "Hey, Mr. Lizard."

Aiden looks at me like I've just spoken Mandarin. "I wouldn't call that thing cute." He shakes his head. Looks at the lizard, and adds, "no offense, buddy."

The lizard closes his eyes, like he's determined that we are, in no way, a threat, and is now simply pained by our inane conversation.

"He takes great offense! He's super cute," I insist. "The uglier the animal, the cuter it is. Fact."

Aiden laughs. "Is that so?"

He's doing that *thing* again. Where he looks at me with those gleaming eyes like he doesn't want to look away.

I swallow. "Yup."

He presses his hand against mine a touch harder, sending a fresh, hot rush of sensation to the area. "It's different for humans, though," he says in a low voice that has no business being as sexy as it is.

"What do you mean?" I ask, slightly breathless.

"Because you are the opposite of ugly, but your stance on animal ugliness is the cutest thing ever." Aiden smiles softly.

All the blood drains from my head, and I'm lost for a response.

Before I can restart my short-circuited brain, Aiden gives me a lingering look, then turns away. Busies himself putting his shoes back on. "Come on, we'd better get out of here."

I nod, still mute.

Cute.

A lot of women don't relish being called cute. But I love the word.

Cute means likeable. Endearing.

Over the years, I've been invited on plenty of first dates. Maybe the man thinks I'm pretty. Or, at minimum, presentable, with my well-executed makeup and fashion-forward clothes. But, the second he sees my personality, he slaps me with all kinds of labels: Weird. Quirky. Different.

Words that are a polite way of saying "freakshow."

Then, there's Aiden—the man I'm supposed to hate—using a word to describe me that has, in my mind, no negative connotations whatsoever.

I let out a long, slow breath as I trudge behind him.

Aiden Shaw thinks I'm cute.

26

COURTNEY

After 359 correct directions from Aiden and zero from me, we emerge from the wilderness, largely unscathed. Save for my pride, which has many wounds to lick this evening. Oh, and the bug bites.

Blaze Crescent Moon and two tall, icy glasses of lemon water are waiting at the finish line.

I chug my water greedily, like I've been in the desert for twenty days instead of in the jungle for two hours. Aiden laughs, takes a few sips, and hands me the rest of his to finish. I'm so thirsty, I don't even question the (actually really kind) gesture.

"Well done, Mr. Shaw, Miss Turner." Blaze claps his hands, and I notice that he's painted his nails a shimmering silver color. "You've completed your task in excellent time due to your teamwork."

"Aiden did all the work," I blurt, surprising myself. Two pairs of curious eyes turn to me, and I don't miss the shadow of a smile that flashes over Aiden's handsome face. Encouraged—and wanting to give credit where credit is due—I continue. "I'm terrible with maps, it turns out. If it wasn't for Aiden, they would've had to send out a search party."

Blaze looks at Aiden, who shrugs. "I like logical things. Maps make sense to me."

"So, I guess we failed this project due to a lack of teamwork," I say, feeling a touch defeated. "I take full responsibility."

Aiden takes my hand, a strangely casual, reflexive action, like he's done it hundreds of times. Our fingers intertwine, and he squeezes softly, which spurs an entire flock of butterflies to burst out of their net and swarm my stomach.

Blaze looks at our hands, then smiles a smile that holds the light of a thousand suns.

"My child," he addresses me directly, not Aiden. Aiden is never "child." Though, given that Aiden is six-foot-two, muscular, manly, and *I'm* the one acting childish today, I'm less bothered by the moniker. "On the contrary, you have passed with flying colors. Teamwork means encouraging each other's strengths, praising each other's successes, and letting your teammate take the lead every once in a while."

I blink, and in the corner of my eye, I notice Aiden's smile.

"To be in a successful partnership, you need to build each other up. And admit your weaknesses when necessary." Blaze nods. "You have been successful on all fronts with this task."

I sneak a sideways glance at Aiden and he's still smiling. Really smiling, his face lit up like Blaze's words mean something to him.

Like this is more than just some daft stunt he's doing for a promotion.

I shiver, then steel myself. Despite how often Aiden has surprised me on this vacation, it would be crazy to think that this is anything other than a temporary truce—a facade —meant to benefit us both.

So, why does his behavior—this sudden, rapidly-growing warm feeling between us—suggest something else entirely?

Blaze swans off and Aiden turns to me, still smiling that smile that hits like a punch to the gut. "Back to the bungalow, I guess?"

"I guess so."

We walk back to our bungalow side by side and I sneak a glance up at him—at his sharp jawline, his handsome, strong profile, the tiny freckle on his top lip.

"Glad to have our first full day of activities over with?" he asks.

"No more yoga or jungle trekking for me."

Aiden chuckles. "Should we hit up the beach restaurant after we shower? I'm starving."

We?

Our programming is over—we're not required to spend another second together until tomorrow morning. But, Aiden's talking like he hasn't considered that. Like it's only natural that we embark on our next activity... together.

Like we're a real team. Choosing to spend time together.

And, if I'm really honest with myself, there's only one answer I want to give.

"I'd love to."

27

AIDEN

The beach is lit up with flickering tiki torches, replacing the sun that's long since set. Along the shoreline, fire spinners dance, throwing balls of flaming light into the night sky and catching them effortlessly. A warm breeze carries off the ocean, making the white tablecloths dance.

Courtney watches the fire spinners, entranced. Meanwhile, I keep catching myself watching her.

Her eyes are wide and curious, and a smile plays on her lips, like this is the most amazing thing she's ever seen. Under the table, she's kicked off her flip flops and her toes draw lines in the sand in time to the steel drum music. I've taken more than a few sneaky photos of her these last few days, but as beautiful as she looks right now, I want to take the night off from thinking about work. Enjoy the moment with her.

"Good evening sir, madam." A waiter appears beside our side and places two huge, tropical cocktails in front of us. "Our special rum punch to start off your dining experience."

Courtney startles, then turns to beam at him. "Thank you. What's it made of?"

The waiter rattles off a long list of ingredients while Courtney listens, head cocked to one side. A small frown appears between her eyebrows for a moment, then disappears.

"Wonderful, thanks so much. Would you mind bringing some sparkling water, too?"

"Coming right up."

As the waiter moves away, I hold up my glass. "A toast?"

Courtney holds up her glass, smirks. "To escaping packs of rabid monkeys?"

"I ain't toasting no monkeys."

"To viral videos winning us dream vacations, then?"

"I'll drink to that."

We clink our glasses, and I take a huge gulp of the delicious concoction. Courtney raises her glass to her lips, but then sets it back down without taking a sip. "Who would've thought a public food-slinging match would send us to paradise together?"

"It was worth wearing pudding for," I say with a smile. "And almost worth having a video of us circulating on the internet for the whole world to see."

The line reappears between Courtney's brows. I want to reach out and smooth it away with my thumb, but I resist.

"Hey, Aiden?" She chews her lower lip, eyelashes fanning her cheeks as she looks down.

"Yeah?"

"I'm, uh, sorry Breanna broke up with you because of me."

"Don't be." I shrug. "It was our second and final date, anyway."

"What do you mean?"

"It wasn't going anywhere. She, um, wasn't really my type."

191

"What is your type then?" Her voice has a strange edge to it, soft but with a sharp undertone.

"I'm... not sure," I eventually answer, surprised by my own abrupt honesty on something I usually hate talking about. She frowns, puzzled, and I shake my head. Rub the heels of my hands into my eyes. "I'm not exactly, um, good with making connections. You know, like, letting my guard down, letting people in. Which, I guess, sounds weird."

Courtney's eyes are laser sharp, her face frozen. Then, she nods stiffly. "Not weird. I get it."

I look at her closely, and realize she's telling the truth. She does get it.

Courtney always acts like nothing bothers her, like she's bulletproof. And before now, I've never gotten close enough to peer through the chinks in all that battle armor of hers. But, for the first time in four years, I'm seeing her in a new light. She's not as hard as she likes to act. Rather, she's a paradox. Tough and soft, sweet and sour, strong and delicate—all at once.

And not for the first time this weekend, I find myself wanting to dive in.

There's a pause and we both shift a tad uncomfortably. Then—thankfully—we're interrupted by the waiter, who reappears at our side with a carafe of sparkling water and a notepad.

"Hi!" we say in unison, way too brightly.

The poor guy, startled by our enthusiasm, smiles feebly. "What can I get for you?"

I order the Surf N' Turf, then wait patiently as Courtney asks a couple of detailed questions. She eventually orders salmon, plain rice and salad. It isn't the first time I've noticed her being careful with what she orders.

"Do you have allergies or something?" I ask, curious, when the waiter strides off.

"Or something," she says, reaching for the water carafe. Her thumb is on her index finger again, picking at the side of her nail.

Somehow, I know that there's more to this. But, as curious as I am, I decide to drop the subject. I don't want to push her, I'd rather give her space and respect. If Courtney wants to share whatever this is with me, I want her to do it of her own accord.

So, Courtney and I eat dinner in the glow of moonlight and spinning strings of fire. We talk, have a real, pleasant conversation. Before this trip, we never used to do this, never used to take the time to actually get to know each other. It's nice.

Courtney tells me about when her dogs escaped her backyard a few months back and took themselves on a walk to a local butcher shop. I tell her stories about Jess and me as teenagers. About the time I may or may not have scared the pants off her eleventh grade braceface boyfriend before their Junior Prom.

"Or," I correct myself, "I should say I scared his pants *on*. At all times."

Courtney laughs, slow and low like warm honey. "If you'd been my brother, you would've had your hand in a bucket of warm water the second you went to sleep that night."

I'm so freaking glad I'm not your brother.

With every conversation we have, every quirk of her smile, every playful, teasing, mischievous shine of her eyes, I'm realizing that this woman is... incredible. Funny, playful and sassy as hell, but man, I kind of dig that.

Too soon, the waiter takes our empty plates and offers us the dessert menu. Courtney politely declines, so I do the same.

I hadn't even noticed that, during our conversation, the

steel drummers finished their set and the jazz band that plays every night took the stage. The band is fronted by a sequin-dressed woman crooning Ella Fitzgerald. But, as objectively pretty as she may be, I can't tear my eyes away from Courtney.

Couples rise from their tables, one by one. Time for the dancing portion of the evening.

Then, I notice that Blaze is nowhere to be seen. Actually, none of the resort staffers are so much as glancing in our direction. Could it be that we've presented such a convincing front that they've given up on scrutinizing us?

It occurs to me that Courtney and I don't have to dance together tonight. We can sit here, watch, continue to talk. But, I find that I *want* to ask her to dance.

And, maybe it's the rum punch or the tropical breeze or the firelight that feels like voodoo magic. But I make a decision. Of the crazy, snap variety.

I swallow, offer Courtney a half-smile as a pit of uncharacteristic nerves gathers in my stomach. Surely this step is going to get magnificently shot down, seeing as no one is paying any attention to us. Courtney will likely just laugh in my face. But, it's worth a try, isn't it?

"Would you like to dance?" I ask quietly.

Courtney blinks, surprised, then takes a look around.

Registers that no one is watching. Blaze is nowhere to be seen. There's nothing driving her to do this.

She lets out a breath. Pauses. Her face is hard, guarded.

Then, she tilts her head, making her beachy curls tumble forward. Her cheeks turn pink, her eyes brighten. And that small change in her expression—the shift to reveal that she might, for a moment, trust me—feels more significant than even the brightest of smiles.

"It would look weird if we didn't, wouldn't it?" she finally says.

I glance around. Plenty of couples are seated. It wouldn't look weird at all if we were among them.

"Yeah, super weird," I find myself saying instead. "We don't want to make anyone suspicious."

Courtney runs her tongue along the edge of her teeth. "Definitely not."

We move towards the dance floor, and nervous anticipation clenches my stomach. This time, when I take her in my arms, she coils her hands behind my neck easily. Our bodies move together, in sync. It's slow, natural, comfortable, and yet, my heart won't stop racing.

The band begins to play a new song—"At Last." And the moment carries me away. I'm holding Courtney close, moving to the music under a velvet canopy of stars, knowing nothing but her warm skin and crystal eyes and the salty-sweet smell of her skin.

It feels good to be spending time with her. No sparring, no games, no animosity. And it might sound crazy, but it almost feels like I've been waiting for this moment. For here and now. Like it was always meant to happen.

She looks up at me, her face questioning. Wordlessly, I smile.

In response, she smiles back. A smile meant just for me.

It's a smile that ignites something in me. Something I've never felt before, something undeniable.

28

COURTNEY

The next morning brings a spatter of warm tropical rain, and the two activities that I've been dreading—couples counseling, and the spa.

While most people might understand my dread to partake in couples counseling with someone who is most definitely not my boyfriend—who actually happens to be my nemesis, but I have the unfortunate side effect of feeling all fluttery around—not many people would dread a free trip to a luxury spa.

For me, though, I'd take thirty killer-monkey-ridden jungle treks before plunging into some romantic hot tub/steam room/couples massage combo with Aiden Shaw.

At this point, I've managed to be on an island with Aiden for two days and two nights without having to bare my body in all its non-glory.

And I definitely mean non-glory.

Don't get me wrong, I'm all for body positivity. I'm in full opposition to society promoting unrealistic beauty standards as the norm, and in full support of each woman embracing her own, God-given shape and size—whatever that may be—and being empowered to feel beautiful in her own unique way.

I know all of this, and I believe all of this. And I know I'm not ugly. But sometimes, when I look in the mirror at my knobby knees, bony, wide shoulders, thin hair, and complete lack of chest, I have a hard time loving what I see.

Diabetes did nothing to enhance my looks. And there's the implant. My life-giving implant that punctures my stomach right where it makes it impossible to wear tight dresses or cute bodysuits or trendy, belly-skimming tops.

A part of me knows I shouldn't care, that I should feel empowered to wear my insulin pump on display with pride. But to me, it's like a beacon announcing my flaws to the world. A neon light illuminating my imperfections, my sickness. A constant reminder that I will never live up to expectations. Never be the romance novel heroine, the sexy woman in the tight, cut-out dress who gets the guy.

So, in shame, I hide it. Disguise it. And another part of me hates myself for doing so.

It's a line I constantly toe. At war with myself and my body, while putting up armor for everyone else to stay away.

Knock, knock!

I jump at the noise, wrenched out of my thoughts.

"Ready?" Aiden calls.

I take a deep breath, give myself one last glance in the mirror. I've braided my hair to one side and donned a pink one-piece bathing suit with ruching on the belly. Hiding hiding hiding. I throw on my sarong and open the door. "Yup."

We eat breakfast at the covered buffet restaurant—pineapples, mangoes, and freshly cracked coconuts with a straw to suck the watery liquid out. Aiden takes less photos this morning. Spends more time talking to me.

When we're done, we leg it through the rain to the

counseling center. Which is actually a beautiful pagoda in the resort's tropical rose gardens. With an ocean view, of course.

Only the best, here at Haven.

Today's goal is to reestablish the "soul" part of our connection. I can't imagine what it might involve.

"Whew," Aiden says as we step into the structure. He shakes his hair, like a dog would (only much more attractive, sorry Cassidy) and shoots me that darned grin.

Those stupid resident butterflies start going all swirly again. They might as well have mainlined a pot of espresso and are now intently bouncing off the walls of my stomach as hard as they can. I'm going to have to drink a liter of pesticide later to get rid of them.

Blaze, who is sporting a fetching purple kaftan and multiple beaded necklaces, waits for us. He's sitting on a bamboo mat, hands resting on his knees in the ohm position, eyes closed.

"Miss Turner, Mr. Shaw," he says without opening his eyes. "Please take a seat."

It appears that the only option we have is to sit on one of the bamboo mats. Sigh.

I wring out my hair and shake my sarong, pulling the damp fabric away from my skin. So much for covering up— the garment is plastered to my body.

Aiden's shirt—blue, this morning—is also damp, clinging to his abs in a way that makes me avert my eyes. He sinks to a seated position, sprawls his long legs in front of him, and leans back on his hands. Which may have given me a glimpse of taut, golden skin on his midsection.

But, I wouldn't know because I wasn't looking. Nope.

On my part, I do an awkward shuffle-crouch, turning my legs sideways in what I hope is a modest, non bathing-suit-flashing position. Newsflash: It's not.

I tuck my legs under me and sit on my knees instead.

Blaze finally opens his eyes, takes in our damp, squelchy appearance, and nods. "Rain is nature's water for the soul."

I'm about to correct him, tell him that rain is actually nature's water for the body, but he continues. "We will now feed your souls with affirmations of your love for one another."

Huh?

Aiden gives me a side-eyed glance. I've never seen him look this unsure before. This cautious.

Probably worried that he's going to have to verbally confess what a terrible human being he is, I think. But the thought isn't convincing, my heart's not in it. It's merely a force of habit.

I shrug at him and turn my attention back to Blaze. Shift on the uncomfortable mat as my heart thuds. What's about to happen?

"Miss Turner, please begin by looking at Mr. Shaw and telling him one thing you love about him."

My stomach twists into a firm, solid knot. I swallow thickly, my mouth like cotton. Blaze nods at me in encouragement.

"I... I don't know." I assess Aiden, crinkling my nose. "I guess I like that he sometimes smells like creme caramel."

Aiden snorts, covers the noise with a cough.

Blaze narrows his eyes. "Very funny, Miss Turner," he says in a way that indicates he doesn't find it funny at all. "Seriously, now."

"All right." I sigh. Look at Aiden again. "He's got... a really nice car."

Once again, Blaze doesn't seem particularly fond of my answer. His nostrils flare slightly. "That is what we call an observation."

"It's a company car, anyways," Aiden mutters helpfully.

Not. I will say I'm surprised, though—I assumed he chose that fancy, flashy Audi himself.

"Now, Miss Turner," Blaze continues, tone uncharacteristically stern. "If you aren't going to take this seriously, I'm afraid—"

"Fine," I say, almost morosely. "I'm sorry, I'll be serious. I guess I like how..." I look at Aiden and trail off. There's a gloss of water over his cheeks, and his damp dark hair falls across his forehead. Frick. He even looks good when he's soaking wet. "I like that Aiden makes me feel like I can be myself and he won't judge me for it."

Wait, what?! Like, solid WTF. Where did THAT come from?

Aiden's eyes widen a touch, and I blink a couple of times, startled by my own words.

"Very good." Blaze smiles at me sagely. "Mr. Shaw, it's your turn. May I please hear *two* things you love about Miss Turner?"

Aiden has a startled, deer-in-the-headlights expression as he turns towards me. The time ticks forward and Aiden runs his fingers back and forth over the ridges of the bamboo, frowning. Like he's thinking. Hard.

Any smugness I might feel about him now being the one in the spotlight disappears.

What's taking so long? Never mind two—can he not think of one nice thing to say about me? This is humiliating... especially after my ridiculous admission.

I run my teeth along my bottom lip, worrying incisor indents into the fleshy pillow as I wait. And wait. My heart inches up my chest cavity until it's in my throat.

This is it. The jig's up. We're meant to be a couple falling in love all over again, and my supposed boyfriend can't come up with a single thing he loves about me. Fake or not.

A deep root of shame takes hold in me. Guess I really am *that* unlovable.

Finally, after both an eternity and an age, Aiden opens his mouth.

"It's hard to know what to say," Aiden says quietly, and my heart sinks further. He finds my eyes. Smiles a very slight, very bashful smile. "There are so many things about Courtney that are unique and special. She's the most loyal, caring friend to my sister—she'd do anything for the people she loves. She's funny and feisty and never scared to challenge me. She has so many sides to her—she's complicated, in a good way. Like a puzzle. And this week, on this vacation, I've seen a new side of her. One that's not afraid to be herself, let her guard down."

I stare at Aiden, open-mouthed, as his wall of words smack me in the face, one by one. I try to steel myself, like I usually do, grit my teeth and bear my armor, but... I can't. The words infiltrate, sliding over my skin and into my pores and sinking into my being. A tear slides down my cheek, unbidden.

Because those words? Words of affirmation, every last one of them. Words I have craved from the people in my life for so long. Words that make me feel seen. Make me feel like it's okay to be me.

And they all spell out an unfortunate little fact that I can no longer ignore: I'm seeing Aiden Shaw in an entirely new light. A good light. A light I like.

A light that's ignited a thousand flares through both my body and my brain.

Which I know is a no-good, very bad, horrible idea.

But it's happening anyway. And the worst part is, I don't think I want to fight it.

29

AIDEN

"Ready for the spa?" I ask, sounding more hopeful than I'd like to.

Our couple's counseling session is finally over, and Blaze has disappeared back into his genie lamp or wherever it is he came from.

Courtney's face pinches. And I get it.

We just went through an hour of serious unloading. For two people who aren't naturally inclined towards raw communication and letting their walls down, we did a lot of honest talking. It was exhausting but satisfying. Worth it.

Now, after spending all morning opening up, I'm surprised to find that I don't want to be alone. Part of me deeply wants to be by her side for whatever comes next (which, according to our official program, is the spa).

I don't think I've ever felt this way with a woman I'm dating, never mind one I'm pretending to date. To get me a promotion. Which is beginning to feel more and more dirty as I realize that there's nobody I'd rather be at Haven with than Courtney. Truce or no truce.

Eventually, Courtney nods slowly. Reluctantly. "Ready as I'll ever be."

"We can skip it?" I offer.

"No, we have to go. It's part of the program." Courtney sounds like she'd rather be tarred and feathered in the street than get a body scrub or mud bath or whatever.

What do people do at spas, anyway? This may come as a shock, but I've never been to one. And I have to assume that, as far as spas go, the Turkish spa here at Haven is pretty fancy-schmancy.

When we arrive, we're greeted at the front door by a lady who embraces us with multiple hugs and kisses.

"Helloooooo!" she coos as she sinks into a little bow. "I am Isadora. Welcome, welcome!"

She looks, and sounds, like a female Blaze. I shoot Courtney an amused glance and she bites her bottom lip to hide her smile. It's an innocent gesture that sends a bolt of lightning through me. Probably meant to smite me down for thinking things I shouldn't about my fake girlfriend.

I seem to keep conveniently forgetting the adjective lately.

To stop my brain from strolling down any inconvenient, clearly insane avenues, I drag my eyes away from her mouth, and pace around the room, taking photos of the spa.

"Today, we will be working on the ancient, sensual erotic art of couple's massage," Isadora announces grandly.

My brain falls out of my body and I just about drop my camera. I look at Isadora, not computing. Her mouth continues to move as she chatters blithely but I don't hear a single word. My brain is in overdrive with what is about to happen. I don't dare look at Courtney.

A few minutes later, Isadora deposits us in a room to "get changed."

The second she leaves, Courtney shrieks, "I'm doing the massaging!"

"Huh?"

203

"Me. I want to be the one learning to give a massage."

"I have literally no idea what you're talking about."

"Did you not listen to a word Isadora said?"

No.

"Yeah..."

Courtney rolls her eyes. "So we're clear, I give the massage, you receive it. Strip off and hop on the table."

"Strip off?!" I say incredulously.

Courtney's cheeks flame but she stands her ground. "You heard me."

"Maybe you should strip off and hop on the table." I suggest with a joking grin. "Do you really want me to get naked?"

Courtney's eyes widen comically, like a cartoon Smurf.

"Keep your shorts on, you big perv," she huffs. "You really weren't listening? Seriously?"

"Honestly? No," I admit a tad sheepishly.

"Well, that decides it. Your punishment is that you're the one getting the massage." Courtney raises her eyebrows, challenging me.

"I feel like we're doing this backwards. Shouldn't we be arguing over who actually *gets* the massage?" I ask.

In all honesty, I have no idea why we're arguing in the first place. We've been getting along so well, I've almost forgotten how we usually interact

Courtney shakes her head. "Who knows where those hands have been?"

Her tone indicates she wants to spar with me, but I don't miss that telltale thumb, picking at her index finger. The way her pupils darken as her voice cracks over her insult.

There's an electric charge in the air, thick and hazy, and a shiver runs down my spine.

This may be the way we usually interact, but we are in

entirely new territory. We're using fighting words, but there's something building between us. Tension mounting at such a rapid rate, it's almost suffocating.

All of our usual feisty back and forth is now backed with the stark realization that, for two days straight, I've been dying to grab her and kiss her.

And the way she's looking at me right now, she wants this as much as I do.

It's like all the hate between us has morphed into something equally sharp and passionate that wants my mouth on hers. And I like it. I don't want to go back to the way things were—I want us to move forwards, not backwards.

I want to kiss her.

Which means that first, I need to show her that the war is over. At least on my end. My weapons are laid down, permanently. She can trust me.

"Fine," I say, my eyes never leaving hers as I concede the argument.

White flag waved.

"Thank you." She smiles her big, bright smile, then puts her hands over her eyes. "Now, strip!"

30

COURTNEY

I just spent an hour rubbing oil on Aiden Shaw's body. I am *not* okay.

That freaking massage altered my brain chemistry, fried my sanity to a crisp.

At the end of the session, Isadora asked if I wanted a turn being massaged. I choked out a very polite "No way in hell!" and bolted for the door.

Now, I am avoiding Aiden for the rest of the afternoon. Making a show of reading in the hammock, frowning at my Kindle with the type of abject concentration I'd need to digest the entire Communist Manifesto in lieu of light holiday reading.

And yes, in reality, I have a swoony romance book loaded up in front of me. But, Aiden doesn't need to know that.

Plus, I can barely concentrate on a single word because every time I read anything about the hero's attractive face, I find myself picturing Aiden. When the hero smiles? Aiden's smug smirk spray-painted in ten-foot-high graffiti on my frontal lobe. And don't even get me started on the biceps... I can still feel them, warm and firm under my shaking hands.

Still hear Aiden's ragged inhale as I slid my fingers along those broad shoulders.

The memory of the sound cuts through me like a knife, setting my skin on fire.

I want... him. This.

Whatever this is, I'm in. Or, so my body keeps telling me that I am.

But, I know that it's more than that. When the heroine in my book speaks of her pounding heart and weak knees, all I can think about is how my heart throbs painfully when Aiden's near me. My physical attraction to him is like a gravitational pull, but that's only one part of it.

Aiden seems to *get* me. Actually get me.

That's scarier than falling in lust with a hot body and ocean eyes, any day of the week. Physical feelings are just feelings, they come and go. But, finding someone you connect with on a deeper level, someone you can communicate with without speaking, someone who makes you laugh without trying to... That's rare.

And, by "rare," I mean that it's never happened to me once in all my thirty years.

It's part of the reason our counseling session freaked me out so much. Blaze's freaking purple kaftan must have spurred on some sort of confessional, because Aiden and I actually managed to have an open, heart-to-heart style conversation. And instead of making fun of me or tearing me down, Aiden listened. Properly listened. Asked thoughtful questions.

He was there for me in a way I've never been supported, but maybe I shouldn't have been surprised. All of our conversations on this trip have been pretty pleasant, with minimal tearing my hair out.

Aiden is actually a... decent human being. A decent friend.

It's throwing me for a loop. When we got to the spa, I realized that I had to be the one to give the massage. The way he was looking at me, I could have sworn he was thinking about kissing me. And it was all I could think about, too. All I wanted in that moment. So, I can't even imagine how my body would have reacted to have his hands gliding over the bare skin of my back and shoulders. The mere thought reduces me to a quivering mess.

But, as it turns out, being the one to give the massage wasn't any less butterfly-inducing.

Which is why I'm doing the very mature, sensible thing and avoiding him. The last thing I want is to let him know how I'm feeling and embarrass myself so badly that I'll have to buy a one-way ticket to Canada. I don't particularly want to move to Saskatchewan or wherever to live out my days as a recluse in a place I'll never be able to spell the name of.

To his credit, Aiden respects my space. My distance.

Or, maybe he's just putting his own distance between us.

It's hard to believe that we're at the end of our trip. Tomorrow, we'll fly back to Atlanta. Share a cab home from the airport. Then, we'll part ways like the Red Sea. Go back to our respective houses and lives. Our ceasefire will be over.

And I'm worried that if I don't wrap myself up in bubble wrap pre-departure, I'm going to be a casualty of my own war.

I feel queasy at the thought.

Nightfall comes too soon, and I make my way to the bungalow, anxious butterflies flying at the thought of seeing Aiden's face. Luckily, he's nowhere to be found. I dart into the bathroom and lock the door. Take my time getting ready for our evening ahead. A final dinner on the beach.

The Last Supper, as I've christened it.

One last feast of the senses before reality comes creeping into my cocoon.

I've chosen my nicest dress for the occasion—floaty pale gold fabric with a low, scooped-out back, and delicate spaghetti straps. I still have no makeup, but I pinch my cheeks and rub Vaseline on my lips and eyelids. Tame my hair with diluted conditioner so it tumbles over my shoulders.

As much armor as I can summon.

I look in the mirror. Take a deep breath.

Go time. One more night of playing pretend.

I step out of the bathroom... And right into Aiden.

"Sorry!" He holds up a hand, takes my arm to—once again—steady me. My anchor in the storm.

No, Courtney. No thinking like that!

He's dressed in charcoal pants and a crisp, white button-down that shows off his killer tan to perfection. The shirt is untucked, only half-buttoned, showing off an isosceles triangle of bare chest. He follows my gaze, shrugs apologetically. "I just finished ironing. I thought I had time to change before you were done in there, and—"

"It's fine," I say shakily.

His fingertips press gently into my arm. "You look incredible."

"Don't say that," I say, some unwanted emotion roaring from deep inside me.

"It's what I think. Why not say it?"

"Maybe you already said enough today."

"What do you mean by that?"

His eyes are intent, gleaming as he looks down at me. What's he thinking?

"It's nothing." I look away, brush off my dress, and try to step around him. Try to pretend I'm not shaking. "Forget about it."

"No." Aiden moves his hand in front of me, effectively blocking my path.

I inhale through my nose, staring at that big, strong hand, splayed just inches from my stomach.

"Excuse me?" I say sharply.

Aiden takes a step towards me, putting his body in the place his hand was. I inhale again, more shakily this time. His proximity, the heady, clean, damp scent rising from under his unbuttoned dress shirt is almost enough to make my knees cave in.

"I said no," Aiden repeats.

I tilt my chin up defiantly, raise my gaze to meet his. It's a mistake. Those midnight blue eyes bore straight into my soul, and my stomach flips over. This is dangerous. Oh, so dangerous.

But, I can't bring myself to take a step backwards. His presence is paralyzing. Never have I ever wanted something so badly that I shouldn't want at all.

"What do you mean, no?" I breathe, not sounding nearly as angry as I mean to. My head is spinning. "You can't just tell me no, like you own me or have—"

"Courtney." He runs one fingertip down my bare arm, leaving a blazing trail of fire and ice in its wake. Goosebumps erupt all over my body. "I mean no, it's not fine. And we both know it."

"What's not fine? I'm fine as... the finest piece of jewelry that ever was. Diamond encrusted in fineness."

"You've been avoiding me all afternoon."

I try to avoid looking at his big hand on my arm. "Well, yeah." My throat clenches. Stomach flutters. "Is that not *fine* with you?"

He shakes his head, eyes riveted on me. Like he can't bear to look away.

"Why not?"

"Because I'm feeling something, and I think you feel it too."

My breath catches. "You are?" I croak.

His eyes drop to my lips and he takes a breath. Moves closer still.

"I am." Aiden's face is close to mine, so close. "And I feel like I'm going to go insane if I wait another second to do this."

"Do what?" My words come out in a breathless gasp. My heart is racing so fast I think it might just take flight.

"First, tell me you feel it too."

Aiden's eyes are intense, powerful waves that threaten to suck me under and spin me around. But, through it all, I feel the most insane sense of clarity.

I could act like I have no idea what he's talking about, but of course, I do. It's all I've been able to think about since the first time I ever saw him.

All I can manage is a nod.

And it's all he needs.

Aiden slides a hand around my back, making every hair stand on end, and pulls me towards him. Roughly. Our bodies slam together, satin dress sliding over his bare torso. Explosive heat rises to the surface of my entire being, and my head swims underwater.

All "DANGER! HIGH VOLTAGE!" thoughts are thrown out the window as Aiden's lips collide with mine and electrocute my body.

A gasp escapes my mouth at the hunger, the sheer desire in his kiss. The sensation shocks me, rocks me to my core, and unfortunately, flips the "off" switch in my brain. As such, my hands develop minds of their own and go for a wander up Aiden's back, tracing the hard, corded bands of hot muscle they find in absolute wonder.

Aiden groans and twists his hand more tightly in my

hair. His other arm wraps around me and finds the small of my back, and he places his hand to steady my body as he guides me towards the edge of the room. He's the Pied Piper, and I am nothing but a hypnotized convert dancing to his mesmerizing tune.

Aiden gently but firmly maneuvers me so I'm pressed against the wall. He moves as close as he can get, covering my body with his as he kisses me more deeply still. His breaths come hard and heavy, matching the erratic rhythm of my heartbeat.

My wandering hands continue their adventure, exploring his shoulders and biceps, one of them even daring to twist into that thick, dark hair. All I know in this moment is him. How he feels, how he smells, how he tastes. And oh, how it's *good*. So, so good.

Aiden Shaw has completely enveloped every one of my senses. I'm totally powerless as his hands move from my back towards my waist, one of them almost brushing my stomach and...

"WAIT!" the shout rips from my mouth as I finally regain control of my hands and use them to shove his broad chest backwards.

Aiden stumbles back a few paces, bangs his ankle on a chair leg. He swears, then he looks at me. His eyes are wide and shocked, and his face pales.

"I'm so sorry," he gasps. He leans forward on the chair, catching his breath. His pupils are so dilated, his midnight eyes look like deep inky blue pools of desire...

No, not pools of desire. His eyes look like black holes, ready to suck me in and crush me, never to escape.

I need to escape. Now.

"Court, I didn't mean to—"

"Don't COURT me!" I yell, suddenly filled with an incandescent urge to hurl something breakable across the room. Smash it to pieces like my stupid, brittle heart. "You can't just... Kiss me like that!"

Aiden sits on the bed, stares at his knees. He shifts to sit on his hands before he looks up at me. The expression on his face is pained, but I will myself not to care. That kiss bust open a massive faultline in my heart, and I'll have to deal with the fallout, and it's all his stupid fault!

"I'm so sorry. I shouldn't have kissed you like that." Aiden's voice is grave, and I hear the shock and pain in his words. "That was dumb, thoughtless. I should have asked you first, I should have been a gentleman and—"

"You should have kept your lips to yourself is what you should have done!" I thunder, my skin heating back up to a million degrees. I can still *feel* him all over me. Like sunshine on my skin, or warm bathwater.

Or, like a... rash. Yup, that's it. Prickly poison ivy. Looks pretty, but it gets all over you and leaves its mark.

"I'm so sorry." He pauses. "Please, just look at me, Court."

I make the mistake of honoring his request. His eyes are raging and stormy, swirling with emotion, and I turn my head away so he can't see the tears forming in my eyes.

I don't know what's worse—that he kissed me in a way that I've never been kissed before in my life, or seeing how much he regrets doing it.

Aiden might go offering his lips to random people in five-star hotel rooms all the time. Maybe that's just another Tuesday freaking night in the glamorous life of Aiden Shaw. Picks up a new conquest in every city. Loves and leaves.

But, that's not me. It never has been, never will be. I'm a thirty-year-old woman who's never had a boyfriend, who wears an insulin pump, and carries a backpack full of medical supplies. Who lives in a house full of dogs with a fridge full of meds that need to be doled out on a daily basis.

I can't be a notch on Aiden's bed post. Someone like Aiden would never give his heart to me. And, if I let my walls down, show him what lies beneath, and he's disgusted by what he sees, I don't know what I'd do.

Stopping him now means that I have a chance to glue the pieces of my heart back together. Getting too close might just grind them all to dust.

31

AIDEN

The rain beats down mercilessly, falling in thick, heavy sheets. It's an uncharacteristically cold and gray fall day in Atlanta, and our Caribbean island paradise feels both a million miles away and a million years ago.

Which is fine by me. The weather matches my mood perfectly.

I close my eyes and lean my head against my seat in the back of Conor's truck. We're currently crawling through the heavy traffic on 85 north, the wipers turned up as high as they go.

Courtney sits in the front seat, her hands folded primly on her lap and her eyes fixed on the road ahead. "Thanks again for coming to get us in this crazy weather, Conor." Her voice is unnaturally strained, overly polite.

But, that one little sentence to my best friend is more than she's said to me since my moment of intense and utter stupidity last night.

Utter stupidity which led to the best kiss of my life.

All I can do is curse myself for being such an idiot. Despite how good that kiss was—how I'm sure we both felt those insane sparks that were more like explosive fireworks

—that doesn't change the fact that she didn't want to kiss me. She wants nothing to do with me. That much is clear. Every word exchanged between us since last night has been painfully polite.

"Are you packed?" "Shall we say goodbye to Blaze?" "Do you have your passport?"

Once again, she disappeared when we got to the airport this morning, putting as much distance between us as possible. But this time, there was no Starbucks apology on the far side of security. No joking or laughing or reaching for my hand on the plane.

My feelings for her—sharp and bright—are a one-way street. And, apparently, there's no space to make a U-Turn. Go back to the way things were. Honestly, I'd take that over this. Give me war and flashing eyes and hurled insults any day. Fire over ice.

Because Courtney hating me with a burning passion feels better than Courtney treating me like she's totally indifferent to me.

Conor casts her a sideways glance as we slow to yet another stop on the highway. "No problem. Jess wouldn't have it any other way."

"How is Jess?" Courtney asks, again super prim and politely.

So politely that Conor gives her another strange look. Shifts in his seat. I'm sure he can feel the uncomfortable tension in the vehicle. "Just fine."

A sudden flash lights the sky purple and silver.

"Whew." Conor whistles through his teeth. He sounds relieved to have a subject change. "Lucky your plane landed when it did. I think we're in for one hell of a storm. Odd for this time of year."

A violent roar of thunder cracks in answer.

I'd quite like to crack my head against the window to end this misery.

After another half hour of awkward, stilted conversation about the freak storm, we finally—*finally*—pull up on our street.

"Are your dogs at home?" Conor asks.

"Still at the sitter's, I'll pick them up tomorrow." Courtney puts a hand on her door, gives a very forced smile. "Thank you so much for the ride, you really didn't have to do that."

Conor, in contrast, smiles easily. "Like I said, no problem."

Courtney hops out of the car, but I'm quicker.

"Thanks, man," I say as I jump out. I walk around the back and extract Courtney's suitcases before she can. Then, run up her front walk to her door.

She appears behind me a few moments later.

"Court—" I start.

She shoots me a strange, furtive look. "Get off my porch, slugboy."

My eyebrows shoot up. She's talking to me again. "We're back to 'slugboy'?"

"Vacation's over, isn't it?" She shrugs, then snorts. "No more truce, we're back to real life again. And in real life, there is no 'we', Aiden."

"What if that doesn't have to be the case?"

"This is the way things are. The way they're meant to be." Her voice is firm, but I swear her lower lip trembles slightly as she speaks.

With one last, pointed look in my direction, she lets herself into her house. Closes the door.

And I'm left alone. In the pouring rain.

Shoes ruined. Again.

Though the thought doesn't bother me nearly as much as Courtney's chilly demeanor does.

By the time I get back to the truck, Conor—bless him—has hoisted my bags to my front door.

"Thanks, dude." I pause for a moment. "You have time to come in for a drink?"

"Sure." He regards me quizzically. "I'll text Jess to let her know."

It pains me to admit how much I don't want to be alone right now. It's pathetic. After three whirlwind days of sea and sunshine and breathing in all that is Courtney, I can't be trusted not to spiral if left with my thoughts.

But, I also don't really want to talk about it, don't even know what I'd say. At least I can trust Conor to slump in front of the TV with me and not ask too many questions.

Or so I hope.

The second I close the door behind us, he rounds on me. "What did you do?"

"What?"

"Don't play dumb, Aiden." Conor takes off his jacket and hangs it up. Kicks off his shoes, then sets them by the door. Like the neat freak he is.

He strides to the fridge. Grabs two beers.

"Help yourself," I say sarcastically as I shrug off my jacket. Drop it on the ground obstinately because I know it'll annoy the crap out of him, and maybe distract him from this firing squad routine.

Yeah. No such luck.

He grins. Pops the top off one beer and takes a long pull. "Now, talk."

"Ughhhh," I groan, accepting a beer from him before I sink onto a barstool by the island.

Conor sits on the island, leans forward. "Well? What was it? Fight over the last cheese scone at the buffet?

Fisticuffs at dawn?" He laughs. "Don't tell me you pushed her in the ocean fully clothed?"

Well, that was a weirdly close guess.

I pick at the label of my beer, not daring to look up. "I kissed her."

Conor chokes on his beer. Coughs. Wipes his mouth with the back of his hand, then gapes at me. "Sorry, I think I may have misheard."

"Nope." I run a hand through my damp hair, making it stick up in every direction.

"What on earth possessed you to do that? Did she try and claw your eyes out after?"

"She kissed me back."

"SHE WHAT?"

"Well, at first she did. It got kinda intense, and then she freaked out and pushed me away. She's barely spoken to me since."

Conor's looking at me like I've told him I have a special, tinfoil-lined room in my basement that I use to communicate with aliens. "I need a moment to process this."

"Good luck with that. I've had a whole day to process it and I still can't make sense of it."

"I do have one question."

"Of course you do."

"Why?"

I meet Conor's curious green gaze. "I think I like her," I admit. "Like, really like her."

"Well, duh," Conor says, sounding just like Jess. "Of course you like her."

I shoot him a *look*. Then, I shrug, feeling downtrodden. "I think I screwed it all up with that kiss."

"Well." For once, my friend is lost for words. He scratches his chin, his calloused fingers like sandpaper against his stubble. "This is... not ideal."

I slump forward and lay my forehead on the countertop, pressing my skin into the cool marble. "Don't I know it."

After an hour of helpfully suggesting Conor go home to his pregnant wife because she might be scared of the storm, and Conor (correctly) insisting that Jess loves storms, I finally get him to leave. The trick was to hint that the oak tree in their front yard might have fallen on their house.

Which it couldn't have. In fact, we *both* know that there is no way on God's green earth that could've happened. That tree is so thick and deeply-rooted, it would take an entire army of giants to knock it over.

But, all I needed was to plant a teeny seed of doubt in his mind that his wife could be in any sort of bizarre hypothetical danger. Once that seed sprouted, he conceded that he "better go check, just in case" and legged it out of here like a bat out of hell. Straight home to Jess, like the doting husband he is.

Was it manipulative to take advantage of how insanely protective he is of my sister? Sure.

Was it also necessary? Yes.

After admitting everything to my best buddy, I realized that I did, in fact, want to be alone. That I needed time to get a grip of what's gone down in the past twenty-four hours.

And so, after Conor makes a break for it through the still-raging storm, I turn the lock on my door, drain the last of my beer, and begin to shed my damp clothes. I leave a trail behind me as I make for the bathroom: shirt, jeans, socks, boxers. It's not like anyone is coming over that I need to tidy up for.

I should embrace the bachelor life because it seems I'm going to be stuck with it.

I yawn, my entire body sagging. It's only 9pm, but I'm tired as could be after all the traveling and worrying I've done today. Best to crawl into bed and call it a day.

I'm halfway to my bedroom when all the lights go out.

Poof! Instant darkness.

Of course. The cherry on top of the sundae that's melted all over me today.

I blindly grasp my way back to the kitchen to find my cell phone, and that's when I realize that all the streetlights outside are off, too. The entire area is having a power outage, by the looks of things.

Only one person comes to mind...

Courtney.

My heart squeezes. Is she okay over there, all alone? Without even the dogs to protect her?

Maybe I could go check on her?

Pants first, Aiden. Showing up there naked would be a *definite* step back given how things are going. And I don't really feel like getting arrested for public indecency at this point.

I eventually locate my phone, turn on the flashlight, and throw on sweats and a hoodie. Then, I go to the pantry and dig out the storm emergency kit Conor put together during his time as my roommate—with candles, firelighters, a storm lantern, and a battery-operated flashlight. Ever the Boy Scout, Conor made some practical improvements around here, alongside his pristine renovations.

I'm suddenly glad I sent him home so Jess isn't alone in this.

I glance through the kitchen window, into Courtney's house. Blinds are down. No flicker of a flashlight in sight.

For some reason, my heart squeezes again.

221

I'm sure she's fine. She doesn't want to see you anyway.

Maybe a text would work? Just a friendly check in that doesn't cross any land boundaries?

Aiden: You okay over there? Got everything you need?

It's a lamesauce text, but better to be ketchup than sriracha. No need to cause an unnecessary flare-up.

Another huge bolt of lightning rips across the sky, bathing my house in a flash of bright white light. The rain is relentless, pounding hard into the rooftop like it's trying to drive right through it.

I check my phone. No reply.

Still no light moving in the kitchen.

Is she asleep? Surely not in this weather.

CRASH!

Thunder claps like a heavenly bowling ball hitting a strike. It's funny, while Jess always loved Atlanta's skyshow storms as a child, I was less keen. Even hid in the closet a time or two. Nothing like being seven years old and having to be soothed by your five year old sister to put an early dent in any attempt at macho-ism. Which, with hindsight, was probably a good thing.

The lightning flashes again, and my stomach is in a peril of knots by now.

I check my phone again. Still nothing from Courtney, and now, I'm getting worried.

Aiden: I know things are weird, but please let me know you're okay. I'm right next door if you need anything.

I lean against the counter, my back to the window. I do everything I can not to look at my phone (watched pot, right?) and yet, my eyes keep slinking over it like the sneaky buggers they are. No screen light, no answer, no word from Courtney.

I wait ten minutes, watching the ticking clock on the far wall.

Something is off. Wrong.

I run my fingers through my hair as my heart thumps. Another crack of thunder shakes the house.

Aiden: Courtney, please respond. I'm worried about you.

Still no answer.

I'd do anything right now to know that she's okay. Even if she tells me to go to hell, I just need to hear from her.

She likely believes that my kissing her was just a move, or that I was playing her. Baiting her and getting one up on her in this ridiculous neighbor war. But, I would never do that. Especially not to Courtney. Especially after realizing just how deep my feelings are for her.

I haven't had a chance to tell her that—I don't know if I should. It's clear that she wants nothing to do with me.

But her lack of response isn't about our kiss. I don't know how I know it, I just do. Deep in my bones, sure as my own name.

Before I can think another thought or talk myself out of it, I'm on my feet and running through the pouring rain.

32

COURTNEY

"COURTNEY!"

Bang bang bang.

"Courtney, open up!"

Aiden. Aiden's shouting for me.

His voice sounds so far away in my dizzy, clammy head. I pull myself up from the couch, still shaking all over. My legs feel like jelly, and it's dark. So, so dark.

I grasp for my phone blindly. No dice.

Stumbling forward, I finally make it to the door, cold sweat pricking my skin.

I open it, and there's the tall, strong, solid outline of Aiden. Drenched to the skin and holding a flashlight, which he shines at me.

"Courtney, finally! Thank God, I was getting wor... What the hell happened to you?"

I wobble, blink against the bright light. My vision is smudged around the edges, like someone put a thumbprint on a lens.

"Aiden," I say, and by the time his name falls out of my mouth, he's in my entryway, holding me.

"What happened?" he repeats, his voice verging on

frantic—a direct contradiction to his strong, steady arms around me.

I try to wave a hand and attempt a laugh. Manage neither. "Just—"

Before I get any further with what I'm trying to say, Aiden springs into action. His hand moves to my forehead, and he oh-so-gently lays a palm flat across it. Despite everything going on with us, I lean into his touch, savoring the coolness of his skin.

"You're freezing" he murmurs, looking at me with an expression so soft, so sweet, I could cry.

He's here for me.

"We need to get you to a hospital," He opens my coat closet and bundles a puffy jacket around my shoulders, wrapping me in it tenderly. He props me up with one arm as he fumbles for shoes with the other. He produces one Ugg boot and one Nike sneaker—both for a right foot—that he then attempts to help me put my feet into. None too successfully, I might add.

"Aiden, wait." I hold up a hand to halt him. The world still isn't right, fraying around the edges, rippling waves through my vision.

"What's up, Court? What can I get for you?" His eyes are wide and worried, God bless his heart.

I shake my head, feeling a little more alert. "I don't need to go to the hospital."

"You're running a fever, your eyes are glazed, you're shaking..."

"It's hypoglycemia."

Aiden blinks. "Hypoglywhatia?"

I sigh. Grit my teeth.

It was totally my fault, what happened. I used to get hypoglycemic attacks all the time—it was one of the reasons I opted for an implant. The pump has been a lifesaver, in general, but today, I was so focused on Aiden, I wasn't paying attention to myself. My blood sugar plummeted, and my alarm went off, but it was too late. The shock was already setting in.

So, here we are. I really, *really* didn't want to do this, never wanted Aiden to find out. But, despite everything that's going on between us, he still came to check on me. And the last thing I want right now is for him to go.

"Diabetic shock, Aiden," I say faintly. "I went into shock. Didn't eat for too long, blood sugar dropped. Takes me a while to come round."

I wait for his reaction. Shock. Pity. Weirdness... Anything.

At the very least, I expect a barrage of a million questions.

Nothing comes. His expression remains the same—impassive and neutral, the Switzerland of facial expressions—and he gently releases me from his hold. Zips up my coat, and pulls the hood over my head, dressing me like I'm five years old. Then, he retrieves my left Ugg boot.

"Come on," he says.

I shake my head. "I told you, I don't need to go to the hospital."

"Not the hospital." Aiden's eyes flash in the darkness. "My place."

"Yeah, no." I chuckle feebly. "That's not happening."

"Court. You can never talk to me again after tonight if you don't want to. I'll leave you alone forever, if you wish. But it's dark, it's stormy, and you just scared the crap out of me. I thought... Just, please let me do one thing right and take care of you tonight. Just one time. Okay?"

A million thoughts run through my head with a million reasons why letting Aiden look after me is a bad idea. More temporary insanity that's only going to cut me deeper when tonight is over.

But, something about the look in his eyes makes me forget the 999,999 reasons why I shouldn't let him take care of me. Focus on the one reason why: because I need him.

"Okay," I say.

His impassive expression cracks, letting through the light of a hesitant, relieved smile. My chest constricts.

"What do you need?" Aiden says. "What can I get for you?"

A new heart.

"Just my backpack."

~

Fifteen minutes later, I'm on Aiden's huge couch, wrapped in a fluffy blanket. I'm sipping a mug of hot, sweet tea that Aiden made using a gas camping stove.

The man is nothing if not resourceful.

Right now, he's lighting candles. Dozens of them. He hasn't asked me a single question, except to repeatedly check that I'm okay, see if he can get me anything.

My hair is in a horrific, damp, ropey topknot, my face is pale and bare of makeup, and I'm wearing a massive old Yellowjackets sweatshirt and t-rex pajama pants. But, for some reason, I don't care.

At all.

It's the most surreal scenario of all time.

"Can you believe we were on a Caribbean island this morning?" I ask.

And that, less than an hour ago, I planned on binge watching Love Island all night while plotting how to never speak to you again?

"Nope. It's been the weirdest day." Aiden goes to the

kitchen, opens a cupboard. "Cheerios or Cinnamon Toast Crunch?"

"What?"

"Gourmet meal, coming right up. You have a cereal preference?"

I chuckle at the sight of him, earnest and sincere, wielding a cereal box in each hand.

"CTC, definitely. My blood sugar's still low so I'll take advantage."

Fifteen grams of carbohydrates every fifteen minutes until it passes. I know the drill.

"The dinner of champions." Aiden fills two huge bowls, sloshes milk in them, then sits next to me on the couch. He leaves about a foot and a half of room between us that I wish wasn't there.

I give him a small smile. "Hey, Aiden?"

"Yeah?" He shovels a huge spoonful of cereal into his mouth.

"Thank you." I take my own bite of food so I don't have to look at him. He's more handsome than ever in the romantic flicker of the candlelight. "For checking on me."

"Is that why you... um, went through security alone at the airport? You had your medical stuff with you?"

I nod. It's so strange, I was so freaked out about him knowing. Didn't want him to see any weakness in me. But, he's barely reacted at all.

"My grandma's diabetic," he says, moving his spoon around his bowl.

"She is?"

He frowns. "Didn't Jess tell you?"

My cheeks heat up. "I, um, never told Jess that I have diabetes. I hate people knowing I'm sick. It's... why I didn't want you to find out."

I don't add that poor Jess—best friend in the world

extraordinaire—has struggled through my disgusting concoctions. I've made her consume my weird, sugar-free cupcakes, cookies and drinks, and she did it all with a cheerful smile and fake enthusiasm.

Aiden nods, like this makes sense. "You don't want one small detail about yourself to define you in the eyes of other people."

I stare at him, shocked once again that this man gets me on this level. "Exactly."

Aiden bites his bottom lip, catching it between his teeth and pulling. I'm instantly jolted back to last night. The graze of those lips, those teeth, on my mouth, my skin...

"Hey, Courtney?"

I snap back to the moment, blush as I stare at my cereal. "Yeah?"

"I really am sorry about last night." Aiden swallows. Sets his bowl on the table. "I crossed a line."

"And now you regret it," I offer with a sad smile. Wrap my blanket around me tighter.

He brings up his knees and rests his chin on them, looking innocent and sweet as a schoolboy. I feel a pang.

"The kiss? No." Aiden's voice is suddenly fierce. "I don't regret the kiss for a second. I just regret that I put you in an uncomfortable position. I'd never do that to anyone, never mind you..."

I'm vaguely stunned. "So you don't regret kissing me?"

"That was the best damn kiss of my life." Aiden knocks his head back against the couch.

I blink, shocked to my core

"Are you mad I don't regret it?" he asks quietly.

I bury my head in my hands. "I don't know." My voice lowers to a whisper. "I don't want to get hurt."

After last night's kiss, I finally had some clarity. Over

the past four years, I did everything I could to hate Aiden, but it was all useless.

I *don't* hate him, as much as I wish I could right now.

"You think I'm capable of hurting you?" Aiden's eyes are darker than I've ever seen them.

"Surprise." I laugh wanly. I've never felt so raw and vulnerable. So exposed. "You don't have to say anything. I'm obviously being stupid and I know you'd never—"

"Courtney, I like you. For real." He screws up his eyes. "I hoped that kiss would communicate that... but it seems to have done the opposite."

I shrug helplessly. "I've seen the women you date, Aiden."

"There's a reason I'm no longer dating them." His lip quirks. "Plus, I don't want one small detail about my life to define me."

I smile a grim smile. "But, say you *did* like me. And I liked you, too. Hypothetically, of course..."

"Of course," Aiden agrees solemnly.

"What would happen after one or two dates? When you get bored and move on, like you always do, and we're stuck living next to each other?"

A shadow crosses Aiden's face. "Bored?"

"You heard me." I feel my temper flaring. But mostly, I feel angry with myself for doing the one thing I said I wouldn't: I caught feelings for Aiden Shaw. "You go through a merry-go-round of women and I refuse to be a part of that. I *can't* be a part of that—"

"Scared," Aiden says suddenly, swiftly cutting off my rant.

"What?"

"I was scared, not bored."

"What in the name of Justin Bieber are you talking about, Shaw?"

"I never let myself get past the first date or two because I was scared. Scared of... commitment, love, all the responsibility that comes with it. Scared of becoming my parents, and putting all my happiness in someone else's hands while neglecting everything else."

I blink, shocked into silence. *This* was the furthest thing I ever expected to hear from Aiden.

He runs a hand through his dark hair. Hair I can't stop thinking about running my own fingers through. "My parents are wonderful people, but I never wanted to end up like them. I've worked hard, so hard, to make sure that Jess had everything she needed when we were growing up. If it was up to our parents, we would have subsisted on fresh air. I love how in love they are, don't get me wrong, but they neglected so many of their everyday responsibilities in the process. It made no sense to me."

He squints, looking pained. Sighs.

"So, I put walls up. Stayed behind them. I was a huge coward. For thirty-two years, I was a coward." He tugs on the ends of his hair before finally meeting my eyes. "Happy?"

I shake my head. "Aiden, I had no idea."

"It was easier to convince myself I only wanted something casual than to let myself fall. Despite what you might think, I don't love and leave women. I'd never intentionally hurt anyone. The problem's never been about the women I'm dating not being good enough. It's my inability to let my walls down and feel anything close to love. It's why I have this house and my stuff and the career I've worked so damn hard for. Staying away from love feels like the safest way to live."

He gives me a fierce look that pierces through to my soul.

"Or so I thought until this weekend," he says quietly.

231

"When I felt things I've never felt before. Things I want to keep feeling."

My heart is racing and I feel light-headed. But this time, not in a bad way. In a shocked, spiraling, excited sort of way.

Aiden likes me? For real?

"I was scared, too," I whisper.

Aiden gives me this defeated smile. "You don't have to say that."

"It's true." I lick my lips, which are suddenly dry. "I put my walls up with you because I didn't think I could trust a guy like you. I... misjudged you. And I'm sorry for that."

He shakes his head. "You don't have to be sorry. I understand why you saw me the way you did."

I nuzzle my face into the blanket, which smells of Aiden—subtle cologne and soap and warmth and sexiness—and find that I want to be vulnerable. I want him to know why I've always acted the way I did. "I think my natural stance is to keep people at arm's length, push them away. That way, I'd be less likely to disappoint anyone. Get disappointed."

"Who could ever be disappointed by you?"

"Everyone."

"What do you mean?" Then, he glances at my face quickly. "You don't have to talk about it if you don't want to."

"I do," I surprise myself by saying. "I think that, despite how strong I always try to be, I have this underlying fear that, if people get too close, they won't like what they see. They'll leave. Maybe it stems from my mom leaving, but I've always found it hard to believe in myself. That's why I stayed at Petit Soleil so long. I was scared to chase my dreams in case I failed. So, I kept putting it off, thinking I'd do it when I had more money. Even though Philippe passed me over time and again for a promotion I knew I deserved, I stayed."

Aiden listens quietly, his handsome face stoic. No judgment. No pity. No disgust or horror. Just a kind, listening ear. He reaches out and runs an index finger along my cheek. "Philippe is an idiot, Courtney. And, believe me when I say that nobody could ever not like what they see when they know who you are. Because who you are is beautiful, Courtney. So damn beautiful."

Entranced by his words, by his eyes locked on mine, something stirs in me that I've never felt before. Something powerful. So much so, I feel myself leaning towards him.

But, he pulls back.

Embarrassment rushes through me, sharp and bitter. "You don't want to kiss me?"

He shakes his head. "I want to kiss you more than anything, Court. But, right now, I think you need to be held more than kissed. And I want to be the one to give you what you want *and* what you need. You deserve it."

With that, Aiden stands, blows out the candles, and returns to the sofa. In the darkness, he reaches for me, pulls me towards him as he lies down. My head comes to his chest, his arm wraps protectively around my body, and I let him hold me close.

We fall asleep on the couch, wrapped around each other.

Sometime in the middle of the night, the power comes back and the lights illuminate the room. But, Aiden makes no move to leave. He simply reaches up, flicks off the light, and keeps right on holding me.

I stay in his arms until the sun comes up.

33

COURTNEY

When I wake, Aiden's not next to me.

I roll over on the couch and squeeze my eyes shut. My chest tightens, an almost automatic reflex against rejection, but then, I take a deep breath. And smell… pancakes?

I open my eyes, look around, and there's Aiden in the kitchen—which literally looks like a bomb exploded in it. He's the diamond in the rough, the calm in the eye of the storm—freshly showered, and clad in sweatpants that sit low on his hips and a navy hoodie the color of his eyes. His hair is damp, his feet are bare, and he's humming softly as he ladles batter in a pan.

The sight makes my heart clench like it's been wrung with a dishcloth.

"Morning, sunshine." He looks at me with that devastating smile of his, the one that plays around his lips knowingly. The smug little smirk that, not three days ago, made me want to rip his head off, but now has me thinking about option B.

Shame on me!

"Coffee?" Aiden quirks a brow, as if to tell me that he sees me staring. Overconfident so-and-so.

"All of the coffee," I mumble in reply, looking away. "Can I use your bathroom first?"

"Down the hall on the left."

"I know." I've been in Aiden's house a few times, back when Jess lived here. But, never since. Without her presence, the house feels more masculine. Stark.

I plod down the hall. Lock myself in the bathroom. Assess the damage.

The results are not excellent.

Hair: Sticking up in every direction

Face: Couch-creased

Breath: Decidedly of the "morning" variety.

I put some toothpaste on my finger and rub it around my gums while using my other hand to fruitlessly attempt to tame my hair. As I'm scrambling around like a mad badger, my phone buzzes.

Aiden: Banana or blueberry pancakes?

I stare at my screen in wonder. How on earth have I arrived at a place in my life where I have a Grade A Hottie making me breakfast after I slept in his arms all night? In an entirely G-Rated, cuddle-fest fashion, of course. *Lizzy Bennet, eat your heart out!*

My phone buzzes again.

Aiden: By the way, you look cute first thing in the morning ;)

I just about choke on my toothpaste finger.

"Court? You okay in there?" Aiden calls.

Of course. He *would* have supersonic hearing.

"Splendid!" I holler back, spitting frantically in the sink.

Who says "splendid" anyway? British people. And me. That's it.

Fantastic.

I hear Aiden's laughter from the kitchen, and blast the

faucet to drown him out. Then, I realize I didn't answer Aiden's question. Oops.

Courtney: *banana emoji*

I set my phone on the bathroom counter. Finish finger-brushing my teeth.

And then, the force of what I've just done hits me. What my text might look like.

Oh no. Oh no, oh no.

Oh no, oh oh oh noooooooooooooooo.

Is the banana emoji even used for... that?

I have no idea. Innocent and sheltered, remember? I rack my brain for anyone I know who would have insight in this area. Aiden (but, obviously, I can't ask him). And...

I dial a number.

"Hi!" Jess answers, slightly breathless. "You're back. Crazy storm last night, wasn't it? Was the power out there, too? I can't wait to hear about—"

"I need to speak with your husband. Is he there?" I whisper loudly.

"What?"

"Conor. I need to speak to Conor."

"Well hello to you, too," Jess retorts, then puts on a fussy old librarian voice. "May I inquire as to why you need to speak with Conor?"

"Guy talk."

"Guy talk," Jess repeats dumbly. "You're calling at 7am to have guy talk with Conor."

"Correct."

Jess pauses, and my phone buzzes once. Twice.

Aiden's texting me back. I dare not look until I work out how big of a faux-pas I've made.

"I'll get him for you," Jess finally says, then adds "you weirdo" loud enough that I can hear. I like to think that she means it affectionately.

"Hello?" Conor's deep voice comes on the line.

I lean against the bathroom counter. The water's still running, and I hope it's loud enough for Aiden to hear none of this.

"Hi. How are you?"

"Good...?" Conor trails off, bemused. Which would make sense. I've known Conor for a couple of years and never once called him.

I get right down to business. "Conor, you're a man of the world, right?"

"Um—"

"I thought so. How's your emoji game?"

"My what?"

Goodness, this is tiring work. "Your emoji game. Like, are you up to date on all the emojis the kids are using these days?"

"Not really, no."

Jeez Louise. "Well, would you happen to know what emoji might be used for a man's... whatsits."

"Whatsits?" Conor snorts with laughter. In the background, I hear Jess demand to know what's going on.

"Yes," I say staunchly. "Whatsits."

"Um, the eggplant emoji usually?"

Oh. Phew.

"So, not the banana?" I say happily, relief flowing through me.

"Oh. I guess the banana could also be used for... whatsits."

My heart plummets. "Really?"

"Courtney, is everything okay?" Conor's beginning to sound concerned. Time to pull the plug on this terrible idea.

"I'm just dandy. Gotta dash!" I hang up before he can reply. Make a mental note to text Jess later to tell her that

I'm not going crazy. Right after I figure out how to explain that particular interaction with her dear husband.

"Courtney?" Aiden knocks on the bathroom door. Oh no. "Are you alright in there?"

"Yes!"

"Pancakes are ready."

"Cool. Cool cool cool." *Shut up, Courtney. Saying "cool" a bunch of times in a row is the literal opposite of cool.*

"Well, they're actually warm. But, they'll be cool if you stay in there much longer."

"Hilarious, Aiden. You're quite the comic."

"I do what I can." A pause. "Are you going to open the door now so we can talk about how you've been in there for twenty minutes on the phone to my best friend?"

"No, thank you," I say in this little mousy voice.

Aiden laughs. "I knew you meant pancakes, Courtney."

Reluctantly, I open the door. He's standing outside, arms folded across his chest, lips twitching at the corners. The man is a vision in sweatpants. I never knew there was such a thing.

"You did?" I ask skeptically.

"Like I said, you're cute in the morning." His voice is low, rough. He takes a step towards me.

My stomach coils, swirling in circles like soft serve ice cream. Here I am, standing in his bathroom with electrocuted hair. No makeup. Wearing t-rex pajama pants. At my worst, stripped of all protective armor. But he's looking at me like he never wants to look away.

He takes another step towards me. Effectively closing the gap between us. I am inches—mere inches—from him.

There's flour on his cheek, and I reach up. Gently brush it away. When my fingers skim his cheekbone, he sighs, and his hand wraps around mine as his eyes lock on my face.

The intense tides are raging in there today, dark and stormy and delicious.

"Courtney."

"Yes?" I gasp.

His free hand moves to my face, and he drags his fingertips slowly, oh-so-slowly, along my jawline, making me see stars. "I'm going to kiss you now."

The soft serve machine in my belly has a malfunction, and my insides liquefy at his words.

"Okay," I manage to croak.

His eyes search mine, intent and serious. "But before I do that, I need you to tell me you believe me when I say that it means something."

I freeze. Swallow. Play his words in my mind again and again. And then, another time.

Aiden waits patiently, not moving a muscle, his eyes trained on me. There's something in the way he looks at me, something in the way he's taking charge, yet letting me lead. Sexy and intense and considerate and sweet, all at once.

At this moment, frozen in time, I choose to trust. Trust the man who I've judged wrongly for so long.

"I believe you," my words come out in a blistered whisper, tender and swollen.

Aiden lets go of my hand, the one he's holding to his cheek. Cups both hands around my face, big and protective and strong, and he moves towards me.

When his lips touch mine, the sensation is spine-tingling. He tastes like summer rain, fresh and sweet. I respond immediately, my lips parting, and he inhales sharply, which sends shivers down my spine. I made him feel like this. Me.

I move my hands to his shoulders, tightening my grip like I'm about to be plunged into freefall and need to hold on for dear life. I expect him to kiss me frantically. Kiss me hard and fast and frenzied.

But this time, he doesn't.

Instead, he gently pulls me closer, holding me to him as he kisses me slowly. Sweetly. Carefully. Like I'm something precious that he doesn't want to break.

He takes his time kissing me, exploring every sensation. And I feel and taste and smell and see and hear everything in that kiss that he's communicating to me.

That I matter.

That he's got me.

When we finally break apart, we're both dazed. Starry-eyed and smiling.

He traces one fingertip along my eyelids, cheekbones, nose, and chin. The feeling of his rough skin along my lips draws a sigh out of me, and Aiden moves to kiss me again.

"What about the pancakes?" I ask as his lips find mine.

"I like cold pancakes," Aiden murmurs against my mouth.

34

COURTNEY

A few hours later, I've picked up my dogs, gone home and showered, and gotten dressed in non-t-rex clothing. Right after I kissed Aiden until my mouth was sore, of course.

My priorities are in check. Because the man kisses like he was born for the job.

Now, Aiden and I are on our way to the arcade for the big birthday party. I'm in the passenger seat of his car, balancing two huge gift boxes on my lap. I got dinosaur Lego for Oliver, which is way cooler than the K'nex rollercoaster Aiden seems so pleased with himself for buying.

Aiden's driving with one hand on the wheel, the other resting on the center console. His index finger draws lazy circles on my knee. It's a mesmerizing motion, sending tingles all over my body.

Jess has been texting me all morning, asking what on earth is going on. I told her I'd explain everything when I see her at the party. Which I am not looking forward to having to do. One, because I can only imagine all the "I told you so"s. And two, because I'm not even sure what I'm going to say. What the correct answer is.

I may not know exactly what this is yet, but Aiden told me that it means *something*.

And, for once in my life, I want to take a risk. Choose to believe.

"You look great, by the way," he says without taking his eyes off the road. "Like, really great."

My hair's in a ponytail and I'm wearing minimal makeup. I'm dressed in a cute lemon-yellow t-shirt dress, a jean jacket for the cooler evening breeze, and bright white sneakers.

It's a far cry from my usual, super polished look, but I feel more myself than I have in a while. I also can't believe how many stolen glances I've gotten from my chauffeur.

"Thank you!" I squeak, blushing from the roots of my hair to my toes. I'm not used to taking compliments, and I have to say, it's nice. Refreshing. A newfound confidence flows through me, strong and bold and sanguine.

Because my armor isn't on right now, and I actually feel good about it.

Like it might be okay to be me.

A few minutes later, we pull up outside Arcadelandia and Aiden kills the engine.

"Ready?" He smiles at me.

I shake my head. Bite my lip. "What am I going to tell Jess?"

Part of me expects him to come back with "there's nothing to tell" or "just make something up." Instead, Aiden's smile grows. A slow, achingly beautiful smile.

"Tell her whatever you like." Aiden brushes a few stray strands of hair off my forehead, gently tucks them behind my ear. "But, just know that I'll be listening because I'm as interested in your answer as she's going to be."

"Guess I'll have to tell her the truth then." My voice comes out so low and flirty, it's almost unrecognizable.

"Oh, yeah?" Aiden says huskily, eyes darkening. "And what's the truth?"

"That I'm not sure which was the best kiss of my life..." I say as I slide a hand onto his denim-clad thigh, surprising myself. I've never been this bold or brazen with a man before, and I'm gratified to hear him make this incredibly sexy noise in his throat. "The kiss at the resort, or the one in your hallway this morning."

"How about this one?" Aiden practically growls as his hand moves to the back of my head, tugging me to him.

Our lips meet, sparking a shock all over my body. My fingers tangle in his hair as his mouth moves against mine, hungry and demanding and oh-so-sexy.

I'm plummeting headfirst into the delicious, all-encompassing sensation of all things Aiden Shaw when—

"YASSSSSSSSSSSSSSSSSS!!!!!!!!!"

We spring apart so fast, Aiden bangs his head against the door. He swears. "What the—?"

And that's when I see her.

Jessica Brady.

She's standing right outside the car, peering in like a pervy old Peeping Tom. Except, unlike most voyeurs who prey on people making out in cars, all five feet, three inches of her full-moon-shaped, very pregnant body is doing what I can only describe as a combination of the floss dance and the running man. While she shrieks like a banshee.

A few paces behind her, Conor is beside himself with laughter.

"Ohhh, boy," Aiden says. He offers me a sheepish grin that makes my heart skip a beat. He looks so cute right now —all mussed-up hair and flushed cheeks. Like a naughty school boy.

Only grown up and freaking sexy.

"Guess I don't have to tell Jess anything." I laugh. Right

243

as Jess herself pries the car door open and climbs into my lap.

"Hello, Jessica," I say, like this is a totally normal occurrence. Aiden snickers. "How are you?"

"Not as good as you two, it seems!" Jess literally looks like she's about to pop. Hopefully with excitement, and not her water breaking. But, at this moment, I can't be too sure.

"We did have a good vacation," I say, deadpan.

"YEAH, YOU DID!" She leans over so she can poke her brother in the chest. "Didn't I tell you?"

My eyebrows shoot up. "Tell him what?"

Jess leans back and loops her arms around my neck, hanging on like an orangutan in overalls. "I have a theory that Aiden's had a crush on you for years, he's just been in denial."

My mouth falls open and I turn to Aiden, who offers me a little shrug. A smile.

No embarrassment. No shh-ing his sister or making excuses.

Aiden Shaw had a crush on me this whole time? Unbelievable.

I feel incredible. On cloud nine.

Then, Jess has to go and spoil it. "And, obviously, Court's been in love with you, Aiden, like, forever. If you guys would've just listened to me earlier—"

"Jess," Aiden cuts her off smoothly while I sit rigidly still, pretty much hyperventilating over the four-letter L word Jess just casually threw out. "Please shut up now."

"Oh, I am never shutting up about this. Ever." Jess uncoils her hands from my neck so she can rub them together in villainous glee.

Aiden shoots Conor, who's still laughing outside the car, a very distinct "please control your wife" look. Thankfully, Conor takes pity on us. Leans into the car, and takes Jess's hand. "Come on babe, we better go. The party's about to start."

"Let's go tell everybody!" Jess yells.

Aiden sneaks a look at me, rolls his eyes. It's an intimate, secret look, meant only for me. We're on the same team. "You might want to check with Court first... whatever it is you're planning on saying."

"That you guys were just making out in the car in broad daylight?"

Aiden's face stays blank, neutral. But I recognize the teasing lilt of his mouth. That mouth that was just on mine. "I can neither confirm, nor deny, that statement."

Jess opens her mouth to retort, but she's cut short by a shriek.

"AUNTIE JESS AND AUNTIE CORNNYYY!"

Oliver comes flying towards us in a Sonic The Hedgehog-style blur of energy. I love that I'm not actually his Auntie—not technically—but he still thinks of me like that. Not having any siblings of my own and being so distant from my own family, this term of endearment fills me with happiness.

"Let's go celebrate Ollie," I say to the group firmly.

Pete and Mia appear behind Oliver just then, Mia carrying their little girl, Addie. I scoop the little princess into my arms and lead our group into the arcade, ready to party.

Thankfully, Jess holds her blabbermouth and manages to get through the afternoon without announcing me and Aiden's wedding or something. It's a wonderful party—full of Pac Man, Pinball, Dance Dance Revolution. And a very, very competitive basketball hoop shooting game between Aiden, Conor and Pete that involves a scary amount of yelling, flexing and smack talk.

Halfway through the afternoon, I'm at the overflowing

food table, drinking a paper cup of Diet Coke. My eyes are glued on Aiden, sitting at one of those race-car games with Ollie in his lap. The two of them are laughing their heads off as Aiden jiggles Ollie up and down, making "vroom" sounds in a way that makes my ovaries shriek with joy.

Aiden in dad-mode might be my favorite Aiden yet.

As if he can feel my eyes on him, he catches my gaze. Smiles that devastating smile. All for me.

We haven't talked about what this "something" between us means, but to be honest, I don't want to think right now. It's worth the risk to just be here, present in this moment.

With him.

Even still, when the cake is finally brought out by a beaming Mia and we all sing *Happy Birthday* to Ollie, I tuck my hand behind my back, out of sight, and cross my fingers as he blows out the candles.

It may not be my birthday, but I make a wish anyway.

It doesn't take long for Jess to corner me. And, I mean *literally* corner me.

She backs me into a corner, using her belly as some kind of crowd-control battering ram.

The corner of the arcade is none too pleasant. My shoes squelch on the carpet in a way that carpet should never squelch (seriously, my sneaker collection is depleting at a rapid rate). It smells like burnt sugar and dusty, stale air conditioning, and there's some suspicious substance splattered across the wall that I refuse to look at too long for fear of it being the hotspot of some newfangled disease.

"Easy, J!" I hold up my hands. "I'll tell you everything you need to know."

"And you'll tell me the truth?"

"When have I ever lied to you?"

Jess's brown eyes light up, big and sparkly. "Have you two kissed more than once?"

"Yes."

She claps her hands in glee. "Do you like her?"

"Yes."

"*Like her* like her?"

I nod. "Yeah, I think so."

"So, she's your girlfriend, then."

"Jess, it's been, like, a day. We haven't discussed labels yet."

This earns me a spectacular eye roll. "Don't you dare pull any too-cool-to-label-it bullcrap with Courtney."

It's not that. Not even a little bit. I want to see where this goes with Courtney, but I want to take it slowly, carefully. This is such new territory for the both of us, and I know we have to establish trust first. Build a firm foundation.

"I wouldn't dare," I say seriously. I even make a little cross my heart motion.

Jess goes serious. More serious than I've ever seen her. "And you promise not to hurt her?"

I nod. "I'll do everything that is humanly possible not to hurt her."

Jess gives me a lazer-death-glare. "Not good enough, big bro. If you hurt her, I'll flux you up!"

"Excuse me?!"

"I said flux!"

She's right. She did.

I look at Jess, stone-faced. "I promise not to hurt her, Jess. This is... different for me. *She's* different."

"And, do you admit that I am always right and you should always listen to me?"

I put my hands on her shoulders. Bend towards her. Look my baby sister in the eye. "Absolutely not."

"But?" she prompts.

"You were right about this one, J."

Jess squeals. "I knew it!"

"You get to be right once in a while, I guess," I concede, smiling.

And I'm glad she was right about this.

My phone buzzes in my pocket, and I slide it out. *Lorna.*

I pat Jess on the head—her absolute favorite move—and she scowls at me. "'Scuse me, J. I gotta get this."

She sighs loudly, rolls her eyes, and steps aside so I can escape my prison.

With a wink in her direction, I walk towards the exit and answer the call. "Lorna, hi."

"Aiden, Aiden, Aiden." Lorna's voice booms. "Congratulations are in order."

"Oh yeah?"

"Ever After put up an Instagram post, announcing you and Courtney were at Haven. Sales of their couple's retreat have gone up 300% in the last twenty-four hours. They're more excited than ever about the new rebrand. Outstanding."

"Cool." I grin, thinking of the escapades Courtney and I were on in the jungle, at yoga, dancing on the beach. "It turned out to be a pretty easy research assignment."

"Well, my boy, keep up the good work. I can't say this on the record yet, but... your future at Zone 6 is looking very bright. *Hollywood* bright."

Lorna's words wipe the smile right off my face.

LA.

My promotion.

The two things that have been furthest from my mind, when really, they should've been front and center. I've just been so busy living and breathing all things Courtney, I've barely thought about anything else.

All my priorities seem to have changed overnight. Because the world didn't end when I finally allowed myself to feel something.

In fact, it got a little brighter.

She makes it brighter.

Not work. Not money. Not security and career growth and logic and reason.

Her.

After a few distracted minutes speaking with Lorna, I finally hang up and search for Courtney. Find her at a flashing game machine, playing Tetris.

Really freaking badly, I might add.

She's hunched over the machine, tongue poking out of the side of her mouth, flipping shapes around at random. Multicolor lines, squares and Ls are piling up in a jumbled mess.

Not one ounce of logic to her method.

I stand behind her, hiding my smile behind my hand. She's adorable. Seriously adorable. Her tan bare legs and sneakers don't hurt, either.

"Agh, no!" Courtney moans as the shapes reach the top of the screen in record time. GAME OVER flashes, big and bright. She turns, sees my face, and plants a hand on one slender hip. "Oh yeah? Think you can do better, Shaw?"

I toss a token in my hand. Move close. "Oh, I *know* I can do better."

She visibly shivers, and it's all I can do to step around her and approach the game instead of dragging her off (willingly, of course) somewhere private so I can kiss her without Jess popping up like a bothersome little whack-a-mole person.

Although, I have to say, it is nice to have my sister *approve* of a romantic decision of mine.

"Do your worst," Courtney teases.

I push my token into the machine and play the game, lining up the shapes, neat and tidy along the bottom.

After a few moments, Courtney gapes. "How did you get so good at this?"

"Practice?"

Courtney peers at me, glee in her eyes. "I had you pegged as a lot of things over the years. A closet nerd wasn't one of them."

I chuckle. "Okay, maybe not so much practice. I guess I just take to logical things," I explain with a shrug. "Things that make sense. Tetris is just a puzzle."

"But you can never win."

"What?"

"Tetris," Courtney says, pointing at the screen. "You can apply logic and reason and problem-solving forever. But, it doesn't get you anywhere. You can never win the game."

I turn to stare at her. I've never lived in a world where logic didn't reign true over everything, a world where I didn't prioritize only the things that make sense.

And yet, here I am, with the most incredible, strong woman I've ever known, and it occurs to me that maybe my life *doesn't* have to be that way. In all my thirty-two years, I chose not to fall in love, not to pursue relationships, because they weren't logical. Love wasn't something I could control, keep orderly and manageable.

But, Courtney's words—intended or not—hit me over the head like a hammer: I can keep trying to control everything, create a security blanket for myself, forever. But, in doing that—on never taking a chance on something else—I can never win. Never get anywhere.

I breathe out slowly. Then, realize I've looked away, lost attention, long enough to lose.

Whomp Whomp Whomp.

GAME OVER.

"Cheer up, buttercup," she says, laughing, as she nudges

me in the ribs. "It's just a game. You can't help the fact that you suck."

I grin. Grab her fingers—that are boring into my side like a drill—and retaliate by tickling her in the ribs, which makes her squeal. She's practically choking with laughter as she wriggles, tries valiantly to jerk away from me. But, I wrap my arms around her in a bear hug, holding her tight so she can't get away.

"Tell me I suck again, I dare you," I growl, gently biting her neck.

She breathes in sharply, then stills for a moment. Then, she twists one arm free and lashes out, whacking my shoulder.

"You... suck!" she wheezes triumphantly, exploding in another fit of giggles.

"Oh, it's on!" I keep mercilessly tickling her, relishing the feeling of having her in my arms. Relishing the fact that all the hate is gone, but what's in its place is still... us. I can't help the smile that spreads across my face as we play-fight and tease, not caring who's watching, or what anyone might say.

I might have just lost the game, but for the first time ever, I feel like I might've actually won.

36

COURTNEY

I thought Haven Resort should be renamed Heaven Resort.

I was wrong.

For the past week, heaven has been right here on our little street in Peachtree Hills, Atlanta.

I know I sound dramatic, but there are plenty of reasons to be dramatic, trust me. Aiden is... nothing like I thought he was (except handsome. I think I grudgingly always knew that one).

It turns out that there are a lot of pros to not hating your hot next-door neighbor. For example, every morning when I step out of my house, dog leashes in hand, Aiden joins me for a walk. On the way back, we stop at the corner cafe to get coffee before he takes off for work. Several evenings this week, he's come over to help me work on my business plan.

And, by "work on my business plan", I mean we do a lot of making out.

One night, we even had dinner at Pete and Mia's with Conor and Jess. It was the hundredth time that the six of us have gotten together, and the first that we were three couples. I liked the change—everything about it. Liked that Aiden and I drove together. Came home together. I invited him in, and we made midnight pancakes, and I put on one of my favorite old records, and he took my hand and twirled me around the kitchen.

He also admitted that he'd watched me doing the same thing from his window just a couple weeks ago. Which, obviously, earned him a swift kick to the shin and the title of "Creep" for the rest of the evening.

In response, I admitted that I had completely misjudged him for four years over a simple misunderstanding with a girl who pulled up outside his house in a sexy dress. He had zero idea who I was talking about, but reassured me that he was only staring at me because he thought I was gorgeous.

I blushed redder than a tomato at that one.

Yesterday, we went to his house. He invited my dogs, which would've been sweet if it wasn't a touch annoying that Cassidy—who's been my partner in crime for the past five years, my supposed ride or die—likes Aiden a little *too* much.

Sue me. I'm the jealous type when it comes to my furballs.

Anyway, Aiden ordered us all take out. And I do mean "all," because UberEats delivers dog treats. Aiden might be the only person sweet and thoughtful enough to have ever ordered takeout delivery for dogs.

Once we were done eating, we sat on his couch and he showed me some of his photography with this bashful smile that made me fall for him a little more.

His photos are unreal. He has the same artistic talent as Jess, channeled into creating these stunning studies of light and color and angles and depth that make you feel warm and cold all over.

He shrugged off my praise, saying the artistic gene ran in his family and he simply chose a medium that he could study in a practical way.

But, I didn't miss the way his eyes lit up when he talked about photography. How his expression became earnest as he explained all kinds of technical terms like "exposure" and "lens flare."

I nodded along like an idiot in response, not listening to a word because I was so focused on how adorable he looked when he got all serious and brow-furrowed and intense.

Today, he's been texting me from work while I'm out shopping. Cute, flirty texts that make me grin like an idiot. Which my friends, very annoyingly, go out of their way to grill me about.

"What's he sayingggg?" Jess whines as she leans over my shoulder to take a peek.

I immediately lock the screen and pocket my cell. "Wouldn't you like to know?"

Mia looks up from the dress she's examining. "I don't ever think I've seen you this happy, Court."

"He makes me happy," I admit bashfully.

"I can't believe it took eighteen months to convince you that my brother wasn't the devil."

"He didn't help his case." I smile to myself at the plentiful memories of Aiden and me, tension crackling around us as we argued and bickered over nothing.

"It's like *Friends*, but if Phoebe and Joey got together at the end." Jess sighs happily. "Stupid Paul Rudd ruined everything for them."

I throw a sweater at Jess. "Don't you diss Paul Rudd. And you really need to find a new TV show to watch."

"No way," Jess says stoutly as she folds up the sweater and places it on a shelf. Conor's clean-freakishness is clearly rubbing off on her.

"Paul Rudd wasn't the culprit, anyhow. The only reason they didn't get together is 'cuz Joey did that spinoff series where he moved to LA, remember?" Mia offers as she rummages through her bag. Produces a tube of Mentos, and wiggles it in our direction. "Candy?"

Jess takes three. I shake my head. "No, thanks. I forgot about the spinoff show. Never watched it."

"Don't," Jess, the official *Friends* representative, tells us through a huge gobful of fruity candy. "It's nowhere near as good as the main show."

"Roger that," I say. Hold up a pair of high-waisted, embroidered jean shorts. "I know it's the wrong season for this, but maybe I'll try these on. They're on sale."

"They'd look fantastic on you," Mia says wistfully. "I wish I had the body for those."

I shake my head again. "You're perfect the way you are."

Mia shoots me a lovely smile. "Thanks. You, too, Courtney."

I love how easily she accepts my compliment, how she can tap into her innate sense of self-worth despite how insecure I know she is about her post-baby body. I need to do more of that. Embrace my flaws, once and for all, instead of hiding them and shielding myself. With the way I've been feeling—filled with hope and optimism—it's an area of my life I should work on.

My next move is to get up the courage to tell Aiden about my insulin pump. We've only ever kissed at this point, and so my secret's still hidden beneath my clothes.

I know it's a stupid thing to be worried about. I know Aiden likes me for me, sees the person I am. And I know my pump is a part of me. But every time I look at it, it just reminds me that I'm far, far from perfect.

"Ready to hit the dressing rooms?" Mia asks.

"Sure," I reply, still lost in thought.

"I'm not trying anything," Jess says, rubbing her belly. "But, I do need to sit down."

In the changing rooms, Jess sinks onto a bench while Mia disappears to try on her armful of clothes. I step into a cubicle. Close the velvety blue curtain. But, instead of trying on the shorts, I look at myself in the gilded mirror. It's one of those fancy, high-end stores with good lighting and air conditioning.

I let my eyes glide over my reflection—my light blond hair that I've always been quick to call "wispy", my pale lips, my tall, statuesque figure. I decide that the girl staring back at me ain't so bad. Cold and goosebump-ridden, perhaps. But, not bad. She's tough, funny and a good friend.

But, is that what Aiden's looking for in a girlfriend? In a partner?

Doubt bubbles up in me. I know that Aiden has dated a lot of women, that many beautiful, flawless specimens would be after him in an instant. It makes me wonder why he would choose me. I might be coming around to my own self-worth, but there's no denying the fact that I will never be flawless.

Not like that chick with the cut-out dress, or Breanna. Not like the women who've paraded themselves around Aiden over the years. How many of them have "slid into his DMs", as the cool kids say these days (which I am not)?

On a whim, I reach for my phone. Against my better judgment, I find the video on Instagram—I haven't looked at it since before our vacay—and scroll down to the comments. Hold my breath.

The comments aren't as bad as expected. There's the odd troll, who I would be delighted to order back into their little hole or under their bridge or wherever trolls reside. But, I am a woman on a mission.

The commenters are, in turn, supportive and nice, mean and scathing, disbelieving and calling it all a "set up." Everyone has an opinion.

But, the overwhelming, overarching theme I see woven through the comments is *Aiden, Aiden, Aiden.* How handsome. How hot. How unfair that such a devastatingly gorgeous man got doused in pudding.

They want their own dates with him. Want him for themselves. These women (and, yes, some men) are aggressive in their wanting. In how Aiden could do "so much better."

As much as Aiden's affirmations to me ring in my head, I can't help but wonder if I am kidding myself with all of this.

"Court?" a voice calls from beyond the curtain. Before I can reply, a bump comes into view followed quickly by Jess herself as she squeezes into the cubicle. "Why aren't you dressed?"

I blink at her, then drop my phone in my purse. "Got distracted by a text from a, um, dog-walking client."

"Are you okay?"

"Yeah."

"Liar."

"Honest."

"Tell me."

I don't want to make this girls' shopping day about me, especially given how wonderful and supportive my friends have been. Besides, the comments don't mean anything and I need to remind myself of that. Some of them are probably bots anyway. Doing bot-like things.

But, Jess is staring at me with those owl eyes of hers, chin tilted down and gaze locked like I'm her prey. I know how she gets when she's like this. There's no sense in fighting it.

"Aiden has just... dated a lot more than me," I mumble, looking at my hands. I run my index fingernail over my thumb, picking at it.

Jess's face turns stormy. I pity the five year old who attempts to bully her child. "Did he say something?"

"No, nothing like that." I hold up my hands. "I just wonder sometimes why he wants to date me."

Jess looks bemused. "Because he likes you, Courtney." She laughs. "He's crazy about you and doesn't even know what to do with that piece of information himself. This is new for him."

"That's what I mean—he's a serial dater. He could have anyone he wants."

"Exactly, Court." Jess grabs my arms. "He could. But, it's *you* he wants."

I nod, because I don't know what else to do. "Okay."

"This is different for him, trust me." Jess shoots me a wink. "I've known him all my life. He's got a heart of gold, but he doesn't get close to people. You're the first woman who's made him act like this."

I smile at Jess feebly and she wraps an arm around me, narrowly avoiding whacking me right out of the changing room with her belly.

As I try to cast all my doubts aside and enjoy the rest of the day with my girls, the same nagging little dirty thought twitches restlessly.

Why me?

And, will it still be me when Aiden sees how imperfect I really am?

37

AIDEN

"Thank you," I say to the Starbucks employee as I hand over a bill. "Keep the change."

The green-haired girl's eyes light up as she takes the money. "Thanks so much!"

"Anytime." I smile, placing the tray of drinks on the passenger seat.

I drive away as carefully as possible—everyone knows cappuccinos and leather don't mix. Crank up the radio and tap my fingers on the steering wheel to the beat of some pop song Jess probably knows every word of.

I don't remember ever being this content while driving to work. A new, inner calm has settled within me. Something is at peace, fulfilled in a way that I've never been before.

The funny thing is, I always thought that I had all the pieces I needed to be happy—the house, the career, the friends, the dates.

Turns out, I was missing the most important piece.

And now that I've found it, I'm clinging to it like a pitbull with a bone. Because I'm never letting Courtney Turner go.

I walk into my office with an extra spring in my step.

"Morning, Kayley," I say brightly. "Coffees for everyone. The usual."

"Thanks, Mr. Shaw—um, Aiden!" My assistant takes the tray from me. "You're the best."

"What's on my schedule this morning?" I take a sip of my Americano and lean my elbows on the reception desk.

But, my mind is already on what Courtney and I will be doing tonight—I'm taking her to my favorite place in all of Atlanta. Somewhere I've never taken anyone on a date before.

I'm loving all these recent "firsts."

A pleasant tingle moves through me as I think about seeing Courtney. About how cute she looked this morning when we went on our dog walk. She was wearing athletic shorts and a tee when she arrived at my house. It was chilly out, so she swiped a hoodie from me. Like went into my house and thieved it from one of my drawers.

I was more than happy to be the robbery victim. And it paid off, because let me tell you, there's nothing sexier than a woman with no makeup, hair in a messy ponytail, wearing one of your oversized hoodies, and a pair of sneakers.

Especially when she's a woman who's as beautiful inside as she is out. A woman who you're falling for. Fast. And you have no desire to step on the brakes or pause and make sense of it, because nothing compares to the high of thinking about her.

This morning, when we walked, she was telling me more about Life is Ruff. Mentioned that she's been saving up for a deposit on a commercial space in the area. She has it all planned out—right down to the color scheme and brands of doggy shampoo they'll stock. Her enthusiasm and passion is inspiring. So inspiring, I find myself wanting her

261

dream to come true for her more than anything I could ever want for myself.

Kayley reads me the schedule for the day and I thank her before going to my office.

Immediately text Courtney.

Aiden: You'd better bring that hoodie tonight.

Courtney: Nice try, Shaw. You're never getting it back. It's mine now.

It is. All hers.

Aiden: I'm feeling generous enough to loan it to you for the evening because it's cold where we're going.

Courtney: Just a friendly reminder that it's illegal to lock people in freezers.

Courtney: Even if they did steal your favorite hoodie.

Aiden: If anything, you're just giving me ideas.

"Knock, knock!" A voice sings from the doorway.

I reluctantly set down my phone. "Lorna. Good morning."

She click-clacks across the room and settles in the chair opposite my desk. "Aiden, Aiden, Aiden."

"What can I do for you?"

Lorna smiles that scarlet Joker smile of hers. "Really, the question is—what can I do for you?"

I frown. "What do you mean?"

Since Courtney and I got back from Haven a week and a half ago, a lot of the hype surrounding our viral video has died down. We've been replaced with new viral sensations of the moment.

With regards to my job, though, every spare moment I've had outside of spending time with Courtney, I've been working on the "Second Chance at Happily Ever After" rebrand.

I came up with the idea of doing an "Instagram vs Reality" approach. Showing that, while the resort is just as beautiful in reality as it is in the photos, a lot of relationships aren't. I made a stunning mood board of all the unfiltered, stripped-back candids I took while at Haven, with an approach of looking at ourselves through an honest lens. Showing that true happiness comes from within.

Zola, one of our web designers, is mocking up a new website for this now. And, my favorite graphic designer at Zone 6, Bill, is using his incredible eye for simple but beautiful design to produce the logo and marketing materials we conceptualized.

Stripped back, stark and pure.

As far as I'm concerned, everything is as it should be. But, Lorna looks like she knows something I don't.

She sighs, tapping her claws on the table rhythmically. "They hate it."

I blink. "Pardon me?"

"Ever After. They hate your concept. It's not aspirational enough. They want glamor. Beauty. Opulence. Relationships that will be glowing and Insta-worthy after a stay at Haven."

"Oh," is all I can say. "I thought they wanted an honest perspective on relationships."

"That's what they thought they wanted," Lorna says simply. "What they actually want is a glow up of that concept. A sexy, marketable spin. But..."

"There's a but?"

"There's always a but, dear boy." Lorna claps her hands. "I took the liberty of going through your files on the cloud. There were a ton of beautiful, polished pictures you took of the premises. And a note that you left: 'Be the best version of yourself.' That's the pitch Ever After want—that coming to Haven will allow you to become your very best self in the most stunning place."

My frown deepens. "The quote is out of context, though. The couples counselor used it during our yoga class. It has to do with working on your own flaws so you can be a better partner for the person you love."

"Aiden, darling, we work in branding. Flaws are airbrushed. Disguised. Never paraded."

My heart sinks. "I guess so."

"I took the liberty of sending over an alternative pitch from you, using your polished photos. My boy, they're eating it up over there! Go with this concept because, if you nail this, the promotion is yours. You'll come back with me to LA, be my right-hand man. Manage a larger team, and have a larger office. It's everything you've worked for."

Everything she's saying sounds great. It's exactly what I wanted. What the old Aiden wanted.

But now? I just feel sick.

Lorna takes my silence to be a good thing. She rises from her chair, bracelets clacking on her wrists. "The sky's the limit for you, Aiden Shaw. There's nothing holding you back from greatness. It's yours for the taking."

Lorna leaves, and I'm left alone with a chasm of thoughts.

Greatness.

Nothing about this feels great.

I worked my butt off to secure this promotion, it was my next logical step. At this point, I've outgrown my position here in Atlanta, my friends are settling down, getting married and having kids... So, it made sense to focus on LA, on getting a fresh start and forwarding my career.

It's everything I've worked for, yes. But, it's nothing I want.

Not anymore.

Now that I've gotten what I *thought* I wanted, I see that it all means nothing. I have a career that lives on the surface.

Focuses on finding the right angles and the perfect spin to make people feel good temporarily. Make things seem more perfect than they really are.

But, perfect is a lie. We're all human—riddled with flaws and imperfections. And I've realized that everything I'm working towards tries to hide that.

I don't want to hide anymore. I'm sick of focusing only on what makes sense in my mind so my heart doesn't have to feel anything. I've been so scared of love coming at the expense of my comfort and security that I've overridden what my heart's been telling me at every turn.

The thing is, though, every human is made up of both heart and mind. And, when these are at war, there can be no peace. No true growth.

I want to live life with another imperfect human by my side. I want something real, a relationship that actually means something. Yes, it might be hard sometimes, but I want to be with someone who challenges me, who inspires me to do better. Be better. And, in turn, I want to inspire them.

I want stormy and chaotic and jumbled and difficult and entirely illogical. Because falling in love might not be logical, but it's worth it.

I don't want perfect.

I want Courtney.

38

COURTNEY

"Nervous?" Aiden asks as I slide into the passenger seat of my Jeep. He tilts his head towards me and smiles. Tonight, he's wearing a black fleece sweatshirt that makes his blue eyes navy.

I shake my head, as though this could shake away the butterflies that are swarming my stomach. "Not in the least. I'd prefer to drive my own vehicle to wherever we're going, though."

"Too bad." Aiden grins, throws the Jeep in reverse.

In the back, Butch, Cassidy and Sundance sit in a perfect row, like little humans.

One big, happy family.

The thought puts an insanely goofy smile on my face. Way too goofy.

I reel it in and arrange my features in a semi-normal expression. "Okay, so where is this 'favorite place' you speak of?"

"'Bout forty-five minutes away. Get comfy."

He reaches for the volume on the radio and I swat his hand away. "My vehicle, my music."

Aiden laughs. "Can't argue with that."

"A month ago, you would have."

"I never would've been in your car a month ago. Unless I was in a body bag and you were off to hide the evidence."

"Yeah, right," I tease. "As if I would've risked getting your gross blood in my car."

"My blood isn't gross, it's a perfect type O negative. Blood banks go crazy for my blood," Aiden retorts, then leans over and pinches my arm.

"Hey!" I squeak. Pinch him back.

He bats my hand away, laughing. "No pinching wars while I'm driving."

"How about no wars at all?"

He looks at me and the smile that lights his face is enough to make me die happy.

"No wars at all," he echoes.

I sit back in my seat with a humongous smile on my face and Aiden's fingers interlocked with mine.

But, exactly forty-five minutes later, I feel like retracting my "no more wars" statement. Because Aiden has brought me to Kennesaw Mountain.

Apparently, he wants us to climb it.

We get out of the Jeep and Aiden puts the dogs on leashes while I stare at the huge uphill trek in front of us and adjust my backpack. The sun isn't quite setting yet, and casts a warm glow over the mountain and its surroundings, but that's pretty much the only thing that's warm. There's a very unwelcome bite in the air, and the wind whistles in the trees as I pull on the hood of Aiden's hoodie. Thank goodness I wore leggings.

I eye the peak skeptically. "*This* is your favorite place in Atlanta?"

Aiden puts on a gray wool beanie. "Sure is."

"I thought we were going ice skating or something."

267

Aiden snorts. "You thought my favorite place was an ice rink?"

"Yes. No. I dunno... maybe you were a childhood figure skater or something."

"Nah, I could never find tights that fit right. Talk about the world's most uncomfortable wedgie." He winks, then smiles. "At the very least, you could've guessed that I was a childhood hockey player."

I look at him sharply. Put my hands on my hips. "Were you?"

"No," Aiden admits. "I've never played hockey in my life. Or figure skated, for that matter."

"But, you like to climb mountains as a pastime."

"I do. It's worth it, I promise."

I sigh, and Aiden quirks a half-smile. "Don't worry, there are no wild monkeys in Atlanta."

"Better not be."

"Do you trust me?" he asks, navy eyes intent. A bottomless pool.

"Should I?"

This makes Aiden laugh. "Oh, you definitely shouldn't."

"In that case..." I grin. Start walking towards the trailhead.

"So contrary." He shakes his head, then follows, a wry smile playing on his lips.

We begin the hike.

Up, up, up, for two whole stupid miles.

It's chilly and damp and the sun is pressing closer to the horizon but Aiden is in his element. He's clearly getting me back for my disparaging comments about his physique at couples yoga, because he's freaking sprinting up the hill. Flanked by my golden retrievers, he looks like he's stepped right out of an LL Bean catalog. All rugged and handsome and outdoorsy, like he's going to build me a log cabin or something.

Meanwhile, I clearly have PTSD from my last hike, because I'm so gassed, I'm unable to breathe. And I keep tripping over my own feet every few steps. Turns out jogging doesn't prepare one for climbing mountains.

Sundance is the only one who seems to understand me. He's walking impossibly slowly—I've seen sloths move faster. He turns indignant eyes on me and I pat his little head. "I know, boy. The bad man is torturing us."

"I heard that!" Aiden calls. But, he slows dutifully. Scoops Sundance up in one arm and grabs my hand with the other. "Come on, I'll drag you up. We gotta hurry."

"Whyyy?" I moan like an annoying child. Whining seems to be the only appropriate way to deal with my feelings right now.

Aiden smiles. "Trust me."

"So you keep saying."

He squeezes my hand. "It'll be worth it."

I squeeze back. Silently let him know that, as long as I'm with him, going *anywhere* is worth it.

We reach the top of the mountain, and I finally see what he means.

The sun is sinking low over the city, casting a magic glow over the world. The skyline appears to be dipped in gold, and illuminated by a halo of pink and orange. The humid air smells like fallen leaves and the wind is cool, but I'm as warm as I need to be with Aiden standing next to me.

"I had no idea you could see all this from up here," I say quietly, in total awe. "It's beautiful."

"Definitely." Aiden moves to stand behind me, loops his strong arms around my body and holds me close, blocking me from the chilly wind. His fingers twist into the material of my (okay, his) hoodie, and he rests his chin in my hair.

"Things are more serene up here. The city looks so perfect, so pristine. You forget that there's, like, five million people down there who are feeling and thinking and going about their lives."

I bite my bottom lip. "All you see is how pretty it is. Nothing more."

"Exactly."

I twist my head to look at Aiden. "Is that why you like to come here? Because it makes things look more perfect than they are?"

Aiden looks thoughtful. He takes a moment to consider my question, and for some reason, this makes my heartbeat quicken. Finally, he shakes his head. "No. I come here because it gives me perspective. Things can look so different if you step back, take another angle."

"Like when we went to the resort?"

Aiden gives me a squeeze. "Exactly. I think we both realized we're very different from what we originally thought."

My heart speeds and I wonder if Aiden can feel it through the hoodie. There's a question I'm dying to ask, but I'm terrified of his answer. Of what he truly thinks. But, as per usual, my mouth blurts out the question anyway. "What if there was an angle you didn't like?"

"I like you from all angles." Aiden loosens his grip and puts his hands on my shoulders. Spins me around gently while pretending to examine me. "Yup. I like that angle... and that angle..."

I giggle at his antics, and then go quiet. "I mean, what if I was less perfect than you thought?"

Aiden stops spinning me so I'm facing him. Looks deep into my eyes. "Courtney, I literally can't get enough of you, but I'm under no illusion that you're perfect. You ruined my Italian loafers."

My tension lifts at his words, and I snort with laughter. "You deserved it."

"Courtney Martha Turner, you take that back!" Aiden tickles me in the ribs.

"Never!" I squirm away from him, breathless with laughter.

As we make our way down the mountain, joking and laughing and shoving each other (okay, the shoving is mostly from my end. Okay, fine. All from my end), I feel lighter than I have in a while.

I've spent my entire life trying, and failing, to be perfect. But maybe I don't have to be perfect. Maybe I can just be me.

I don't like to take risks. But, buoyed by Aiden's simple words—"I'm under no illusion that you're perfect"—I'm ready to take one.

39

COURTNEY

We're back on the highway when I finally say, "Aiden, you know how I'm diabetic?"

"Yup. I vaguely recall that time you scared the pants off me by nearly dying rather than telling me the truth." He looks at me, eyes twinkling, but I look at him seriously.

My thoughts are rushing faster than a freight train. I think I might be sick. Careen right off the tracks. But, I push on, determined.

"Ihaveaninsulinpump," I mumble.

Aiden quirks an eyebrow, runs his fingertips along the bottom of the steering wheel. "What?"

"In my stomach, aninsulinpump." My voice isn't any louder.

"You're going to throw up?" Aiden asks, suddenly alarmed.

I take a deep, deep breath. Force the air to leave my lungs in the form of loud, clear words. "I have an insulin pump."

"Oh. What's that?" He sounds casual, conversational.

I, meanwhile, feel like my entire head is on fire. "A

medical device. I had it implanted in my stomach a couple years back. It gives me insulin when I need it."

Aiden goes silent, and my heart stops. Like, officially stops beating. Hopefully Aiden packed a defibrillator in his hiking backpack because I may well be dead before we get home.

I clench my fists in my lap. Wait for awkwardness, disgust, or worst of all, pity.

Instead, he takes his eyes off the road again. Grins. "Man, science is awesome."

"It's in my stomach," I reiterate, peering at him to see if he gets it. "Permanently,"

"Does it hurt?" He changes lanes, zipping around a slow-moving VW bug being driven by an elderly guy who's got to be in his nineties. Gives the old man a cheery wave as he passes.

"Well, no," I say slowly. His lack of a reaction has knocked me for six. "But it's always there."

"Cool."

"Cool?"

"Well, not cool that you're ill, obviously," Aiden back-tracks. "But, cool that there's something that makes your illness easier to live with, right?"

I blink, still not fully comprehending his words. "You're not weirded out by it?"

"No." He frowns. "Why? Should I be?"

I stare at the man beside me, his profile lit in the fading golden rays of the glorious sunset. This beautiful man who's cocky and smug and sarcastic and way too pleased with himself most of the time.

I've never met anyone so absolutely, totally, unequivocally imperfectly perfect in my life.

"No," I say softly. "I guess not."

A few minutes later, we pull up at my house. Get out of the Jeep. Walk up my driveway together, dogs in tow.

"Thank you for tonight," I say.

"Thank *you*."

We're standing on my doorstep, looking at each other.

I open my front door. Let the dogs in, one by one.

Then, after the longest pause known to humanity, I take a step towards the door myself. Coyly look over my shoulder. "You coming or what?"

Aiden laughs, the sound deep and gravelly, before I grab his hand. Yank him over the threshold.

The door barely has time to close before we're tangled up in each other.

We laugh as we kiss, making our way to the living room, utilizing several walls before we finally end up on my couch.

Kissing him is beautiful. Perfect. Every touch of his lips, every caress of his hands, is a declaration of a new era. No more me versus Aiden. But Aiden *and* me, against the world.

"Courtney," Aiden pulls back to whisper, and a word that used to sound like a curse on his lips now sounds reverent. His large hand cups my chin, and the sensation of calloused roughness on the sensitive skin lining my jaw coaxes a gasp out of me. "You're so beautiful."

He expertly tilts my head back so his lips can claim mine, and I gasp again as he pulls me close, wraps those arms around me and holds me tight, pressed against him. My heartbeat reverberates around every inch of my body, thumping like a bass drum as I lose myself to his kiss, drunk on the sensation of him.

I reach up and twist my hands in his hair, running them along his scalp. He makes a noise deep in his throat and his fingertips tighten on my back as he deepens the kiss. My stomach curls with desire.

Like a woman possessed, my hands slide over Aiden's chest, then fumble for his shirt collar. I undo his buttons, one by one, breaking our kiss so I can press my lips to his hot skin. Right above his heart.

Aiden groans, plants an open-mouthed kiss above my collarbone that sends shivers down my spine. Then, he pulls back to look at me. His navy eyes swim with desire, hazy and dilated and full.

Eyes you could drown in.

I lean forward to kiss him again, but he moves away, rests his head against my shoulder.

"We should stop," he murmurs as he catches his breath.

A pit forms in my stomach. Reality comes crashing on me like a lead weight. A weight that I'm unable to carry alone.

"I understand," I say numbly. Defeated.

His head snaps back and his eyes come back into focus. "Quit that!" he orders suddenly.

I blink in surprise at his tone.

Aiden sits straight. Tense and rigid. When he looks at me again, the passionate desire in his eyes has been replaced with what almost looks like anger.

"Courtney." He puts his hands on my arms, looks deep into my eyes. "I'm not stopping for me, I'm stopping for you. I want you more than you could even imagine, but what I want more is for you to believe in yourself. I know people have hurt you in the past, but you have to stop beating your-self up and believe me when I tell you you're amazing. Special. And so, I want to take this slow, one step at a time. Until you truly understand how special I think you are, and that I'm not going anywhere. Unless you tell me to go and you really mean it, I'll be right here, at your side, taking each step with you. Okay?"

The breath leaves my lungs in one fell swoop. This is so different from anything I could've expected from Aiden Shaw. The womanizer who is not a womanizer whatsoever.

"I'm sorry for unbuttoning your shirt," I say quietly.

Aiden laughs gently, wraps his hands around mine. "Don't be. There are so many things I want to do with you, share with you. But, we don't have to do them all tonight."

"I thought you were having second thoughts about my insulin pump," I admit, not looking at him. "A part of me is scared I won't live up to your expectations."

"Expectations?" Aiden's voice is rough. "You think I have expectations of you?"

I bite my bottom lip. Hard enough for my mouth to fill with an acrid, metallic taste. "Look at me. I'm sick. The evidence is right there on my stomach."

"Courtney, you're beautiful," Aiden says softly. "That medical device you have on you is beautiful, too. It keeps you safe, keeps you healthy. All I want is for you to be safe and healthy."

I peek up at him through my eyelashes. "Really?"

"Always," he says without a moment of hesitation. He takes a couple of breaths, like he's trying to stay calm, but his eyes are on fire. "And as for expectations, I have none of you. Except for you to be happy. You need to know that it's always okay for you to set boundaries. Whatever those may be, it's your job to set them, and other people's job to respect them. And I will always respect them. Respect you."

His words hit home, and I fall into them. They feel like balm on a wound. A true depiction of Aiden Shaw's character—selfless, kind and entirely beautiful, inside and out.

But, it doesn't quite stop the fear that's currently lapping at my insides.

"What if I'm not enough for you?" I speak my greatest fear aloud, my voice barely above a whisper. But the sound echoes around the room like the loudest crash of cymbals.

Aiden gently takes my chin, forces me to look at him. When he speaks, his voice cracks with emotion. "Courtney, you're everything I never knew I could want. You are more than enough."

Waking up with Courtney in my arms makes a lifetime of waking up alone feel like a lot of wasted time.

Before last week, I'd never held a woman in my arms all night before. Just *sleeping*. Sleeping with someone beside you is super underrated. Why did no one ever tell me?

And sure, we slept on the couch together when she had her hypoglycemic episode, but this was different. That time, I was worried about her, stressed and restless because I needed to know that she was okay.

Last night? It was easy. We fell asleep in each others' arms like it was the most natural thing in the world.

I take a moment to look at her now, my eyes scanning her face to memorize her every feature. She's beautiful when she sleeps—her face screwed up in the cutest little nose-scrunch, her hair spilling all over the pillows.

Reluctantly, I disentangle my arms from around her body, and kiss her on the forehead. She's been working so hard lately, she needs to sleep.

I slip downstairs, the three furry amigos at my heels. Decide to feed the dogs and put on a pot of coffee for her before I leave for work.

I take the doggos' medication out of the fridge, and dole it out like she showed me to. I can't help but think how her care of her dogs reflects who she is as a person—she loves these animals, who all have a similar health condition to her, with all her heart. Giving them their shots is the least I can do, and I want to keep doing this. Every morning for as long as she'll let me.

Because she loves me. I know, in my heart of hearts, she loves me.

And I love her, too.

Which is terrifying. But at the same time, it isn't.

I think about love as I let myself out of her house and walk next door. Collect my mail, which is mostly for Courtney anyway. I shower, change into one of my favorite suits—slate gray with a light blue button-down underneath—and, as I'm cracking eggs in a pan for breakfast, I whip out my phone and dial a number.

"AIDEN!" Moments later, the blurry image of my mother, clad in a hot pink bikini, appears on the screen. "My one and only son! Om suastiastu!"

"What does that mean?"

My mom peers at the screen like she's raised a half-wit. "That's 'hello' in Balinese."

"Of course it is." I smile at the screen fondly. "You're in Indonesia now, then?"

She angles the phone to show me the beautiful ocean views behind her. "On Gili Trangawan island, just off the coast of Bali. We went to quite the party last night. Your father is off getting his gear ready for his night dive on the reef."

Yup. Most fathers his age are into reading the newspaper and watching old reruns of Seinfeld. My dad mud wrestles and scuba dives.

"So tell me about your new love," Mom says, super casually.

I freeze mid egg-stir. "Pardon?"

"The new lady in your life. There *is* a new lady in your life, right?"

I think back to our last conversation. "What did your third eye tell you now?" I ask suspiciously.

Jess and her big mouth, more like...

I expect Mom to launch into a big explanation about some mystical thing she's dreamed up, but she surprises me by smiling. "Nothing. You just look happier than I've seen you in a long time."

I grin back, entirely involuntarily. "I *am* happy."

"Love will do that to a person. I see so much of your father in you, Aiden." Mom's eyes are soft and gooey, her tone fluttery. She and Dad have been together for about a million years, but she still talks about him like he's the best thing since sliced bread.

And for the first time ever, I understand. Love can fill you so full, it's like everything you'll ever need is right in front of you.

Something about this revelation reaches deep inside of me, like an invisible hand, and twists open the top of the bottle I've kept buried beneath the surface all these years. All the feelings I've kept bottled up rise to the surface, like a Coke that's been shaken.

"I never thought I was capable of having love like you and Dad have," I say quietly. "One where you care so much, everything else becomes insignificant."

I feel ridiculous saying this, and how I feel as I say it makes me feel even more ridiculous. I know I had a happy upbringing, I was given so much in terms of care and family. But a raw, sharp sting tinges my throat as the words leave my mouth.

Mom's eyes become brighter, more focused. "Love isn't just about finding the right person, Aiden. It's about being the best you can be for that person, choosing them every single day when you wake up. Love isn't just a feeling, it's a decision. Your father and I decided long ago to love each other better, every day."

Mom scratches at her cheek and I realize that her eyes are gleaming. Shiny. For some reason, this makes my throat close up. We've never had a conversation like this. Never been open and honest.

Or at least, I've never been.

"We may not have had a lot, but we had each other," she goes on, and her voice wavers. "And then, we were blessed with you and Jess. And we had everything we ever wanted and needed. I don't want you to think that we believed everything else was insignificant. That truly wasn't the case. It was just that it didn't take priority. Not over making sure you and Jess were happy. Not over being a family."

My mother's words run over me like water over hot coals. And I'm instantly cooled, soothed.

For so long, I've had it all wrong. I've tried to replace love with security. But, I can collect as many material things as I like, work jobs that might furnish me with everything I think I need. All in order to feel a sense of control over my circumstances, but at the end of the day, it's empty. Hollow.

Maybe love doesn't have to mean spiralling out of control, like I always thought it did.

"Thanks, Mom," I whisper, my throat hoarse.

"We love you, Aiden. So much."

"I love you, too. You and Dad. You've taught me so much, and I'm lucky you're my mom."

"I'm lucky you're my son," my mom replies. Then, suddenly, she smiles bright, looking at a point just over the screen. "Ooh, look at that! A rainbow lorikeet."

281

She swivels her phone around to show me a brightly colored bird in a nearby tree. I chuckle at her enthusiasm.

"Better go get my sketchbook," she chortles happily. "Are you okay, Aiden?"

"Yeah, Mom. All good here."

My mother and I say our goodbyes and hang up, and I proceed to scrape my very burnt eggs into the trash. But, I'm filled with a brand new sense of warmth, hopefulness and assuredness.

Falling in love is nothing like I thought it would be. It doesn't mean sacrificing everything else. It means choosing one person over everything else. Every single day.

Love doesn't mean becoming my parents. They did things in the way that worked for them, and I can do the same for myself. I can still have other dreams and aspirations. And so can Courtney. But in the end, being the best for each other is the best thing we can do for *us*.

It's all I want to do for the rest of my life. Be better for her.

Because I love her.

I *choose* her.

With both my heart, and my mind.

Which is why, this morning, I'm going to work and officially telling Lorna that I politely decline the promotion.

Decline the move to LA and all of the benefits that come with it.

Because I have everything I want and need, right here in Atlanta.

41

COURTNEY

I am enough.

I can do anything I want in life. I can be who I am, proudly, without being perfect. I can reach for the stars. I can... probably go another three minutes before my need to pee becomes catastrophic.

Definitely should've gone before leaving the house, but I was too fired up and excited.

I clench my pelvic floor muscles and will my bladder to hang on a few more moments. Almost there...

Unfortunately, my bladder protests violently.

"You got this," I say aloud as I swerve my Jeep into Petit Soleil's parking lot. The jerky motion makes my cell phone slide right off my lap, down between the seat and the center console.

Ughhh. I'll have to grab that later. No time now.

It's 11am, the doors will be opening for brunch. The tables will be set immaculately. The pianist will be singing her heart out in French. And Philippe will be in the kitchen, barking at the staff.

A nervous shiver passes through me as I hop out of my vehicle. Show time!

"Morning, Diana!" I call as I stride into the restaurant. "Feeling better after your surgery?"

"Courtney!" She gives me a hug. "I am, thank you. How are you? I heard about... everything. You doing okay?"

I laugh. "Great, actually. Better than I've ever been. Is Philippe in the kitchen?"

Diana looks a little frightened. "He is. Do you want me to get him?"

"I'll find him myself."

Bladder momentarily forgotten in my adrenaline rush, I let myself into the kitchen. Locate Philippe immediately. He's holding court in the middle of the brunch prep, terrorizing everyone.

"Philippe!" I call happily.

"Courtney," he startles, dropping the spoon he was just tapping some poor busboy on the arm with. "I wasn't expecting you this morning. You're not back on the schedule until next week."

"I'm here to tell you that I don't *want* to be back on the schedule, please and thank you," I say sweetly.

Sudden silence falls over the normally-bustling kitchen.

"Pardonnez-moi?" Philippe squeaks, shooting me a scathing look. Probably not a good look for him that I'm essentially quitting in front of everyone.

I smile confidently. The humidity in the kitchen is probably making my hair frizz, I'm dressed in old leggings, and my hair's in a messy ponytail, but it doesn't matter. None of it matters. I don't need my armor anymore. I am enough. I am worth more than this crappy job with a boss that I'm done making excuses for.

"I am here to respectfully decline your offer to return to the Petit Soleil team," I repeat.

Philippe's face turns puce. "Why would you do that?"

It's a valid question. A question the Courtney of a

month ago would've been demanding the answer to, over and over again. But, I'm not that Courtney anymore.

Sure, I may not have enough money saved to be totally secure in my new business venture. I don't even have enough to put down a deposit on a commercial space I can make my own. But, I can start small and expand gradually. Maybe use my house. Work towards my goals slowly, but put everything into achieving them.

No more excuses, it's time to believe in myself. Take a risk, and make a bet on me.

Because I believe I can, and will, succeed.

I *am* good enough.

So, to Philippe's question, I answer calmly. "You passed me over time and again for a promotion and only offered me what I deserved when there was something in it for you." I cross my arms and look him dead in the eye. "For so many years, I fought hard to be good enough in your eyes. I was an excellent employee, and you never appreciated me."

You could hear a pin drop in the kitchen. Philippe just smirks. How insane to think that I used to believe that smirk drove me wild. "Is that so?"

I nod once. Firmly. "It is."

Seeing that I'm not wavering, that he has no power over me anymore, Philippe's smirk turns ugly. "You walk out that door and you've burned all your bridges." he seethes, pointing a finger at me. "Mark my words, you'll lose everything."

"I won't. This is *your* loss, Philippe. Not mine."

Philippe gapes at me. Behind him, Trainee Waitress silently claps. I shoot her an encouraging smile, hope that I might've inspired her to stand up for herself.

"Au revoir, Philippe!" I smile.

With that, I make a beeline for the bathroom.

42

AIDEN

"Petit Soleil?" I ask uneasily, swiveling on my chair.

I've watched enough *Law and Order* to know you should never return to the scene of the crime. Or in this case, the scene of the creme caramel.

"That's what they've requested." Lorna's tone is brusque. "Brunch at the place where it all started. Now, chop chop! Let's get going. I'll drive."

"Okay," I relent with a sigh. This is *not* what I wanted to speak with Lorna about, but I guess I can tell her about LA after brunch.

Right now, keeping Ever After happy and making this rebrand a success is the best thing I can do for Lorna and Zone 6. I've made my peace with the fact that I don't want the promotion, but that doesn't mean I want to throw my coworkers under the bus.

Lorna and I are meeting with John Andersen and I'll play it his way. Abandon my candid idea and give the client what they want—glitz and glamor. I'll ace the meeting, won't let Lorna down.

Then, once we're back at the office, I'll let her know I'm not taking the promotion. That I'll still give my all to my accounts, especially Ever After. But, I can't go to LA with her.

Feeling good about my decision, I smile at Lorna. "I can drive, if you'd prefer."

She shakes her head, diamond earrings flashing in the light. "We both know I have a faster car."

She does, actually.

And, because of the speed of said Ferrari (seriously, what do they pay her?), we make it to Petit Soleil in a record time. Speed limits apparently do not apply to Lorna Strummings. Nor do Stop signs.

I'm personally delighted I'm alive.

Petit Soleil is just as bougie and stuffy as I remember. It smells like steak and fresh flowers, the oddest combination. The only major difference from the last time I was here is that it's even *more* packed. And the average age of patrons has dropped by about two decades.

Which, I guess, Courtney, Breanna and I likely had something to do with.

John Andersen is already waiting for us at a table in the corner. He's in another steel-gray suit, and he's sipping on a Martini with about six olives bobbing in it—even though it's barely 11am.

"Aiden Shaw!" he booms, standing to shake my hand (firm grip, which I always appreciate). He then moves to kiss Lorna's powdered cheeks.

We sit around the table and exchange pleasantries, order a coffee for me, and a Martini to match John's for Lorna. She does seem to hate being left out. Then, we dive in. I open my laptop and begin taking John through a few ideas for Ever After's future.

Polished. Perfect. Flawless. The opposite pitch to the one I'd originally made.

With my years of experience, I was used to this, used to

airbrushing and putting a gloss on things. So why did this particular discussion feel so weird?

Somewhere in the middle of everything, Philippe pulls up a chair. Uninvited.

The guy bugs the crap outta me.

He kisses Lorna, then turns to me. Extends a hand. "Hello again, Aiden."

There's a razor-sharp edge to his voice I don't like one bit. Lorna and John fall into a discussion about Petit Soleil's decor, leaving me to deal with Philippe and his absurdly white teeth.

"Philippe," I say through a forced smile, shaking his hand a tad too hard. Just enough to make his eyes water.

He peers obviously, almost rudely, at my computer. "How're things?"

"Great. I was just taking your dad through the plan for the color scheme and logo—"

"I mean with Courtney," he cuts me off. Grabs a bread roll off the table, rips it clean in half.

What is this guy's deal? I thought he'd never shown interest in her, romantically. Which, obviously, makes him a fool. But, that's beside the point.

"Courtney's great," I say crisply.

"Blaze sent over the staff's full report from your time at Haven." Philippe grins. "Seems you two are *very* much in love."

Despite Philippe being the human equivalent of a toilet brush, I go momentarily soft as the fresh bread rolls on the table at the mention of Courtney and me being in love.

Love. Something I've finally found and embraced with open arms.

"We are," I say with a smile.

Philippe takes a huge bite of bread. Chews aggressively, then swallows. He doesn't break eye contact as a slow,

288

triumphant smile spreads across his face. "Ah, love. I guess that means you've asked her to move to LA with you?"

I blink. Suddenly, both Lorna and John are listening. "I, uh..." I fumble.

"Aiden," Lorna interrupts suddenly, her eyes urgent.

"Oh!" Philippe gasps theatrically. "Have I put my foot in it?"

"No, no." I shake my head, heat gathering on the back of my neck. A trail of curse words travel through my head. This is *not* how I wanted Lorna to find out. Damage control time. "It's just—"

"Aiden!" Lorna says again, more loudly. She's looking at Philippe like she could stick her steak knife in him.

"Lorna, I can explain—"

"I'm not the one who needs an explanation." Lorna points behind me.

I turn around and catch a flash of dark clothes—and a familiar blond ponytail—dart out of the restaurant. My blood goes ice-cold and I half-stand, my heart banging frantically around my chest. "Courtney!"

"Oh, no." Philippe tuts behind me. I whirl around in time to see him bite back a vicious smile. "Was she not supposed to know that?"

꙳

I'm halfway to the door of the restaurant when Lorna catches up with me. Guilt floods my body for leaving her in the lurch, but I have no choice.

"Lorna, I'm so sorry to leave like this," I call over my shoulder. "But I need to go after her."

Lorna shakes her head vehemently. "I'm not here to ask you to stay."

I hand the coat check boy my stub. Damn it, what was I

thinking, checking my jacket? It's cold outside for this time of year and I only have a dress shirt on. I look out the window for Courtney, distracted. "You're not?"

"Aiden, Aiden, Aiden." Lorna puts a wrinkled hand—violet nails, today—on my sleeve. "I know you're not taking the promotion."

Now, she has my attention.

"Lorna, I..." I trail off, lost for words.

This is not how I wanted her to find out. I look back at the Andersens, still seated at our table and staring at us. Uh oh.

"It's okay." She pats my arm, smiling a surprisingly sweet smile. "I understand. I see it all over your face that this girl means the world to you, but it's not only that. The job's wrong for you. Your candid work is spectacular, and a promotion at Zone 6 will mean dampening your creativity, selling perfectly-branded photography to big companies who want 'flawless.' You, my dear boy, specialize in flaws."

I blink. "Thank you?"

"You celebrate flaws," she goes on. "Showcase things that are real and honest and meaningful."

I'm not sure where she's going with this.

As I stare at her, confused, her red-lipped mouth stretches into a smile. "What do you really care about, Aiden? What do you believe? Want to pursue in life?"

I think back to the conversation with my mom this morning, and immediately, I know. See everything clearly.

My priorities are in the correct order now. And it may not be logical, or reasonable, or make the most financial sense, but my heart knows it's *right*.

Lorna smiles knowingly at my expression. "You're wasted at Zone 6, churning out work that doesn't reflect who you really are."

"Are you telling me to quit?" I frown.

She laughs, and the sound echoes like a tinkling bell. "I can fire you, if you'd prefer?"

"What about Ever After?"

"Pshhh! John and that little weasel Philippe are no match for Lorna Strummings. They'll live!"

Before I can think about what I'm doing, I throw my arms around Lorna and give her a hug. "Thank you, Lorna."

She hugs me back, warm and sincere. "You'd better be thankful," she mutters. "Now I'm going to have to take Winston back to LA with me."

"Sorry about that," I say, then laugh. "Happy trainspotting, I guess."

"Over my dead body." She gives me one last affectionate little squeeze. "Go get the girl, Aiden."

Courtney. I need to find her.

Explain that I'm really not going anywhere, unless she's by my side.

But first, I have one thing I need to do.

"Thank you for everything, Lorna!" I throw on my jacket, which the coat check worker finally—*finally*—found and take a few strides towards the door.

Then, the realization hits me that I don't have any way to follow Courtney. Reflexively, I whirl around.

And Lorna's standing in the same spot, hand outstretched and smiling like a Cheshire Cat. "You might need these."

She tosses me the keys. To her freaking Ferrari.

I gape at her, and she winks. "Do me proud, dear boy."

I intend to.

43

COURTNEY

I run into my house and slam the door. Fly up the stairs and into my bedroom, my pups hot on my heels. My heart pounds at a million miles an hour as I open a suitcase and set it on the bed.

When I woke up in this bed this morning, I had every-thing I wanted in the world right beside me.

My dogs, of course. And a man who inspires me to believe in myself. A man who wants me to be happy, wants me to succeed.

A man I want more than anything.

Since Marina Cicero's 14th birthday bash more than half my life ago, I've tried to live without the things I want.

I believed that, if I never wanted a relationship, it couldn't hurt me, couldn't affect me negatively, when someone didn't want me back. On reflection, I see now that I convinced myself I had a crush on Philippe because it offered a distraction from pursuing anything that might've actually been meaningful.

I was scared of anything "meaningful." It was easier to have an unrequited crush than let anyone get close.

Same goes for my business. I could've started a long

time ago, in all honesty. I had the means and resources to get things started, build it from the ground up. But, I was scared of what I wanted. What if I failed? What if my failure proved that I wasn't good enough?

I hid behind excuses about money instead. Made endless lists of pros and cons to justify my stance.

But, Aiden has taught me that it's okay to want things, to pursue my dreams even when there are potential pitfalls. Because it's okay to fail. I have built-in value whether I succeed at things or not.

I'm choosing to believe that.

Earlier today, I took a risk by not taking my job back at Petit Soleil. Now, I'm taking a risk on Aiden Shaw. Crumpling up every possible list I could make about what I should do next, because only one thing matters:

1. I've fallen in love with him. And I believe he loves me, too. Truly believe it, to my very core.

Apparently, that same Aiden Shaw that I love is moving to LA.

2187 miles away, or a thirty-two hour drive. Google Maps confirmed this.

What it did *not* confirm is why Aiden didn't tell me that he was moving across the country. But, I'm not going to doubt him—I spent four years trying to hate him on a weak assumption that built nothing but a house of cards. A house of cards that toppled the second I got to know him.

He has been unwavering in his belief in me, so it's my turn to believe in him.

I stuff clothes, underwear, shampoo, pretty much everything I can get my hands on into an oversized case. Obviously, I can come back later and repack. But right now, it's all about the gesture.

I've read enough romance books to know that every good love story has one.

Mine and Aiden's love story?

It's better than good.

It's the best thing that's ever happened to me.

Three dog leashes, two overstuffed suitcases, and one sweaty, panting Courtney later, I'm outside and on my way next door.

I puff my way up his steps, then ring the doorbell urgently. Again. A third time.

A massive wave of uncertainty crashes over me. He's not home. I haven't heard from him all afternoon. I don't think he saw me dash out of Petit Soleil earlier, but what if he did?

What if he didn't come after me?

Oh, no!

I swallow all of my doubts in one big gulp. I'm not doing this anymore. Not going to conjure the worst case scenario in my mind and drown in it.

I've since learned to swim.

Resourceful as ever, I lift the ugly, googly-eyed garden gnome on the porch. I know, for a fact, that Aiden has a spare key stowed under there. Jess (perhaps unwisely) told me about it back when Aiden and I were locked into our war.

I've never used it until now. Promise!

Feeling slightly like a home invader, I gingerly turn the key in the lock, push open the front door. Step inside.

Butch, Cassidy and Sundance skid across the floor in joy. They dart from room to room as they search for Aiden, their new favorite person. Which I get. He's mine, too.

I stop in the entryway, inhaling the faint scent of him that mingles sweetly in the air. As I wrestle my suitcases into the corner, I notice that the closet door is wide open. Aiden's enormous shoe collection is absent.

At first, I stifle a snort. Of course his beloved sneakers would be the first thing he packed. Probably wrapped them all up in cotton wool and tissue paper before placing them in their original boxes.

Then, reality hits me. Hard.

He's really leaving. Already packed.

At that moment, the door flies open, and I'm suddenly face to face with a breathless, disheveled, slightly frantic Aiden. His eyes were wild and worried, but as soon as he sees me, his face lights up brighter than a Christmas tree. "Courtney! You're here!"

"Hey," I say slowly. Drink him in as he stands before me. "Is everything okay?"

"I've been calling you. I thought when you didn't answer, you were mad..." He trails off as he registers the suitcases by the closet. "What's going on?"

"Aiden." I take a breath. Take a step forward. Take my biggest risk yet. "I heard your conversation in Petit Soleil earlier."

"Court, it's not what it—"

"I want to come with you!" I blurt. "If you'll have me, that is. Or, we can make it work long distance, I'll do whatever it takes. I'd never ask you to give up your dreams for me, so I'd never ask you to stay. But I don't want to lose you."

Aiden stares at me for a few long moments, stunned into apparent silence. When he eventually unfreezes, his voice is croaky. "You're not going to lose me. I'm not going anywhere."

"What?"

"That's why I didn't tell you about LA," he says softly. "I decided not to go."

"Aiden," I say seriously. "I never want you to give up anything on account of me..."

"Don't you get it? I'd give up anything in a heartbeat for you. Anything."

I blink, breathless by the sheer force in his words, the sincerity in that simple sentence. "I can't let you do that. This job is what you want, everything you've been working for."

"You were about to do the same thing for me," he says in that calm, reasonable tone of his. "But, your dream of opening Life is Ruff is *actually* what you want. My promotion at Zone 6 turned out to be the opposite of what I want. What I want is you. And me. Together. Right here in Atlanta."

"Me too," I say softly.

He takes my hands, a small smile playing on his lips. "Growing up, I watched my parents love each other more than anything in the world. I could never fathom having a love like that. I didn't want a love like that. I was worried it would swallow me whole. That I'd lose sight of what's important. Lose myself in it. I didn't want love. But then, I found you."

Aiden's eyes smoulder as he stares at me, full of care and desire and support. Life support.

"So, what's happening with your job? With Ever After?" I whisper.

"I quit." He shrugs. "It's not my future. You're my future, Courtney. You changed everything for me. You make me a better man—the man I've always wanted to be but didn't know how. And that's why I did this."

He hands me an envelope.

With shaking hands, I open it. Stare blankly at the page.

296

"What is this?" I ask, breathless.

"My declaration that I believe in you. That you've got this."

"How did you...?"

Aiden smiles. Puts his hands on my arms. "There was a catalog that came in the mail for you this morning, full of commercial spaces for lease. I saw one in the area that looked perfect, everything you said you wanted, so I put a deposit on it."

I look at him. Then at his empty shoe closet.

My mouth goes dry. "You didn't."

"I did. And I wanted to. My shoes don't mean anything to me anymore, not compared to you." His fingers trace concentric circles on my skin, each a little stroke of love and tenderness. "*You're* important to me."

"I don't know what to say," I breathe, tears collecting in my eyes. This is so much more than anyone has ever done for me and I'm blown away. I intended to follow Aiden to LA, to support him in his dreams. But, he's flipped the script. "This is so much. Too much."

Aiden blows out a long breath. A solitary tear runs down his cheek, but he makes no move to brush it away. "You've taught me so much, Court, and I know I still have a lot to learn. But I promise, if you trust me with your heart, I'll take care of it like it's the most precious thing on this earth. I'll never use or abuse it, or make you feel like you're not good or worthy enough. I love you *for* all the things that make you who you are, not in spite of them. All of your imperfections are perfect to me, because they're what make *you* perfect for me."

I stare at him, entranced. I can barely breathe, hardly dare to imagine that this is true, this is real.

"You don't have to love me back," Aiden's voice lowers, cracking slightly. "You don't have to say a word. But, you need to know that, no matter what you say or what you do, I love you. I'm not going anywhere."

Everything I've ever wanted, everything I've ever needed, is right there in his words. Etched on his beautiful face. A partner. A teammate. An equal. Someone who sees the best in me, but accepts me at my worst. Encourages me to be my best. Who isn't going to run when the road gets bumpy.

"I love you, too, Aiden," I blurt, tears flowing freely down my face. "I love you so much."

A smile brighter than sunshine spreads over his face.

And I just love him all the more for it.

He pulls me close to him, leans towards me, but just before his lips meet mine, I see a flash of red outside his open front door.

"Aiden?"

"Yes, Courtney?"

"Why in the name of all three Jonas Brothers is there a Ferrari out front?"

44

COURTNEY

One Year Later...

The rain comes in droves, pounding and unrelenting.

The sky is stark, gray, cold and bleak. Raindrops bounce from rooftops in erratic, frantic drum beats. Puddles form in drains, and the surrounding sidewalk floods.

"What a beautiful day!" Jess, ever the optimist, flings open the curtains and peers outside at the unseasonably gross early fall weather.

Baby Freddie (Freddie Caiden Brady, to be exact—yup, she did it), who's strapped to a carrier on her chest, gurgles. Then, grabs her boob through her sage-colored silk dress.

"Owww," she complains.

Freddie giggles. I join him in his laughter.

"I agree, it's perfect." I lace my custom-made, glittery white sneakers, then pet Cassidy—who's at my feet, as per usual—on his golden head. "No amount of rain could ruin it."

Mia comes into the room, a cloud of hairspray hanging around her head. Ollie and Addie toddle at her feet, suckers in their mouths. Butch and Sundance trot stealthily behind little Addie, having correctly identified her as the weakest food link.

Mia sees me eyeing the kids' candy and shrugs. "Call me a bad mom but it keeps the tears away."

"I'd never call you a bad mom," I say fiercely. "I was more worried about Addie sharing with Butch."

"Thanks." My friend smiles. "You look beautiful, Courtney."

"So do you guys." I stand and let my white satin dress—floor length, with a scooped back, and oh-so-delicate spaghetti straps—fall to the ground, over my sneakers. It's form-fitting and fabulous and totally, 100% me. "Now, let's do this thing!"

I reach out to hug Jess and Mia, who *do* look gorgeous in their matching bridesmaids dresses, and we have a big cuddle-puddle of a group hug.

Today, I'm marrying Aiden Shaw.

And I've never been more ready for anything.

After a lot of running and screaming while holding multiple umbrellas, Jess, Mia, the kids, the dogs and I pile into the waiting town car outside my house.

I glance left. A little peek at my next door neighbor's house.

Soon to be *our* house.

It made sense for us to move into his place: it's bigger and more modern. My compromise was that all my fluffy crap comes with me. All my throw pillows, blankets, house plants. Even Piggie Smalls and every useless Billy Mays-punted tool I've ever ordered from an infomercial.

Aiden pretended to grouch about this, but we were both

fully aware that he's been dying to get his hands on my old record player for months.

Over the past year, Aiden and I have gone from strength to strength. His photography company—specializing in frank candids that are both unfiltered and unapologetically honest—has developed a sort of cult following. Particularly with brands looking to connect with savvy, modern customers seeking transparency when they shop.

I've also seen a ton of success with Life is Ruff. Every week, more owners sign up with their pups, and I've had to employ two more staff to keep up with the demand. Aiden, through every challenge and obstacle, is my biggest cheerleader, unwavering in his belief that I can do it.

Sure, we've had our ups and downs, like every couple does. We're two imperfect people in love. Sometimes, I'm stubborn as a mule and convinced that I'm right when I'm absolutely not. And sometimes, Aiden will watch a video on his phone at full volume when the TV is on. Apparently, he can legitimately watch two things at once. It's like some kind of entirely annoying superpower.

At the end of the day, imperfect as we are, we are perfect for each other. The ups are way more plentiful than the downs. Aiden supports me, believes in me, encourages me to pursue my dreams. He makes me feel cherished and safe and free to be me.

In turn, I show Aiden that love can be something positive. Something that enriches all areas of your life without drowning you.

When we do hit a down—a.k.a any time I get fearful that I'm not enough for him, or any time he's scared to be vulnerable or let his walls down—we go back to the first thing Blaze Half Moon ever taught us: we work on being the best versions of ourselves so that we can be the best we can be for each other.

Because falling in love with the best person you could imagine being with? It's better than your wildest dreams.

And worth fighting for and working on. Every. Single. Day.

We pull up at the church, and Mia gets the kids out. Jess squeezes my hand. "Ready?"

"As I'll ever be."

She laughs, and on a whim, I grab her. Hug her. Hard.

"Jess?"

"Yes, Courtney?"

"Thank you for being the best friend, maid of honor, and now sister that a girl could ask for." I sniff, trying not to get too choked up. Don't want to ruin that eye makeup I spent forty-five minutes perfecting. I still love wearing makeup on special occasions, and this occasion is the most special. "I always wanted a sister."

Jess's smile puts the sun to shame. She bats at my hand, bashful. "Me too, Court. I'm... glad it's you."

Our friend group has this little toast we always make: *To friends who feel like family*. Now, with Jess and Aiden, and Conor and Mia being siblings, all three of us couples are not only friends who feel like family... We're friends who are *also* family.

I hold onto Jess for a few more moments, and then it's time.

Lights, camera, action.

I face the open doors of the chapel, butterflies flying in my stomach. The church is lit with flickering candles and lanterns, and a pianist plays soft notes that carry through the fragrant, floral-tinged air.

Mia walks up the aisle first, flanked by her kiddos. Ollie looks gravely serious, while Addie flings fistfuls of rose petals with abandon. Jess is next, Freddie strapped to her chest. She holds three special, wedding-bedazzled dog leashes.

My furry boys look spectacular in their little doggie tuxedos. You really can find everything on Amazon.

Then, it's my turn.

The music changes, and the congregation stands.

I take a deep breath, and I step forward. To walk myself down the aisle.

I'm nobody's to give away. I've belonged solely to myself for a long time. Now, I belong with Aiden.

The pews are filled with the people nearest and dearest to us. I spot Mr. and Mrs. Shaw in the front row, sporting what look like matching gold togas. A bunch of Aiden's college friends and colleagues are here, a few of my cousins, and some girls I waitressed with. Lorna and her husband, who have flown in from LA for the wedding, sit near the front, beaming, her white pups on her lap. They each have a sequined headband for the occasion.

At the front of the church are Pete and Conor, each looking handsome in a dark gray suit with a little daffodil blossom pinned to the lapel.

New beginnings.

I see Aiden and everything else fades as those navy eyes find mine.

He's breathtaking in his three-piece charcoal suit, hair mussed just enough for it to look like it was an intentional, chic fashion choice—though I know it's because he's been tugging on it. He always does that when he's nervous.

As soon as he sees me, those nerves visibly fall away, and his face breaks into the most beautiful smile, eyes crinkling at the corners.

I reach the top of the aisle and he practically jogs towards me to grab my hand. We step forwards together, linked by the hand, and ready to take the plunge. Commit.

Blaze Crescent Moon steps forwards, hands raised. He's dressed in a yellow tunic that's brighter than sunshine. "Dearly beloved, we are gathered here today..."

I shoot a sideways glance at Aiden, smile. He grins back at me, a secret smile meant just for me. Filled with nothing but love, love, love.

Enough for a lifetime.

Thank you so much for reading Aiden and Courtney's story!

If you enjoyed this book, please leave me a review. As a new author, reviews mean everything to me. I appreciate each and every one of them.

A NOTE FROM KATIE

Hello,

If you're reading this, first of all, a massive, gigantic, enormous THANK YOU is in order! Seriously, thank you so much for reading this book. I really hope you enjoyed it.

The Neighbor War was a lot of fun to write, but simultaneously, was very difficult. I really felt a sadness in Courtney's character as I started writing her, and it felt authentic to lean into this for her, and have her take a journey of finding self-acceptance and self-belief.

I hope I did her character justice, and I hope I did her life with diabetes justice. I did a ton of research on the illness, and I'm hoping the portrayal is as accurate as possible. My intention when writing this was never, ever to bring any sense of shame or stigma to anyone living with a disease, but rather for this story to be one of empowerment and owning who you are.

And this doesn't just apply to physical diseases or impairments, it also speaks to mental health struggles and emotional struggles. There's so much pressure out there for women to conform to a societal idea of beauty or character, and I wanted Courtney to walk out from under this weight on her journey.

So, to any woman out there who has ever been made to feel like she's not good enough, not smart enough, not pretty enough... this one's for you. You are enough. Just the way you are.

I also wanted to take a moment to thank a few people without whom The Neighbor War would never have been possible.

SJ - You're the bomb diggity. I seriously love you. Thank you for making this book make sense (somewhat).

To my ARC readers - I can't thank you all enough. Your encouragement, support, kind words and love for my characters means the world to me. You're incredible, each and every one of you.

And to everyone who took a chance on reading this book. I hope it gave you a few laughs, and maybe tears, along the way.

I love you all.

Gratefully,

Katie B x

ALSO BY KATIE BAILEY

Donovan Family

So That Happened

I Think He Knows

Only in Atlanta

The Roommate Situation

The Neighbor War

Made in the USA
Columbia, SC
19 November 2023

26736001R00186